BOOK ONE

OF THE

KATZENSTEIN KIDS TRILOGY

BOOKS BY A.G. SULLIVAN

THE KATZENSTEIN KIDS AND THE EYE OF HORUS

THE KATZENSTEIN KIDS AND THE 12 MINOTAURS

TRYPOPHOBIA – A NOVEL

TATOOS & POETRY

THE
KATZENSTEIN
KIDS
AND THE EYE OF HORUS

A.G. SULLIVAN

Cover Design by Extended Imagery
Illustrations by Michael Gregory Suarez & Surya Nair

www.thekatzensteinkids.com

Out of a dream came a plot…

Sprinkled with history and imagination…

Then told like an adventure out of my childhood…

To become an amazing story.

Dedicated to Kaitlyn & Trevor,

You are my heroes.

CONTENTS

CHAPTER 1
THE DEVIL'S GARDENS
El Alamein, Egypt – 1942

"I already told you; he put the gun to his head and pulled the trigger!" Otto, a regular in the German 21st Panzer Division, yelled the words once again.

With a mouth hoarse and dry from repeating himself, he was reluctant to continue his bizarre story – the same one which had led to the death of his fallen comrade. Sitting before his interrogators, Otto's tan and unshaven face looked as haggard as he felt. He was little more than a shell of the man he'd been only three days earlier. The body in the chair, weak and lifeless, didn't feel like his anymore. It was all drained out.

"What else do you want me to say?" He looked between the interrogators, squinting into the darkness. "I've told you everything!"

In the darkest corner of the windowless room, a shadowed figure loaded a blank page into the typewriter before him, eager to record everything. His fingers danced across the machine and the hammering sound the keys made was the only sound in the room. They spelled out: *"Interrogation Report."*

A second figure appeared, emerging from the shadows. The man stood tall, but his was a face made for the shadows, distinguishable by the ominous scar that marred it. The cut tore across his left eye, long and jagged. "Tell us what happened," he said sternly, his breath hot and menacing as he leaned across the table. "This time, from the beginning…"

Bewildered by what he had to describe, Otto dropped his head, pausing for some time. With every second that passed, he was forced to relive the moment again. Finally, he drew in a long, shaky breath.

Where do I begin?

The room seemed to freeze with anticipation, hanging in the air like a palpable cloud that everyone could feel. Exasperated as he was, Otto knew he had no choice and so, his mouth cracked open to retell the tale once more.

◆ ◆ ◆

A mere seventy-two hours earlier, the KFZ – an armored reconnaissance vehicle – was battered by the force of nature as harsh desert sand blew against it in a roaring wind. Inside its belly, the crew of two remained hunkered down, resigned to the fact that they were going nowhere at that point in time. A sandstorm – not unusual for this region – whipped across the vast undulating oceans of sand known as Northern Egypt. Quiet emptiness had transformed into a raging beast determined to bury everything beneath the sand. Nothing was safe from its wrath, least of all the reconnaissance vehicle.

Loyal to their need for radio silence, the crew carefully logged their waypoints along the route. It was the only way they were able to keep track of their position. They knew they were approximately thirty miles south-west of El Alamein, along the southern edge of the Devil's Gardens, an array of minefields used to protect the German defensive positions against British Forces. Named, rather appropriately, by none other than General Rommel himself.

Their mission was one of routine. They were to conduct visual recon along the fortified line, beginning from their northern position with the 21st Panzer Division and continuing south along the Devil's Gardens all the way out to the Qattara Depression. It was an important and exhausting job, far easier said than done, but it was of the utmost importance. Their responsibility was to ensure that the southern access was clear of any and all kinds of possible outflanking maneuvers the British offensive might make. If the Brits did decide to move in, they would come from the east, where they were meant to find resistance.

After what seemed like an age, they could hear the sound of the storm unwinding and dying down. The welcome, albeit gradual, development garnered a sense of relief from the squashed two-man crew within the KFZ. Overhead, the sky had cleared and, in its vacancy, there wasn't so much as a hint of a cloud in sight. The burning sun beat down cruelly, but the passing storm faded further and further away, disappearing into the distance. It came as a glad tiding.

It was only midday, but the crew had a lot of work to do and a limited amount of time to do it in. The wheels needed to be dug out from beneath the sand and they needed to complete their final waypoint before they could turn back. It was going to be a tight schedule.

"Finally!" Hans shouted in relief as he pushed open the top hatch. He brushed back his chestnut hair and climbed out of the vehicle, grateful for the opportunity to stretch his narrow shoulders and reedy body.

The sight of the desert before him was incredible and mighty. Desolate and barren, the rolling hills and dunes remained unmoving, save for the gentle wisps of sand that blew to and fro in the dry heat. The unending blue sky, stagnant and devoid of clouds, looked like wallpaper and the sun resembled a blinding spotlight as it burned mercilessly.

"Get the shovels! I want to return to the 21st before dark," Hans said, feeling optimistic.

Otto jerked awake from a well-needed nap. His short blonde hair was messy, wet with sweat. The smoldering heat of September was made worse by the fact that he'd been cooped up in the driver's quarters for nearly two hours. Needless to say, it was stuffy and cramped. Grumbling, Otto lifted himself out of the seat and reached toward the open hatch. The armor was hot to the touch. Every joint popped and crunched with the effort of moving as Otto pulled his stiff body through the hole.

Squinting in the brightness, Otto was greeted by a clear afternoon and scorching hot air. The stiff wind blew particles of sand against him. His clothes were hot and sticky, distracting enough that he almost didn't notice his comrade in the sand.

"Otto," Hans called excitedly. "Otto, get the binoculars!"

Jarred by the urgency in Hans' voice, Otto dropped back down to grab the Dienstglas Binoculars they'd brought with them. Once he had them, he scuttled back to the opening. His eyes were still adjusting to the light of day as he reached forward to hand the binoculars off to Hans.

"What is it?" He asked. "Have we been spotted?"

This was a grave concern… being spotted.

Without responding, Hans took a few steps forward. His tattered boots sunk into the vacuum of loose sand as he raised the binoculars to his eyes and worked the focus wheel. In that moment all his senses started working once again. Squinting across the landscape, he observed a strange object in the distance through the shimmery refraction reflecting off the dunes.

Hans continued to look through the binoculars, using his trained eyes to identify the object. "It looks to be the bones of a wooden ship," he called upward. He turned back to the KFZ and Otto paid close attention to what he had to say. "Let's get a closer look."

That was enough for Otto to jump into action. Working together, the two dug through the fine sand, clearing it away from their four-wheeler as quickly as they could. The moment they were done, Otto climbed back into the driver's quarters and powered up the V-8 petrol engine. It ground into low gear, rumbling into action. Meanwhile, Hans braced himself on the standing platform near the roof hatch. Using both hands, he locked down the L/55 autocannon and took his position as scout commander.

The KFZ jolted forward and the four wheels freed themselves of the sand as the two began their drive southward toward the mysterious object in the distance.

"I don't understand," Otto called back as he drove. "We've definitely been this far south before. How have we never seen this thing?"

"Maybe it was the sandstorm. It could have been exposed when the terrain shifted."

Otto furrowed his brow. He supposed it was possible that the object could have been buried beneath the sand for a long time. He double-checked the waypoint log. Based on their entries, the object was within the northern boundaries of the Qattara Depression, which was a large expanse known to be well below sea level. It was believed to have once joined with the Mediterranean Sea some thousand years ago. Otto couldn't help recalling Hans' words. His comrade had said the object looked like the bones of a ship. Could it really be?

They were about to find out.

The KFZ traveled quickly, easily carving its way through the sandy valleys. Slopes formed by the wind seemed to carry them like waves toward their destination. At last, they arrived at the site of the mysterious object.

"Halt," Hans commanded from his look-out position, his voice raw with dehydration. He pulled his field goggles back to look at the object with his own eyes. "It's massive indeed!"

Otto returned the engine to idle and turned off the ignition, eager to join Hans. "I want to get a better look for myself."

"And so you will, my friend," Hans smiled.

The pair climbed out of the KFZ, but the men were not prepared for the sight before them. They froze where they stood, the moment their boots sunk into the sand below the KFZ. They could only stare at the object, wide-eyed. They had a clear view of it where it protruded out of the recently shifted sand, dripping particles like an unsealed hourglass. Otto's eyes were done adjusting to the sunshine, but he didn't know if he would ever adjust to this peculiar discovery.

"Astonishing," Hans breathed.

The enormous wooden hull was at least twenty feet tall, towering above their heads. The siding was mostly gone and the wood was weathered, revealing the mangled remains of an ancient ship. Its structural bones were bare for the world to see.

Hans turned to Otto, a hint of a smile playing at the corners of his lips. "Do you think it was carrying gold?"

"I can only hope," Otto replied with a tinge of humor in his voice. Beneath that humor, however, was a sense of hope that only Hans could recognize. "We could take it and get far away from this dastardly war."

Hans ventured closer to the ship. Squatting before it, he peered into the vessel, looking beyond what was left of the outer hull. He cried out suddenly, "There's something inside!"

Otto jolted forward to join his comrade. "What do you see?"

"Look…" Hans pointed his finger into the thing. "I can see the glitter of something silver between the cracks of that wall."

Otto followed the direction of Hans' pointing finger. "Gold, silver," he muttered, hopeful once more. "I would take either at this point."

Inside the structure of the vessel's once water-tight hull, the men could see a wooden cargo chamber. It was cast in shadow by the surrounding structure and, for the most part, still buried in the sand. Nevertheless, it appeared to be intact and Hans cautiously moved toward it. The scale of the ship was such that he couldn't help gazing overhead at the size and shape of it even as he went to investigate. He tugged a pair of tan leather gloves off of his belt and slipped them onto his hands, pulling back on the cuff to ensure they fit tightly.

"What are you doing?" Otto asked quietly.

"I'm going to dig into the chamber," Hans reached forward and wedged his fingers into a joint between the planks, giving a strong tug.

The brittle wood splintered and pulled away with little effort. The dust dissipated into the surrounding air, wisps of it circling like a cloud and threatening to make Otto cough. As it cleared, it revealed a better view of what lay within the ship and both men took an involuntary step toward it. They ached to satisfy their curiosity and the anticipation hung between them thickly.

Otto crouched behind Hans in order to get a better look. Behind the wooden planks, the glittering silver object Hans had spotted appeared to be a rectangular box of some sort. Otto could hardly contain his excitement. Though its finish was unusual, its shape and size matched that of a tomb or coffin. The two men felt no guilt in wondering whether its contents would be valuable.

"I think it's been here for ages," Hans murmured. "Perhaps for thousands of years."

"Perhaps," Otto remembered the region was once below sea level.

Hans reached in once again, pulling away yet another plank, and then another after that. Each disturbance he made caused the ship to spit out a fresh puff of dust. Hans shielded himself by cupping his hands over his mouth every time one of the planks broke free, choosing to squint through the dust since they had no goggles.

Finally, he ripped the final board free and broke through the wooden chamber, revealing the silver object in its full splendor.

"Astounding," Otto breathed. "Simply astounding!"

The men were awestruck by the sight before them. Finished with a polished silver surface, even after years beneath the sand, every side of the box was engraved in row upon row of strange symbols. Hans and Otto moved in, peering closely at the symbols in an attempt to comprehend their meaning.

Centered on the top of the box, a larger and more prominent symbol stood out to Hans. He scanned the decorated surface of the thing and leaned in toward the prominent symbol. The bold, engraved lines stood out and it wasn't long before Hans' gloved fingers followed his eyes, tracing gently over the strokes. They formed the shape of a crude eye with a large pupil, a curved eyebrow above it, and a curved teardrop below.

Intrigued by the symbol, Hans removed the glove from his right hand and extended his palm over the symbol. Otto didn't notice what his comrade was doing, preoccupied with the symbols on the side of the box. As Hans' bare skin came into contact with the cold surface, some kind of electric discharge ignited and lines of static current sparked across the box. Otto gave a startled gasp, but Hans made no movement, save for the widening of his eyes. Energized by this strange force, a field of glowing black energy crept towards Hans' hand. Thin tendrils of black smoke wrapped themselves around his fingers.

"Get back!" Otto shouted, jumping back from both the box and Hans.

Before either of them could make another move, a sharp ray of light descended from the sky above, splitting through the horizon as if it were the Hand of God reaching down to where they stood. It was sudden and unexpected, resembling a bolt of lightning. Otto stumbled backward onto the ground, petrified by what he was seeing. He watched, terrified and helpless, as the brilliant ray of light shimmered over the silver object. Goosebumps rose on his skin and, despite the fact that he was in the desert, he suddenly felt cold and unnerved. Every part of him wanted to move toward his friend, to drag Hans away from that thing, but he couldn't risk going near that awful bright light.

"Hans!" He called once more. "Get back! Get away from it!"

Hans made no move. His frozen figure remained eerily still and Otto got the feeling that something was very wrong. Hans' body reminded him of a statue, lifeless and unmoving, his palm still pressed to the top of the object.

Beyond the silhouette of his friend, Otto could still see the iridescent phenomenon. The strange beam of light that shone down from the heavens continued to shine with an intensity that was nearly blinding. As he stared into it, Otto's hands began to shake uncontrollably. In an effort to regain control, he tore his gaze away from his friend and the ray of light. He stretched his fingers out and then balled them into a fist, repeating the action several times.

"Everything..." He murmured to himself, furrowing his brow as he stared down at his hands. For reasons he couldn't fathom, they felt as though they belonged to someone else. His eyes narrowed as he watched his fingers release and clench, his thoughts muddled as they floated around his mind. "Everything seems so strange."

Glancing around the terrain, Otto noticed that things looked different. The sand was a glowing orange and the sky had an unfamiliar shade to it. It was almost as if someone had played with the contrast and saturation of their surroundings. Fear gripped his heart like a vice, causing it to race against the inside of his chest until he could barely breathe. Sweat gathered on Otto's brow and he raised a trembling arm to wipe it away.

Otto never thought any of this would happen. Now that

he was in this situation, desperation to get out of it rose from his throat, acrid as bile. The only thing that seemed to feel real was his own body and he could feel warmth flushing his face as panic swirled inside him. The sandstorm was over, but he had to deal with an entirely different storm now.

Searching within himself, Otto couldn't find the words he wanted to say. His lips were dry and cracked. To open them would be painful.

Something is terribly wrong...

Before he could gather his words or his thoughts, the ray of light vanished. All at once, it simply disappeared; a retracted bolt of lightning, returning from whence it came. With its disappearance, the colors of the world returned to normal and Otto barely had a moment to blink in realization that everything was once again calm. It was as though nothing had happened.

That was when Otto noticed Hans. His otherwise motionless body gave a bit and his posture shifted, just enough that the scuffle of sand caused Otto's head to snap back toward him. Hans lowered his hand slowly and gave a subtle turn of his head, looking back at Otto with a glazed expression.

"Hans?" Otto breathed. He was still shaken from the whole ordeal, still confused by what strange thing they'd discovered, and most certainly still unnerved by his friend's behavior. As Otto took Hans in, he couldn't help but think Hans looked strangely blurry around the edges. "Are you... Are you okay?"

It was quite clear that Hans was not okay. Though he faced Otto and his eyes were on Otto, he seemed far away. The glazed expression hadn't vanished and there was a darkness in his eyes as he squinted at Otto. Only, he didn't appear to be looking at Otto at all. It was as though he was looking at something just behind Otto. He took a slow step forward and then another, coming into focus with each move he made.

Otto found himself praying that Hans would be okay, but as he looked into those eyes, he saw an uncharacteristic depth. He could barely breathe as Hans moved toward him, could barely even move. "Hans?"

Grinning lopsidedly, Hans asked the most unexpected question; "Did you see the darkness?"

"Darkness?" Otto asked, taken aback. "No… I only saw the light?"

Otto didn't know what happened to Hans and he didn't know what he could do to fix it. As he thought about this, Hans took several more steps. His motions were stiff and awkward, as though he didn't remember how to walk. Hans' eyes remained glossy, but his expression grew more intense as he came to a stop in front of Otto. Dropping the glove to the ground, he reached for Otto's face, taking it with both hands.

"What light?" Hans breathed, tilting his head forward until they were nose to nose. His voice deepened. "All I saw was darkness… Darkness that covered me… Darkness that got inside of me…"

Alarmed, Otto wrenched himself free of Hans' grip and backed up toward the KFZ. Hans stared at him, perplexed. "Have you… Have you lost your mind?!" Otto yelled out in distress. He could barely get the words out, his mouth and tongue fumbling over his speech. "Something is wrong! That thing… That thing did something!"

Hans turned suddenly, facing the strange object.

Absently, his hands found their way to his belt, where he unsnapped his holster and removed his Luger sidearm. Without hesitation, he lifted it and pressed the barrel to the side of his head. His body swayed slightly as he stared at the object. "The darkness is inside me," he mumbled calmly. "All I see is darkness."

In that instant, the sound of a gunshot broke through the air and rang through Otto's ears, deafening and abrupt. Hans fell face-first into the sand, spraying it in every direction. In the eerie silence that followed, Otto could hardly breathe for the deep pounding of his heart in his chest. His nerves were shot and the hairs on the back of his neck stood on end. He gulped down the lump that formed in his throat, his mouth drier than ever before. Otto knew he must be as pale as a ghost because he felt the blood drain from his face.

For the longest time, nothing happened. The world was silent and Otto didn't move. He could only stare straight ahead. Eventually, his eyes fell to the limp body on the ground before him and he crawled backward, distancing himself from Hans' lifeless form. It seemed as though everything had slowed down. Nothing seemed real anymore, least of all that dreaded vessel and its horrible contents. A tear ran across Otto's cheek, hot against his cold skin, and dripped down onto his dusty clothes. With one last glance at Hans' body, he had an unrealistic hope that Hans might suddenly move and come back to him, but no… Hans remained motionless.

Otto eventually climbed back into the KFZ, aghast. In the back of his hazy mind, he knew that he was in shock, but he hastily made his way to the medium-range radio transceiver. His hands were shaking as he grabbed ahold of the mouthpiece and powered on the unit. Static filled the confined space. Otto twisted the frequency knob slightly and it faded. Then, feeling far from ready, he squeezed the microphone button and transmitted.

"KFZ 49... Waypoint 30-18/27-51... Man down... Red Ruby... Repeat," Otto closed his eyes and pressed down on the button, static breaking the silence again. "KFZ 49... Waypoint 30-18/27-51... Red Ruby... Over."

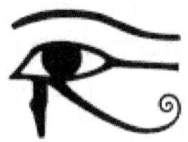

CHAPTER 2
RED RUBY

Twenty miles north-east, a radio officer hastily recorded the message onto a small piece of paper. He folded it in half and handed it to his messenger with a sense of urgency. "They found a Red Ruby. Deliver this to Rommel at once!"

Moments later, the messenger burst through the door of General Rommel's command post. The general was reviewing battle preparations and looked up with an arched eyebrow at the interruption. The messenger greeted the general with a traditional Nazi salute, raising his right arm into the air with a flat palm and straightened fingers. He held the note out to the general with his opposite hand.

The general stood from his seat and grabbed the slip of paper without returning the salute. The messenger knew this was a signal that he should stay and wait. The general would give further orders when he was ready.

Rommel was a deliberate and calculated man with a lot on his mind. As he read the note, however, all that troubled him faded away. If one didn't know the man, they might not have noticed any reaction at all. That didn't stop the tiny muscle in his jaw from twitching as he realized that a new priority had taken precedence over all others.

"Are you sure they said Red Ruby?" General Rommel spat harshly, looking up from the note.

The messenger nodded his head curtly. "Yes, sir."

Red Ruby referred to the discovery of unusual artifacts, equipment, or technology. The purpose of the code was to alert the Germans that there might be something out there that could aid their quest for world domination. These discoveries were to be reported and secured the moment they were found. The general knew the Red Ruby was to be investigated, protected, and extracted to German territories at once. These were not just any orders – they came from Hitler himself, a man who the general owed his first loyalties to.

General Rommel sat back down at his field desk, grabbed a pen and paper, and began writing. The room was silent, save for the sound of his pen as it scrawled unforgivingly across the page. Once his message was complete, he handed it to the messenger, dismissing him with a high salute of his own.

"This message must be sent to Berlin immediately," Rommel murmured.

Once again, the messenger nodded. With that, he

scurried out of the room to do his job.

The general returned to his plans, though they had changed. Before the end of the day, Rommel knew he would have to send a lightning division to the Qattara Depression to ensure the protection of the Red Ruby. He also knew that within a few short hours, Berlin would be dispatching an emissary from the Archaeological Division known as SSA to come investigate and identify whatever the Red Ruby might be.

◆ ◆ ◆

The new day broke across the sky with a flash of blinding sunlight. Over the blue waters of the Mediterranean Sea, the horizon gave way to the display of an incoming ship. Atop its gigantic steel structure, a flag billowed in the wind. The Swastika brandished its red, white, and black pattern ominously, standing out against the clear blue sky.

Within the depths of the vessel, Lieutenant Edmund Himmel woke from a somber sleep, jostled by the sudden easing of the ship's twin steam turbines. The crew was hard at work on the upper deck and it was a welcome sound to the lieutenant's waking ears. It was a sure sign that the Light Cruiser Kurmark had reached its destination.

A knock echoed off the cabin door and the lieutenant raised his head.

"Enter!"

A young, uniformed sailor burst through the door and greeted the lieutenant with a high salute and a grin on his face. "Heil Hitler," the sailor eagerly began. "We have arrived at El Daba. The ship is preparing to dock and we should be ready to disembark by zero eight-hundred hours."

Himmel returned the salute before stepping off of his bunk and making his way toward the small stainless-steel sink in the corner of his cabin. It was mounted below a small mirror, behind which was a cabinet. The lieutenant opened it and grabbed a brown leather case from within, unzipped it, and began removing the contents of a shaving kit.

"You are dismissed," the lieutenant added, glancing back over his shoulder at the young sailor.

"Yes, sir," the boy murmured, but he made no move to leave. He paused, hesitant, before he finally asked, "May I ask you a question?"

Himmel ripped open a small packet of shaving cream and emptied it into a waiting cup. He added water to the cup and began stirring the foaming cream with a boar's hair brush. "What is your question?" Himmel snapped, clearly bristled by the intrusion.

More reluctantly than before, the sailor asked his question. "Why do they call you Falcon Sky?"

Himmel's eyes flicked sharply toward the sailor, breaking his gaze away from the mirror. He couldn't help but think that his reputation preceded him. Without looking away from the mirror, he began brushing shaving cream over three-day old growth, responding with a question of his own. "Why do they call Rommel the Desert Fox?"

The sailor shifted from foot to foot; he'd grown visibly uncomfortable in the fear that he may have offended one of his authoritarians. "I'm sorry, sir," he stammered. "I... I didn't mean anything by it. I just heard some of the crew talking about it."

Himmel reached for the butterfly razor on the sink and looked intently into the mirror, carefully dragging the blade over his chin, leaving behind a smooth strip of skin. "Don't fret, boy," he murmured. "I will tell you what you want to know. But after that, I will have to throw you to the sharks."

The lieutenant paused long enough that the young sailor's eyes widened in fear before a smile broke across his cream-covered face. The smile quickly transformed into laughter and the sailor released a breath, realizing it was a joke. His shoulders remained tense.

"They call me the Falcon Sky," Himmel chuckled, "because I am a hunter. Much like the falcon, I swoop in with my talons and sink them into whatever it is that I seek." He dragged the razor down over his chin once more. "That last part is simple. In Middle High German, Himmel means sky."

"I see," the sailor nodded, far more relaxed than before. "Thank you, sir."

Soon, Himmel's every stroke had cleared the shaving cream from his face, leaving behind an expanse of smooth skin. With a splash of water against his face, he rinsed the remains of his efforts and grabbed a towel off the hook beside the sink. He turned to the sailor, drying his face off. "I need a message sent to Berlin."

Hurriedly, the sailor pulled a notepad and pencil from his front pocket.

"Tell them," The lieutenant murmured. "The Falcon Sky has landed."

"Yes, sir," the sailor took down the message and departed from the cabin.

Lieutenant Himmel turned to the uniform awaiting him on a set of redwood hangers. He began to prepare himself for the day ahead. A few days earlier, he'd left the security of his post at the Port of Kirkenes, Norway. He'd been dispatched under direct orders of the Supreme Leader of the SSA and sent to the battle zone of North Africa. It wasn't exactly what he would consider an ideal mission, but he'd been assured by the Supreme Leader that this was no ordinary archaeological inquiry.

Hitler himself had taken an interest in this particular discovery.

The lieutenant recalled the way Hitler had dispatched the cruiser within a mere twelve hours. He'd ordered Rommel, the Desert Fox, to hold El Alamein at all costs. The Red Ruby had quickly become the first priority and it was to be extracted at the soonest opportunity. What made this discovery so intriguing was the inexplicable event that occurred; one which included a death and an eyewitness.

Before long, Himmel was ready. He stood fully dressed in a grey-green field uniform, which went along with the soft embroidered cap on his head. He felt immense pride as he looked at his reflection, standing with his back and shoulders straight. The sharp shirt was defined by three insignias. The Nazi national emblem, an eagle clenching a wreath of oak leaf over a red Swastika, sat atop his right breast pocket, his rank was marked by shoulder straps, and his collars bore colored tabs with double braids. Unlike the traditional insignias, the red Swastika was unique to the SSA. Himmel speculated that it might have been designed to reflect the symbolism of Red Ruby. Some believed that it might be in honor of the blood moon, significant to the SSA.

There was a story about the SSA. It was said to be born out of the Waffen SS during a total eclipse over Germany in 1938. The eclipse appeared red in the skies over Berlin. The story was carefully thought out and was engineered in such a way that it made people think of majesty when they thought of the SSA.

The sound of the ship's horn echoed from above, alerting the crew members that they could disembark at will. A gold lapel depicting a falcon in a striking pose, talons extended, sat on Himmel's bedside. He picked it up and pinned it above his left breast pocket. Right before leaving the cabin for the gangway, he retrieved his service pistol and snapped it onto his leather holster. He was ready.

Outside, the air was dry and hot. It reminded Himmel of an oven. The only relief was the gentle breeze coming off the coastline, but even that couldn't cool him. He dreaded stepping away from the shore, knowing that the deeper he ventured into the scorching hot desert, the stickier his uniform would become.

"Heil Hitler," rung out as Himmel stepped off the gangway.

The lieutenant returned the gesture.

"I'm here to escort you to the site," a uniformed officer spoke. "Warrant Officer Kirk, sir."

Himmel nodded curtly and the two walked along the floating dock toward an open-top military car that waited for them. The warrant officer rushed to open the rear door, allowing the lieutenant to climb into the car before he jumped into the driver's seat. He opened the glove box and removed an envelope, handing it back to Himmel.

"That's the interrogation report from the eye-witness," he met Himmel's eyes in the rearview mirror.

Himmel took the document and was quick to break the seal and remove the report.

"Where to, sir?" Kirk asked.

"To the site," Himmel muttered. "Immediately."

Kirk pulled back the choke, depressed the clutch, and powered on the engine. As the vehicle began to roll forward, he used his free hand to flag a waiting KFZ, signaling that they take the lead. He called out to the KFZ's scout commander, "To the site!"

In the backseat, Himmel unfolded the report and began to read it. The details surrounding the strange event were scattered. It quickly became clear why he was sent for as he read the report. This was not any ordinary discovery. The eyewitness, Otto Berger, and his deceased comrade had stumbled upon something that, based on what he was reading, caused a massive surge of energy. This same powerful force seemed to have had some kind of an effect on the mental state of the deceased, Hans Mayer.

Himmel grew anxious as he read the report, but he remained skeptical, albeit fascinated. He was a man of science. As a physicist, he was knowledgeable in the study of matter and energy. He was educated in Berlin with an associate degree in Archeology and he was recruited by the SSA at the start of the war.

The SSA doctrine carried an underlying theory, Hitler's theory, that ancient artifacts may contain the power of the gods and the supernatural. Should that be the case, the Third Reich believed that it was destined to obtain this power and rule the world for a millennium. Himmel wasn't beholden to the full Nazi vision, unhappy with some of the things happening in his beloved Germany. He couldn't afford to speak his mind though. In these tumultuous times, the only path he could risk was one of party loyalty, if only for the sake of his wife and daughter.

As they traveled across the vast desert, they noticed several armed KFZ vehicles positioned along the route. They were stationed like guards. Himmel supposed that was exactly what they were.

"A camp and perimeter have been established around the Red Ruby," Kirk called to be heard over the engine. "General Rommel has dispatched tanks and artillery guns to the area."

"I see," Himmel muttered, glancing out of the car.

The desert began to prove how hot it could truly get as the cooler morning temperature gave way to midday. The sun, now high in the sky, beat down upon the earth and all those beneath it could feel their pores begin to open. As if it could get any worse, the closer they got the more Himmel's anxiety grew.

"The site is just ahead," Kirk gestured.

The vehicle was about to breach the peak of a large hill. Himmel looked onward, rising out of his seat with a gasp.

The towering form of the ancient ship had come into view and the lieutenant could scarcely believe his own eyes. This was no ordinary ruin after all.

With years of field experience behind him, Himmel knew what he was looking at. Before they pulled onto the site, he'd already begun his visual assessment. Ancient ships such as this one had been found near the great pyramids and the wooden structure was much the same. Nevertheless, this one was obviously much larger than anything discovered before. Unlike the previous findings, the hull construction was devised of a structural framework. Others had used hollow hull pits.

Upon their arrival, Kirk flagged the KFZ escort to remain at a distance. All the while, he scoped out the site. The perimeter of vehicles and armed soldiers was positioned about one hundred yards out. He brought the car to a stop and switched off the ignition, jumping out to open the door for Himmel. He needn't have worried. Himmel moved with a sense of urgency and had already stepped out of the car. This was most unusual for someone of his rank and Kirk was unable to mask his bewilderment. The lieutenant didn't notice; he was already making his way toward the ship with growing interest and curiosity.

"Amazing, isn't it?" Kirk turned to Himmel, walking beside him. "No one has been allowed this near until your arrival."

Himmel nodded, more out of courtesy than anything else, before redirecting his attention to the great vessel ahead. His first impression was that it was remarkably similar to the Solar Ships once used to honor the dead during the First Dynasty of Ancient Egypt. Walking beneath the hull, he closely examined the dry wood, quickly identifying it as cedar.

"Just as I expected," he muttered to no one in particular.

The wood was commonly used some five thousand years earlier, imported from Lebanon in order to build such ships. As he looked up at the towering hull, he saw nothing but a clear blue sky. It took a moment for Himmel to notice the exposed cargo chamber, but once he looked beyond the hull, his breath caught in his throat. The object inside glinted as he approached.

A silver sarcophagus. Himmel could hardly contain his excitement. He'd never seen anything like this in all his years.

Glancing over his shoulder at Kirk, he pointed toward the sarcophagus. "That right there. That's our Red Ruby."

"Remember not to touch it," Kirk murmured as they moved closer.

"Of course," Himmel muttered, recalling the report. Whatever happened to Hans was the result of physical human contact with the surface of the sarcophagus. Wary of the risk of physical contact, he breathed, "*Amazing.*"

Kirk stayed slightly behind him, eerily silent.

"This is no cargo hold," Himmel muttered. He'd made a noteworthy observation of the placement of the sarcophagus. "It's a death chamber." Who knew what lay within? There may have been a dead body or it may be used to transport dead bodies.

"A death chamber?" Kirk repeated.

"Yes," Himmel responded.

Solar Ships usually had an open roof above the death chamber. This was a part of the funeral ritual. It was designed to allow the Sun God, Ra, to rain in upon the sarcophagi. In order to pass on, Ancient Egyptians believed that the dead should be exposed to the heavens. This chamber, for reasons not yet known, was fully enclosed.

This ship was designed to hide the sarcophagus. For some reason, they didn't want Ra to see what was inside.

The thought sent a shiver through Himmel's spine. He wasn't an easily shaken man and at that moment, he was both intrigued and apprehensive. In an attempt to redirect his focus, he examined the engraved skin of the sarcophagus. It was instantly apparent that the strange symbols described in the interrogation report were hieroglyphics. They covered the entire surface of the box and he'd never seen anything like this on an Egyptian artifact before.

As the report described, a larger symbol was centered on the top of the sarcophagus. The lieutenant pulled a magnifying glass out of his back pocket and leaned in to take a closer look. This was the spot that Hans touched, triggering a burst of light from the sky.

An uneasy feeling ran through Himmel as he tried to comprehend what it was that he was seeing. "How is this possible?"

The symbol was no mystery to the lieutenant. It was quite recognizable and common among ancient hieroglyphics. The symbol was the Eye of Horus, commonly associated with one of the Ancient Egyptian deities. It was thought to be a large gemstone that possessed great power. The thing that disturbed Himmel had nothing to do with this, but rather with the fact that Horus was commonly depicted as a man with a falcon head.

The Falcon Sky stood in disbelief. It was a mighty strange coincidence if it was one. He couldn't help but wonder if the falcon symbolism meant his role was predestined.

"How should we proceed, sir?" Kirk asked, breaking into Himmel's thoughts.

The lieutenant stepped back from the sarcophagus and turned to Kirk, shaking off the thoughts that plagued his weary mind. He set aside all trepidation and executed his prime directive. "Get your men. We need to remove the Red Ruby. Bring ropes and pulleys." He paused and gave the box a sideways glance. "And under no circumstances is anyone to touch the artifact. That's an order!"

CHAPTER 3
MILTON'S BOX
Dennis Port, Massachusetts – 1979

The predawn sky was touched with grey and orange along the horizon as night surrendered to the oncoming day. Tiny sparkling droplets of dew covered the white and weathered sign. Upon its dewy face, black painted letters spelled out the words *"Welcome to the Dennis Port."*

The sign was visible to all who traveled down Cape Cod's East Main Street. A traditional Cape Cod house was located just beyond the sign. It was only a stone's throw away from the corner of Sea Street and Center Street. To those driving past, nothing about the house seemed unusual. No one would think it a special place, yet the walls of the Cape Cod house hid a decades' old mystery.

As one moved into the house, one would find a cardboard box sitting stubbornly on the bottom step of the staircase to the attic. It was coated with a layer of dust. Written in magic marker along the side of the cardboard box was the name, "*Milton.*"

Up the hall, in the back bedroom, a woman slept soundly. Hair, long and white, was splayed out over her pillow, and her face, soft and friendly, was lined with wrinkles noticeable even in sleep. A lightweight quilted blanket covered her body. Marjorie Weatherbourne, around seventy years old, was lucid and young at heart. She was the sort of woman most people would mistake to be simple and naïve. Little did they know Marjorie was filled with years of wisdom, gathered from a long life full of experiences.

In the garden beds beneath the windows, one could hear the persistent chirping of crickets. Early in the morning, the sound would fade down to nothing, only to be replaced by the insect life of day. The buzz of June bugs fluttering around the outside light couldn't be heard on this particular morning. Instead, the sound of chirping crickets gave way to a moment of eerie silence. It was the kind of silence that had an undertone of something sinister lurking within.

Mrs. Weatherbourne woke to the distinct crash of steel trash cans. It's a ruckus that sends her cat Seymour scurrying off the bed and out of the room, the hairs on his furry body standing on end, right down to his bristly puffed-up tail. Mrs. Weatherbourne switched the lamp on and climbed out of bed, stepping into her slippers. She retrieved her robe and wrapped it around herself, fastening the strap while walking down the hall toward the kitchen.

It was the best window to get a view of the trash cans in her yard.

Had it been any earlier in the evening, Mrs. Weatherbourne might have missed the silhouette creeping across the open yard. As it was, however, she could make out the shadowed form beneath the orange glow of the streetlights. The cold hands of fear grasped her heart and she reached for the doorknob. She twisted it as softly as she could, concerned that she might alert the stranger in the yard to her presence. The fact that the doorknob didn't give offered her a sense of relief.

The shadow seemed to be fading further away, disappearing into the grey of the early morning and out of her line of sight. A chill coursed through her body at the idea that someone may have been watching her and she tried to shake off the sensation. There was no guarantee that that was the case. For all she knew, the early morning tiredness had her feeling paranoid. In the distance, she could see one of the trash can lids lying on the ground. It was probably what woke her. It could have been anything. Perhaps it was a raccoon. Mrs. Weatherbourne tried to ease the discomfort growing inside her, swelling like a balloon, by telling herself that there was nothing to worry about.

Just then, Mrs. Weatherbourne's ears perked up as she heard the unmistakable sound of a car start up. The skid as the car sped away echoed through her ears. Still, she tried to calm her mind, repeating reassuring thoughts to herself.

It's June and neither a raccoon in the trash nor a hurried departure is unusual this time of the year.

When she turned around, Mrs. Weatherbourne was

greeted by her cat Seymour, sitting patiently on the floor. He looked up at her expectantly, as if waiting for some kind of explanation as to what was going on. If not that, some filling up would have to do. Mrs. Weatherbourne placed her hands on her hips, looking sternly at her cat.

"I see the commotion outside didn't stop you from wanting some food," there was a morning rasp to her voice.

"*Meow,*" Seymour gave a lick of his lips and Mrs. Weatherbourne recognized the hungry stare in his eyes.

Smiling, the elderly woman turned to one of the cupboards and grabbed the container of cat food. She poured some of it into the empty bowl on the floor and watched as her cat began lapping at the contents of the bowl. While Seymour ate, Mrs. Weatherbourne caressed her cat's spine with an open palm.

"What would I do without you?" She whispered.

The cat brought a sense of ease and comfort to the elderly woman. He was a welcomed companion, particularly in times when Mrs. Weatherbourne was socially aloof, which was most of the time. She was a generally lonely woman and without the cat, it might have driven her insane. As it was, he spent the better part of his life by her side, a solemn and considerate companion. Throughout her daily activities, he was there. If Mrs. Weatherbourne so much as sat on the porch with a book and a hot cup of tea, he was there to keep her company. Were it not for Seymour, Mrs. Weatherbourne would be left with an overbearing number of thoughts to sift through on a daily basis.

"Here I am chasing shadows," Mrs. Weatherbourne said to Seymour. "Do you know what Milton would say? *Go back to bed! Everything is fine, my dear!*"

The cat was the only one she could share the remembrance of Milton with and, purring, the cat seemed to like it when she did. Once the name fell off her lips, Mrs. Weatherbourne turned away from Seymour and made her way into the living room. From there, she could see the dusty cardboard box sitting on at the base of the staircase to the attic. It was Milton's box. There were a number of his boxes scattered throughout the dusty attic, but this was the only one she was able to retrieve on her own.

Mrs. Weatherbourne glanced back at the cat. He was still gobbling up his food, teeth crunching as he worked his way through the dry kibble. "Well, Seymour," she murmured. "There's no sense in going back to bed now. How about we see what's in this here box?"

Moving across the room and toward the box, the woman moved with a gracefulness not commonly associated with a woman of her age. She picked the box up and moved into the living room with it. There, she pulled open the flaps to peek inside, her heart racing.

At first glance, Mrs. Weatherbourne could already tell this particular box was one of the older ones. She was greeted with a pile of black and white photographs, mixed with letters so old the envelopes had yellowed. The anticipation and anxiety faded away as she went through the box's contents. A delighted smile played at the corners of her mouth and the crow's feet around her eyes as she realized she knew these letters well. They were the same ones she'd written to Milton while he was away in the Navy.

My Milton, she thought. *You saved all my letters.*

As if he could tell she was going through the box, Seymour approached Mrs. Weatherbourne. He brushed his furry body up against her leg, mewling for attention. Mrs. Weatherbourne responded to his request by reaching down to gently stroke the cat's head, massaging the spot she knew he liked most, right behind the ears. The furry creature began purring loudly.

"I know how you feel," Mrs. Weatherbourne sighed. "I miss him too."

It had only been five months since Milton passed away and the Cape Cod house seemed to carry the echo of his presence, engraved into the foundations of it. The house hadn't quite returned to its normalcy, and Mrs. Weatherbourne thought that it may never do so. She and Seymour still saw the shadow of Milton; there were times where they would see him in the living room where he enjoyed reading the morning paper, other times they'd spot him in his study where he used to enjoy a glass of whiskey in the evenings, and sometimes they'd spot him in the kitchen as though nothing had changed.

Of course, *everything* had changed. Mrs. Weatherbourne didn't think much of her life without his presence. Any life she'd ever thought of living had always been associated with Milton. They'd spent a lifetime together and neither of them had ever considered the possibility that they might finish that journey apart from one another. It wasn't a part of the plan. Then again, did anyone ever plan for that?

Thankfully, Seymour was always around. He did what he could to help. Cats had a way of sensing a change in mood and at such times, they seemed to know what to do to help make one feel better. In Mrs. Weatherbourne's case, Seymour gave her something to take care of. With this sense of responsibility, she couldn't wallow in sadness and self-pity. She was forced to get out of bed each day, if only to fill his food and water bowls up. It didn't hurt that the purring noises he emitted each time she scratched that special spot behind his ear brought a lightness to her chest and a smile to her mouth.

Seymour was the man of the house now that Milton was gone. It was kind of ironic, really. Milton was the one who'd brought Seymour home when he was a mere kitten. Several years earlier, Milton had been on his way home. He'd gone out to drop off an old lawnmower – the son of an old friend planned to use it to make some extra cash over the summer. It was as he was driving past Seymour Pond that Milton spotted a handmade sign on the side of the road that read, "*Free Kittens.*"

Well, how does one ignore a sign that offers free kittens? Milton certainly couldn't, especially considering he'd spotted the sign at Seymour Pond. As far as he was concerned, it was fate. He took the very next right turn and followed the road that would surely lead him to the free kittens.

Seymour Pond was a significant location for Milton and Marjorie Weatherbourne. Many years before, they'd discovered the beautiful location while exploring the backroads of the area. They'd found the place right in time to witness one of the most beautiful sunsets they'd ever had the pleasure of witnessing and that was when they decided they were going to do their best to make sure they saw more of them. It became a regular spot for picnics. Marjorie loved picnics to such an extent that she even owned an authentic picnic basket, complete with separate compartments for silverware, porcelain crockery, a corkscrew, and wine glass holders. Needless to say, making Seymour Pond their picnic location marked the start of what would be a special place for many years to come.

The last time the couple had a picnic at Seymour Pond, Marjorie had suggested they get a cat. They'd had a dog for many years, but as all creatures must, their dog grew old. When he was too weak and frail to handle life without pain, they made the tough decision to euthanize him. It was best for the dog that they said goodbye. Still, the couple missed having a pet to care for and love. Marjorie was certain a cat would bring joy into their lives.

Milton spotted the *Free Kittens* sign only months later and so, he simply had to stop for them.

Milton had been a man who believed destiny led him. In his eyes, there was a predetermined path that everyone followed. His had brought him good fortune in the past and, regardless of the risk, he'd become a man that jumped into each decision without giving it much thought. In his mind, he believed the decisions had already been made for him, somewhere deep within his subconscious. Strangers believed the man was guided by intuition and intuition alone.

It quickly became clear to Mrs. Weatherbourne that she

would have to sit to sort through Milton's cardboard box. It was going to take some time and standing wouldn't be good for her back. She set the box down in front of her favorite armchair and made her way back toward the kitchen to prepare the kettle for some tea, Seymour hot on her heels.

The cat was delighted by the attention Mrs. Weatherbourne gave him and the verbal banter brought him joy too, if the vibrations rumbling through his belly were anything to go by.

"Oh, Seymour," she sighed as she poured hot water into her mug. "It's been so many years now. Perhaps this was why you came into our lives after all. My Milton might have been right about fate, you know."

If not for that fateful day, Mrs. Weatherbourne would be all alone. Seymour gave a mewl as if to say they needn't worry about what would have happened if Milton hadn't picked the kitten up. He was there. That was all that mattered now.

With her tea and a biscuit, Mrs. Weatherbourne returned to the living room. She settled into the armchair and retrieved a handful of letters and photographs from the top of the box, sorting through them as she went. One by one, several small piles began to form on the surface of the coffee table. Mrs. Weatherbourne sorted them by the year they were postmarked, quietly busying herself. She smiled as Seymour hopped onto the armchair and curled up into a ball beside her leg while she stacked the piles neatly, continuing to sift through the layers and layers of photographs and letters.

By the time the elderly lady reached the end of her first cup of tea, she had made a great deal of progress. The coffee table before her was laden with the sorted memories of Milton's past. The smile had all but faded and Mrs. Weatherbourne felt her chest tighten as she looked over the piles on the table. How could it be that a person was reduced to a collection of mementos like this one? The thought made its way to the surface of her mind before she could stop it and she couldn't hold back the tears that threatened to spill over the waterline of her eyes. She considered swiping the hot, salty moisture away but ended up giving in to her emotions and letting them flow down her worn cheeks.

Though she was crying, she continued to go through the memories of the late Milton. She reached into the bottom of the box and pulled back yet another layer of photographs. Mrs. Weatherbourne had taken out the majority of the letters, but she spotted one more at the very bottom of the box. It was a rather old, folded letter and, unlike the others, it was not in an envelope. The edges of the letter were worn and moisture-damaged, causing the ink to bleed. She wondered if it was still legible and, captivated, she put the photographs down on the table and tugged it out so that she could take a closer look.

Mrs. Weatherbourne slipped her reading glasses on and cautiously unfolded the letter, glad to see that she was indeed able to read it.

> Dear Commander Weatherbourne,
>
> I leave behind the love of my daughter and

an incomplete promise...

It only took the first few lines before Mrs. Weatherbourne had to stop. She set the letter down on the table and grabbed a tissue instead. The tears flowed freely. "All these years," Mrs. Weatherbourne sniffled. "And I've never seen this letter before..."

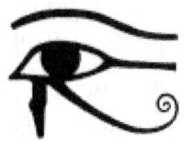

CHAPTER 4
WILL

The grey of the partly cloudy morning gave way to brilliant rays of oranges, pinks, and purples as the sun broke through the early morning clouds. It rose and began to break through the day in the same way all the early risers did, stretching their limbs out until they let out that satisfying sigh of wakefulness. Once they got out of the house, they'd shine as proudly as the sun did over Dennis Port.

Found on the corner of Sea Street and Mill Road, the McMurphy home was vintage in style. Its two-story stature dated back to the early 1900s and the creaking wood of those halls, resembling the joints of the elderly, showed its age. The foundations of the house were strong – they don't make them like they did in those days, people would always say – but that didn't change the fact that it was rickety and rusty and brittle in other places.

One such place was the double-hung window on the second floor. It was kept open to let in the fresh sea breeze from the ocean, wobbly and rickety all at once. The room belonged to a young boy named Will. At that point in time, the boy was sleeping peacefully. As with most kids, he had an innocence to his features that almost always only revealed itself in sleep. He wore an expression of soft contentment, visible only at the corners of his mouth as they threatened to flourish into a full-blown smile.

With the break of dawn came the noise. It happened out of nowhere. A peaceful morning had suddenly turned into a cacophony of noise as the room erupted with the sound of various alarm clocks. The ear-piercing sound of a digital alarm, combined with an assortment of ringing bells and vibrating buzzing, was loud and painful. It would have been enough to bring the dead back to life.

Will sprung out of bed with the kind of energy that only a kid could maintain. His feet hit the wooden floorboards with a thud and raced toward the open window. The sight before him brought about that full-blown smile. The boy was excited for the tarmac before him, the sidewalks and even the grass in their yard were dry. The rain that plagued the little port had finally come to an end and, still moving ever higher into the sky, the sun shone down brightly.

The only priority Will had in mind was playing. When it rained, he couldn't do that. This was a good day to play.

Thump, thump, thump...

The sound echoed through the wood and into his

room, barely audible over all the alarm clocks. Will already knew what the cause was and hurried to turn off all the alarms. The thumping didn't stop while he did his work. It was only once the last alarm had been turned off that the wood fell as silent as his room and he could breathe a sigh of relief. His sister's room was right next door to his.

"I'm sorry, Beth!" Will called out.

There was no response, but that was as good as any. The thumping had stopped, after all. Will could picture his sister rolling her eyes and turning over to go back to sleep. He, on the other hand, had other plans. They didn't involve staying in bed for a single second longer. He hastily got dressed, put a worn baseball cap on his head, and raced to the stairs.

The boy was eager to start his day. It wasn't every day he set various alarm clocks up to ring at the same early hour of the morning. Today, however, was a rather special day for him. Since school ended and the summer holidays began, this was the first day without rain. That meant it was the first day he could finally meet with his friends Isaac and Dez. They had a special treehouse where they would hang out. It had been rather inaccessible with the sky pouring down on them each day since the start of summer.

"Will!" Beth's voice rung out from her bedroom door and Will could hear the agitation in it. "I'm telling mom you woke me with all those alarm clocks!"

For a moment, Will made no movement. He simply listened to the house, paused on the top step of the staircase, but all was quiet downstairs. With a sigh of relief, he realized his mother hadn't heard either the alarms or his sister. If Will's mother had been awake downstairs, she would have surely yelled up the stairs when she heard the alarms, but that was not the case.

If it had been, Will's pleasant day would have come to an end before it had even begun.

The old house creaked and breathed as the boy made his way down the stairs. The walls were covered with wallpaper older than he was, perhaps older than his parents were, and the yellowed edges exposed plaster and wood lath here and there. These intermittent areas needed to be patched, as established by the endless to-do list his father carried. On his way, Will passed through a few empty rooms that his parents were in the process of remodeling. The old house was partially updated. It was his mother's idea to purchase and remodel an old house.

Will's mother was a second-generation Italian woman and, as such, she had distinct taste and a particular way of making choices. She'd grown up in an old house in Cambridge. The moment the couple saw this particular house, an old house on the corner of Sea Street and Mill Road, she picked it immediately. It reminded her of her childhood home and, upon telling her husband what she wanted, he made it happen. Her wish to remodel the home slowly came to fruition.

Mr. McMurphy, Will's father, was a second-generation Irish man. For the most part, he led a fairly simple life. He worked full-time at the local Post Office and his salary was sufficient enough to meet the family's needs, granting a tweak in the expenses here and there. If it were up to him, he would have left the house the way it was when he first arrived. The only reason he put in all the hard work — and the funds for that matter — is for the sake of his beloved wife. Otherwise, he was most certainly not pleased with the great deal of work the house required of him.

Remodeling and renovating a home came with an enormous amount of stress, in more than one way. In the case of Will's father, everything about the home had worn down his patience. He considered it more of a burden than anything else, made worse by the hard labor and the financial strain it put on him.

This attitude brought about many a disruption in the home of the McMurphy's. The burden of the house became an immense pressure that Will's father carried on his shoulders every day. He grew grumpy and angry, moods not as easily eased by his new habit of drinking as he would like to think. The alcohol brought about an atmosphere of unease and discomfort. Will's father had a mood that would make anyone in the house want to leave it and so, with the end of the rain upon them, Will was all-too-excited for the chance to finally escape its creaking hallways.

A sadness came over Will as he walked through the living room. The TV was still on from the previous night, the only light source in a room where the curtains were closed, as though that could mask the shame of last night's binge drinking session. There were several small bottles on the floor and Will recognized them as the vodka bottles his father referred to as *nips*. Hurriedly, Will switched the TV off and collected the bottles from around the room. He didn't want his mother and sister seeing them, so he buried them beneath the other items in the trash can. This was routine. Will had gotten used to it, but that didn't make things any better than they were.

The kitchen was one of the first rooms to be completely remodeled and as such, it was the prettiest room in the house, complete with modern finishes that matched the overall vintage feel of the house. Will felt his belly grumble the moment he walked into the room. He hadn't eaten much the previous evening and he was in dire need of sustenance. He retrieved a box of cereal, milk, a bowl, and a spoon. Without further ado, he prepared breakfast for himself.

Will barely had a moment to look up from his food at the sound of footsteps approaching from outside. His mother opened the screen door off the kitchen and walked in with a beautiful smile on her face. "Good morning, Will," she said warmly, brushing her hand lovingly across his shoulder.

Will had been in the process of taking in a rather large spoonful of cereal and mumbled back an embarrassed, "Morning, Mom," over a mouthful of food.

His mother didn't seem to notice. From a paper bag, she pulled out a package of chocolate chip muffins. Once he was finished chewing and swallowing his mouthful, a grin broke out across Will's face. They were his favorite. As he watched, his mother opened the package, cut one of the muffins in half, and popped it into the toaster oven. She waited with her hands neatly folded as Will continued munching on his cereal.

When the toaster dinged, Will's mother buttered both

halves, set them on a dish, and placed them on the table in front of Will. With a smile, she asked, "What do you say?"

"Thank you, Mom!" Will responded without hesitation.

At that moment, Will and his mother were joined by Beth. "Mom," she began sternly, without so much as a greeting. "Will…"

Knowing what was about to happen, Will interrupted her. "Good morning, little sis. Would you like me to make you a chocolate chip muffin?" He raised his eyebrows pointedly as if to dare her to continue with her complaint.

Beth paused for a moment and looked at Will, tilting her head slightly. "Yes," she nodded, turning back to their mother. "Will woke me up with the sound of a hundred alarm clocks!"

"Will," their mother said, already preparing a second muffin for Beth. "That was not very nice, was it?"

Will was staring at his sister, his mouth agape. He hadn't expected her to tattle after the offer of a muffin. He wouldn't have. "*Oh my God, I offer to make her a muffin and she still throws me under the bus,*" he mumbled in an attempt to pacify the situation. "Ugh."

"Okay, that's enough," their mother snaps. "Apologize to your sister. Now."

"Fine," Will responded, looking at his sister unapologetically. "I'm sorry!"

The look on his face didn't matter to Beth. He'd gotten in trouble and that was all she could have hoped for. With a smile, she took her plate with its freshly heated and buttered muffin and made her way back to the comfort of her room. Will didn't miss the satisfaction written on her face.

"What are your plans for the day?" Will's mother asked, looking back at him.

Of course, Will knew exactly what he had planned for the day, but his mouth was full. Thinking about his plans brought a faint smile to his face. He'd been cooped up indoors for three days, one of which included his birthday, and it was finally his time to have some fun outside in the sun.

"Are you going to see Isaac and Dez?" His mom asked when he didn't respond.

Will nodded his head as he chewed the last bite of his chocolate chip muffin.

"Good," Will's mother clapped her hands. "I need you boys to do me a favor. Mrs. Weatherbourne asked if I could send you over to help move some boxes out of her attic."

Free of food, Will's mouth dropped open in surprise. The last thing he wanted to do was spend his day helping Mrs. Weatherbourne. He was supposed to be having a *fun* day.

"Don't you look at me like that, Will," his mother wiggled her index finger sternly. "You and Isaac have helped her out before and she is always very grateful for it. It will be good for the three of you to do something nice for someone in need." She paused. "Besides, you know she lost her husband last winter."

His mom sat down on a chair in front of him and waited for him to give in. The only problem was that Will didn't actually mind helping Mrs. Weatherbourne at all. In fact, he would have done it happily if his mother had asked him on any other day. He simply didn't expect to have to do it today. In the past, he and Isaac had completed a few favors for the Weatherbournes. They made a bit of money shoveling snow in the winter and raking leaves in the fall.

That was when the thought started to settle and it occurred to him that this could actually work out for him and his friends. They could all stand to earn a few bucks, money they could use at Davenports, the local Five and Dime store.

He stood to put his dishes in the sink and looked over at his mother. "Okay, Mom. We'll stop over and help. Don't worry about it."

Will was rewarded with a smile and a hug as his mother pulled him into her arms. "I can't believe you're already thirteen. You're growing up so fast."

Smiling, Will surrendered to his mom's hug. As much as he complained, he secretly enjoyed his mother's warmth. "I know, I know," he muttered. "I better get going, Mom. I don't want to be late."

"Okay," his mom released him. As he left, she added a quick, "I love you!"

"Love you too, Mom!" Will called as he walked away, heading back up the stairs.

He had a few things to grab before he headed out. Will didn't even need to call on Isaac to know that his friend would have the same thing on his mind. With the sun out, all three boys would gravitate toward their official hangout.

Dez lived one street over, on Center Street. His house was situated right beside a wooded area and it was the perfect place for the boys to find a retreat. Over the previous summer, the three of them got together and built the coolest treehouse they had ever laid eyes on. It took most of the summer and they'd had to borrow tools and equipment from all of their parents, but it was well worth it. The place was special and it offered them an escape that was theirs and theirs alone. That was why it became their official hangout.

Since Dez lived so close to the treehouse, they ran an extension cord from his main house across the yard and into the treehouse, with permission, of course. This meant that their treehouse was equipped with a light, a radio, and a fan for when the temperatures got too high in Dennis Port. It couldn't get any better.

In no time, Will was ready to go. The side door of the old house led onto a covered patio and it was there that he picked up his bike. Hopping on, he barely remembered to yell out a quick goodbye as he rode away from home.

"Be back later!" He called out, hoping someone had heard him.

Will peddled up Sea Street. As per its name, this was the road one would take if they wanted to find the local beaches. With the weather being as miserable as it had for the past few days, Will knew that there would be a few people flocking down to the sandy shores to bask in the warm sun. The beach side was on his left and on his right, Will rode passed Mrs. Weatherbourne's house. He knew these roads well, he had grown up riding his bicycle on them, and he swerved right onto Center Street not too long after passing Mrs. Weatherbourne's house.

Dez lived a mere six houses down Center Street. His house was on the left side of the street, a relatively old one-story and sporting black shutters on each side of the front windows.

Meanwhile, Isaac lived three streets to the east on Depot Road.

For the boys, Dennis Port was an adventure waiting to happen in and of itself. There were plenty of things for three boys on bicycles to get into, especially if they had a few bucks in their pockets. They had beaches, the town square, a fair share of local stores, and the Best Ice-Cream Shoppe on all of Cape Cod.

What more could they possibly wish for?

CHAPTER 5
ISAAC

In the Goffman home, the phone had hardly begun to ring when Isaac raced down the hallway to answer it, his stomps causing dust to spring upward from the old carpet. He'd been anticipating a phone call all morning – or at the very least, he'd been hoping he might receive one. The phone came off the hook with a loud click and Isaac, in his hurry, nearly dropped it. Thankfully, he caught hold of the cord and pressed the phone to his ear.

Isaac responded to the caller with plain one-word replies. "Yup," he said. "Okay. No."

His mother watched on with a smirk on her face, one that spoke of knowing. There was no doubt that she knew who her son was talking to. She couldn't help but think her son adorable as he continued with his cryptic conversation.

"Yes," Isaac continued. "Soon. Bye." The call ended abruptly and Isaac hung up the phone. He turned to look at his mother. "I just spoke with Dez and we are meeting at his house. I need to leave as soon as possible."

Isaac was an only child. His father was a self-employed accountant at his own firm, Goffman Accounting Services, and he had an office located right beside the family home. It had once been a garage, but the family had had it converted for the purposes of his father's business. His mother, Anne, was a housewife who spent the better part of her time caring for the family's needs. She was a quiet and orderly woman and a loving mother to a fault. That fault was that she was often overprotective of her son, but who could blame her when he was her only child? Though she disapproved of some of his adventures with his best friends Will and Dez, Anne wouldn't stop them from having their fun, so long as she was assured no one would get hurt.

Though she was a stay-at-home mom, Isaac's mother occasionally did volunteer work at the local library. As a result, the hallways of the house were often littered with piles of books. Isaac's mother enjoyed bringing her *work* home with her, particularly if she couldn't make the trek into town. The library was near the town square, off Main Street. The dismal weather of the last little while made it impossible to visit. How could she take books back to their rightful home when it was raining? Books were not meant to get wet, after all. Isaac had a feeling that his mother secretly enjoyed the rain, for she could curl up in an armchair with a book and make an excuse about taking it back. The pitter-patter of rain against the rooftops made for a relaxing ambient sound as one lost themselves to the pages of a book.

Isaac rushed to ready himself for the day ahead. Once he was dressed, he spent some time looking at his reflection and, using his hands, did the best job he could of straightening his rich brown hair. He knew it wouldn't stay neat for long, as his hair never did, but at least he could say he tried. Satisfied with his work, he headed into the kitchen, where his mother was already waiting for him.

"Good morning, young man," she greeted him as if he hadn't just been on the phone with his friend. "I made you some breakfast."

A plate of pancakes topped with sliced bananas waited for Isaac, but he was eager to leave. It was the first week of summer and none of the boys wanted to miss a second of it. As far as they were concerned, the rain had already kept them from too much. They were excited to get on with it. Isaac, however, knew that his mother wouldn't allow him to leave until he'd eaten and so he began to gobble the food.

"Thank you, Mom," he mumbled as he gulped down mouthfuls of pancakes, sitting at the table.

"Did you wash your hands first?" She asked.

"Yes," he nodded.

"What about your teeth?" His mother continued. "Did you brush them?"

Isaac had never understood the concept of brushing one's teeth *before* the meal, but he nodded his head nonetheless. "Yes."

"And did you plan on chewing your food or was it always your intention to swallow it whole?" She raised her eyebrows.

Isaac grinned sheepishly, knowing the question was rhetorical. He'd been so eager to get out of the house and play with his friends that he must have eaten the entire plate of pancakes in only three bites, if not less. His cheeks had the gentle, warm flush of embarrassment to them.

"I'll stay out of trouble."

Once he was finally ready to leave the house, he gave his mother a tight hug. He was well aware of the fact that his mother was protective and that she worried about him. He couldn't blame her because he was also well aware that his mother had lost her family at a young age and her concern was rooted in her from her childhood.

As he turned away from his mother, setting his eyes on the door, it seemed he hadn't yet heard the end of it.

"Wait a minute," his mother's voice rang out.

Ugh, he thought. *Here come the words of a slow and sure death.*

Isaac plastered a smile onto his face in the hopes that he could hide the concern that his mother was about to delay his departure. He turned back to his mother to find out what it was that he was waiting for. He couldn't stand to know what the full brunt of this delay might mean. His day was already perfectly planned out and all he wanted was to do was get on with it already.

"*Here it comes,*" he mumbled to himself, quiet enough that his mother wouldn't hear him. It was all Isaac could do not to scream in agony as he looked upon his mother's face, anxious to know what was in store for him.

His mother reached into a basket of papers on the counter and retrieved a business card. As she handed it over to her son, he read the name, "*Chatham Jewish Center.*"

"I need you to stop by Mrs. Weatherbourne's house today. Drop this off. She told me she wants to donate some of her husband's old items."

"No problem," Isaac nodded, unable to stop the smile from coming to his lips. "I will."

He was rewarded with a smile and he took it as permission to leave. This time, his mother didn't stop him when he walked toward the door. Relief washed over him as he finally stepped outside into the warm summer air.

Phew. That wasn't so bad.

CHAPTER 6
DEZ

Will pulled into Dez' driveway and came to a skidding stop. A few months earlier, Will and his friends would have simply allowed his bicycle to drop to the ground with a clatter and run off to play, but Dez' grandmother had asked that the boys remove their bikes from the driveway. That way, they wouldn't get damaged, and they would be out of the way if anyone needed to get in or out of the garage. Will rolled the bike up to the maple tree beside the garage and propped it up.

Walking up the wooden steps of Dez' porch, he could hardly contain his excitement and he knew anyone who looked his way would recognize the grin on his face. Once he'd reached the side door, he rang the doorbell. Inside, Will heard the pitchy barking of the Pomeranian. There was a distinct rumbling from the people within the house, a mixture of movement toward the door and the shushing of the dog's persistent barking.

The longer he waited, the more Will's anxiety grew. He was concerned that all the noise might have woken Dez' ill mother. That was the last thing he wanted to do. Peeking through the window, he could see the Pomeranian running and jumping at the door like a wild animal. Why was it always the small dogs that made such a big fuss?

Cocoa, the Pomeranian, belonged to Dez' grandmother and accompanied her everywhere she went, as a constant companion. "Cocoa, stop!"

Moments after she'd told her dog off, Dez' grandmother, Ruth, opened the door. "Come in, Will," she smiled at him. Grandma Ruth was a warm and soft-spoken woman. "Cocoa, calm down. It's only Will. You remember Will."

Will held his hand out for Cocoa and she stopped barking to take a sniff of his offering. She had a liking for Will, which was apparently rare. Will didn't understand why a family would keep a dog if it didn't like anyone else, but he didn't complain and he didn't ask questions. Cocoa licked his hand and Will smiled, petting the small dog's fluffy head.

"Hey Will-bo," Emilio Fernandez or Dez for short, walked into the kitchen with a grin as big as Will's on his face. The boy was taller and chunkier than most boys his age, but he had an infectious sense of humor. He greeted his friend with a high-five. "What's up?"

"Hey Dez," Will stood up straight to return the high-five.

"Isaac just called," Dez grinned even wider than before.

Dez was of Portuguese descent and he had deep brown skin, while his hair was thick and black, right down to the bushy eyebrows on his face. The hair on his head was still wet from a shower but was neatly combed to one side. His usual attire hadn't changed over the last few days, rain and all, and he wore an alligator shirt a tiny bit too small, along with a pair of beige cargo pants. The only reason he wore them all the time was that they were packed with pockets upon pockets. Will could tell he was ready for the day's adventures.

"Dude," he continued cheerfully. "The boys are back in town!"

From another room, they heard a faint, crackling voice calling out. "Emilio!"

Grandma Ruth, who'd been watching the boys interact, turned to her grandson. "Go see what your mother wants, Emilio."

Will didn't miss the change in his friend's expression, which had shifted from cheerful and excited to somber and worried. As selfish as it was, neither of the boys wanted anything to spoil the fun day they had planned ahead.

"I'll be right back," Dez murmured.

Will nodded his head. He knew what it was. The voice that called him spoke for itself, weaker and huskier than usual. Dez' mother, Silvia, had been sick for some time now. Over Thanksgiving the previous year, she'd been diagnosed with some form of cancer. Will wasn't privy to the details, but he knew that the Fernandez family had spent the better part of the holidays in the hospital. His friend didn't speak about it much, but Will knew that his mother had been bedridden ever since. Dez' father was killed in the Vietnam War when he was only three years old – Grandma Ruth and his mother was all he had left.

Each of the three boys carried a dark secret with them, each one pertaining to the things going on at home. They didn't share their troubles with anyone but each other. After all, how could they? What would they say? Who would possibly understand them? They were only kids. Their bond of friendship was tied as tightly as it was due to the fact that they were the only ones who understood one another and the things they were going through. They found comfort in that.

In Will's case, he felt as though he could speak to no one else. His friends Dez and Isaac were the only ones who seemed to understand him. As such, they were the ones he shared his concerns with. If he didn't have them, he would have had no one else to share the concerns about his father's excessive drinking. They were the only ones who knew that his father's habits grew more frightening as time passed. Sometimes his rage even got physical.

Isaac, on the other hand, expressed anxiety. There was more to his and his mother's relationship than mere overprotectiveness. The older he got, the more he came to terms with the fact that his mother was deeply sad and he couldn't help but wonder if he was responsible for her brokenness.

Both Will and Isaac knew that they could never compare to the horrible things happening to their friend

Dez. They hadn't seen Silvia in a long time. These days, she was nothing more than a voice that occasionally called out from a back room. Gone were the days where she served them fresh lemonade and bifanas, traditional Portuguese sandwiches. Dez' mother was dying and he refused to talk about it, but they could see the pain of it in every smile and laugh. As much as he joked around, his friends could tell that he was suffering and they couldn't imagine anything worse.

A few moments later, Dez returned to the kitchen with a small stack of comic books in his hands. "Are you ready?"

Will nodded and, after saying goodbye to Grandma Ruth, they headed outside. Cocoa barked at them on their way out. As much as the dog had complained about Will's arrival, the Pomeranian didn't want them to leave. She was rather enjoying the company and it didn't hurt that Will always gave her attention – even if it was simply so she would stop barking at him. They ignored Cocoa and, once they were out of earshot, heard her eventually stop barking for them to return. The first stop was the garage. There, Dez dropped his stack of comic books onto a makeshift workbench.

"Dude," Dez whispered. His voice was filled with the hush of excitement. "Check it out. I got the last edition of Howard the Duck, Number Thirty-one and…" Dez paused for effect, tugging one specific comic book out of the pile, slow enough that Will couldn't see what it was until Dez was ready to reveal it. "The last Human Fly, Number Nineteen."

"Wow!" Will's eyes widened at the sight of the cover.

"That's awesome. These are totally collectibles." He reached for the stack, knowing far less about comic books than Dez did, and pulled out the one at the bottom of the pile. He had seen Dez' collection before and he could tell this one was a new one. "What about this one?"

"Oh," Dez murmured dismissively. "That's just a reprint of Superman 1938. It's not actually worth anything."

Will set the comic down and shrugged. "I just started reading the Super Boy Series. Isaac traded all his DC Super Boys for all my Detective Comics."

Dez raised his eyebrows and the corner of his mouth lifted into a smirk. "Lame!"

Their laughter was interrupted by the unmistakable sound of a bicycle's tires skidding to a stop on Dez' driveway. The boys looked at one another with wide eyes, realizing what it must mean. They gave each other a high-five and, at the same time, yelled out Isaac's nickname.

"G-Man!" It was derived from his last name, Goffman, and it sounded really cool to the boys.

Dez shoved the stack of comic books into a backpack and passed them over to Will. "Go ahead," he inclined his head toward the door.

Grabbing the backpack, Will ran for the side door and went out to greet Isaac. Meanwhile, Dez took a moment to grab a few things from the garage. Much like Will, he had to pick up a few things before they went on their adventures too. This was almost always the case. Dez pulled out one of the step ladders and climbed it carefully. He reached for one of the various shelves so that he could grab a jelly jar full of nails. Climbing down, he'd barely stepped off of the ladder when he used his opposite hand to grab the hammer lying on one of the wooden workbenches.

"Isaac," Will greeted their friend at the door. "What took you so long?"

"Breakfast," Isaac answered. "Where's Dez?"

Dez chose that moment to walk around the corner, his face glowing with anticipation. This time, it was the good kind. "Hey bonehead," he grinned at Isaac. "What took you so long? Did your pubes get stuck in your zipper again?"

Isaac and Will snickered before Will whispered, "You better keep it down, man." He glanced over at the main house. "If Grandma Ruth hears you talking like that, we're all screwed."

Dez gave a chuckle and walked toward the back gate without another word, juggling the hammer and the jar of nails as he went. The other two boys were close behind him, but not before Isaac propped his bike up against the maple tree with Will's. They walked past an opening in the stockade fence and then they were in the grassy backyard. Will could tell he'd been right about the weather changing and the grass crunching under their feet only served to prove as much.

Along the edge of Dez' backyard was a beautiful, wooded area. It was dense with a myriad of trees including pine, oak, and maple. The treehouse was located only a few feet in, beneath the canopy of trees. It was constructed between three large pines, eight feet off of the ground. The boys had built it with the knowledge that even when they were older, the treehouse would still be taller than they were, even if it was a marginal height difference.

Despite the fact that the boys believed this to be the best treehouse in the world, it was rather shabby-looking. This was largely because the sides were made using hodge-podge scraps of wood they'd found in the garage. The roof itself wasn't made of anything solid, but of nothing more than a green tarp drabbed over the wooden framing of the treehouse and stapled securely into place.

The three gathered beneath one of the tall pine trees, below the treehouse. On this particular tree, small wooden rungs had been nailed up along the trunk to create a makeshift ladder. The boys could simply climb up the trees like a group of wild animals, but this made it easier and it was a little safer. They could only imagine what their respective guardians might say or think if they saw the boys climbing eight feet up into the trees without some kind of safety net. As it was, the ladder would take them up to the treehouse, but it was weak. Some of the wooden rungs were loose and unstable, made worse by the atrocious weather of the winter months.

As soon as they got there, Dez opened up the jelly jar and set it down on the soft ground. He reached in and took a handful of nails out. Isaac and Will could only watch. It wasn't as though there was enough room for them all to work around one tree trunk and Dez was the only one with a hammer. He began nailing additional fixes to the first few rungs, the ones that was the most unstable.

Once he was done, he stepped back to admire his

handiwork. He smiled confidently and closed the jelly jar of nails. Walking around Will, he unzipped the backpack and tossed both the hammer and jelly jar into the bag before zipping it up.

"That should do the trick."

With that, the boys each climbed the newly repaired ladder, one after the other. Each of them found that, upon reaching into the opening on the side of the treehouse, the wood on the inside was damp.

"It looks like the scrap wood took most of the water damage," Will called out as Dez was still climbing the last few steps into the treehouse.

Glancing around the inside of their hangout, they found that their comforts appeared to be intact and free of water damage. It was a miracle. Rugs covered the floor and each corner had a bean bag chair, sufficient enough for each boy to enjoy. In the center of the small room, between the chairs, sat a plastic milk crate and atop it, a lamp without a lampshade. Inside the milk crate was a stack of magazines and comic books for light reading.

One of the walls had a small square cut in the wood to make an easy window opening, one that faced the main house and gave the boys a good lookout point. From there, they could easily see anyone approaching the treehouse. Right beside the window, an old radio hung from a nail that the boys had hammered into the trunk of one of the pine trees.

It wasn't the shoddy exterior that made this treehouse the best one the boys had ever seen. It was the inside, the comfort, and the secret escape that it offered them. They could ask for nothing more or less than the ability to spend time with one another in a place no one else knew about.

Satisfied that nothing was damaged, Will turned on the small lamp in the center of the room and the treehouse lit up. He plopped down onto his bean bag chair and looked at the other boys with a smile of utter contentment. With that, he reached into the milk crate and pulled out one of the comic books.

While Will read his comic book, Isaac hesitated. He didn't sit immediately and instead, decided to conduct a bug hunt. The moment the boys entered the treehouse, he'd noticed a spider web above his spot and he knew he wouldn't be able to settle down until he'd cleared the area. Isaac wasn't the biggest fan of insects, especially spiders. He grabbed one of the comic books in the milk crate and, unlike Will, it was not with the intention of reading it. Instead, he knocked away the spider web above his bean bag chair right in time for Dez to tell him off.

"Dude!" Dez cried out. "That better not be the Penthouse."

Isaac rolled his eyes and looked back at his friend. "It's a comic, bonehead."

"Phew," Dez sighed in relief. He began digging through the pile of magazines and pulled out the beloved Penthouse before sitting back and relaxing in his own seat.

The only sound that could be heard in the treehouse for some time was the gentle flipping of pages as Will read his comic book and Dez fanned through the pages of his magazine. He stopped on the centerfold, held it open, and stared down at the model. His wide eyes and the way his mouth kept opening and closing as though he was going to say something gave away his excitement.

"Dude," Dez murmured breathlessly. "Check this out."

Will looked up from his comic book to breathe out,

"She's amazing, dude."

Isaac looked up to take a good long look at the centerfold model and when he responded, he had a smirk on his face. "In your dreams."

It was Dez' turn to roll his eyes and he did, sitting back in his chair and admiring the Penthouse models on his own.

Beside Will, there was a shoebox filled with old cassette tapes. He opened the lid and rummaged through them, naming the musicians as he went, mostly to himself more than anyone else. "Floyd… Queen… The Stones…"

He made his choice with a low grunt, took the cassette out, and placed the box back in its spot beside his seat. Will was the only one who could reach the radio without having to stand and so he was generally in charge of the music. It did help that the majority of the tapes came from his house anyway. He loaded the cassette into the player.

"Turn the volume up so my grandmother can't hear us talk," Dez chortled.

Will followed the orders and the sound of a cash register reverberated from the speaker, vibrating through the wood of the treehouse. A steady beat started and all at once, the three boys began singing along with the song. They knew these songs well.

"Money… Get away."

"Get a good job with good pay and you're okay…"

The moment they realized they were all singing in synchronization with the lyrics, humming to the beat, they met one another's eyes from their respective chairs and burst into laughter. In this moment, with one another, they were as happy as ever. They were in their favorite spot with their favorite people. This was what the treehouse was all about. Their eagerness to leave their not-so-ideal home life was made better by the chance to escape their reality. Nothing and nowhere else gave them that chance.

"Speaking of money," Will started, looking at the other two boys. "I kind of made a deal with my mom. If you guys are up for it, I figured all we have to do is go help Mrs. Weatherbourne, earn some cash, and hit the store."

"What kind of help, dude?" Dez raised his eyebrows. All he ever did was help out around the house these days.

"She just wants us to move some old boxes from her attic. Apparently, they belonged to Mr. Weatherbourne."

"Oh, hey," Isaac joined, remembering his own morning. "That reminds me. I was supposed to give Mrs. Weatherbourne a business card from my mom."

"All right," Will smiled. "So, we're going over there anyway."

The other two nodded in agreement. They'd head to Mrs. Weatherbourne's house in a few hours.

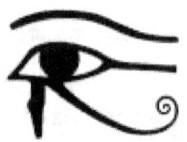

CHAPTER 7
THE WEATHERBOURNE'S

Milton Weatherbourne grew up in New Bedford, Massachusetts. His family was not a wealthy one. In fact, he and his two younger sisters grew up in poverty, living in a modest basement apartment of a two-story brownstone.

After World War I, Milton's father settled into the fishing industry of New Bedford. It was a tough job, but one that allowed him to provide the basics for his family. No one would say he brought home the bacon, but he certainly kept a roof over the heads of his children. He was a veteran of World War I, carrying scars both on the inside and the outside. They were jagged cracks that he struggled to hide and he went through his days wondering why it was necessary for him to do so.

Milton's mother was a Portuguese woman who'd been raised as a strong woman by her equally strong single mother. Those weren't the only footsteps she followed either. Like her mother before her, Milton's mother worked as a baker at a local deli. It was a job that provided a steady supply of Portuguese sweet bread – often the leftovers that had failed to sell for two days or more – and discounted linguica sausage.

The Great Depression had taken a heavy toll on Milton's parents and due to it, Milton quickly learned the lesson of a hard day's work. Before most kids his age, his father had him working as a deck boy on a contracted fishing boat. It was one of the few that managed to do well during the depression. It was hard work and there wasn't much in the way of payment, but Milton couldn't complain. He knew it was more than most people got in these tough times. One of the benefits of being a hand on a fishing boat was that they always had food on the table.

The other men on the boat had a saying and they lived by it; "You make your own way or you die trying."

Milton carried the pains, hard work, and happiness of his childhood everywhere he went. He was a decent man, though he often appeared staunch and unapproachable to those who did not know him. The man knew what a day's work meant and he never once shied away from the challenges of the time he lived in. It made him a hardened man, albeit a hardworking one.

If there was one person with the ability to open up his closed off and hardened heart, it would be his first and only love, Marjorie Wilson. The two met outside a Captain's

Ball held in the banquet room of the Red Inn on Commercial Street. The ball was one of the most prestigious events that week, though there were many that took place during the annual blessing of the fleet in Provincetown, a big fishing community located at the very tip of Cape Cod's hook-shaped peninsula landmass. The blessing of the fleet was the most celebrated ceremony to fisherman for miles around.

At the young age of twenty-two, Milton Weatherbourne was not the type to be invited to events such as the Captain's Ball. It was because of this, and this was not an uncommon occurrence, that he and his buddies instead planted themselves on the pier wall across from the venue. There, they watched the ladies in fancy dresses and the neatly uniformed men attending the ball. It was difficult for any of them to take the situation seriously.

"Oh, why thank you," Hudson, one of Milton's work friends, hopped up onto the wall and gave a deep bow. "I'm honored to be attending such a prestigious event."

"Heavens," another one, Michael, said. "You do look rather dashing in your expensive suit, Mister Hudson. Wherever did you get it? I've been meaning to get some new threads."

"Whatever do you mean?" Milton joined in, adding an extra pitch and a high accent for extra effect. Both his friends stared at him, worried that he might break their roleplay. With a grin, he stood and took a bow of his own. "You look absolutely marvelous this evening!"

The other two, surprised by his outburst, couldn't help

but burst into fits of guffaws that had them clutching their stomachs for breath. Milton laughed with them, sitting back down on the wall. He went back to watching the event as his buddies took their places on the wall.

"Wouldn't it be great if we really were invited to gigs like this?" Michael asked wistfully.

"Maybe one day, old boy," Hudson blew a kiss into the sky. He was the type of man that had big dreams and even bigger plans to make those dreams a reality. None of them involved staying in this little town.

Milton barely caught the rest of their conversation. In glancing across the street, he had caught the eye of a beautiful woman with soft features. She and a girlfriend were standing outside the big building as though they were taking it in. From where he sat, Milton thought they might have been doing the same thing he and his buddies were, dreaming of a day where they might one day be able to attend such an event, imagining what it might be like to enter the building with an invitation in their hands.

The women were taking a casual evening stroll along the brick walkway that weaved between the grassy landscapes outside the building. They had a lilt to their steps, as though they were dancing rather than walking, moving to their own music. Milton supposed they could have been dancing to actual music. He and his buddies were at a distance where no such music could be heard, but it was more than possible that the two women could hear the music of the event. They were close enough to steal a peek through the windows of the Red Inn and they turned chastely away, almost as if they were guilty about stealing glances at the elegance within. That didn't stop them from doing it one more time, giggling with one another before turning away once more.

It was after the second glance that she looked up and across the road. Perhaps it was because she felt the eyes of someone watching her or perhaps she simply wanted to gaze upon the moon as it shone down on the beach. Whatever the reason, she knew she had been caught peeping and she caught someone else peeking at her. Milton's face hid none of what he felt, the attraction that practically pulled him across the road toward her, and he gave her an inviting smile as they looked over at one another. Was it him or did she linger a little longer than necessary? Her eyes were as inviting as his smile, even as she lowered her eyes and allowed long black lashes to brush the tops of her cheekbones. With another giggle, she turned away, looking down at the bricks beneath her feet.

Milton could scarcely believe his eyes. This moment felt significant to him. He wasn't sure what it was. It could have been the setting, beautiful as it was, and it could have been the delicate laughter he could hear even from the pier. It resembled, in its own way, something from a movie. As silly as it may have been – and it certainly didn't *feel* silly – he felt as though he'd walked onto the set of a Hollywood film. The feelings going through him were things he'd only heard others speak of: the flutter of his heart and the tightening of his belly.

At that, Milton knew he couldn't ignore the strange pull any longer. This wasn't a chance he could afford to miss.

"I'll be right back," Milton suddenly murmured to his

friends. He could hardly get the words out for staring at her. "There's this... *girl*..."

Marjorie Wilson was the daughter of a Chatham lobster boat captain. Her family lived a good, sweet life in a modest house in Harwich Port. While her father led a crew on a boat, her mother helped manage the ledgers for her uncle's cranberry bog. Her parents were currently in attendance at the ball that evening and it was because of this that Marjorie could be found lingering outside the windows of the Red Inn.

Milton had never been the type of man to do this sort of thing. It was why he'd never been with another woman before. Work had always been the most important thing in his life, if only because he had no other choice than to prioritize it growing up. Nevertheless, he found himself making his way across the crowded road, filled with other party guests, toward the white picket fence in front of the Red Inn. She'd been watching him walk across and when he reached the fence, they met one another's eyes and he raised his hand to gesture for her to come toward him.

"Come closer," he murmured, but she couldn't possibly have heard him over the hustle and bustle of the busy street. He took a deep breath through his mouth and exhaled through his nose, desperate to quell the nervousness as his heart pounded against his chest.

The boat hand could not recall a time when he had ever been as nervous as he was at that moment. It was a miracle that he didn't trip over his own feet, flustered as he was by the beauty across the road. He told himself that he needed to slow down because he didn't know what he would do when she finally made the trek toward him. He wasn't one for conversation and he had no idea what he would do or say when she finally came toward him.

As he breathed in, the salty ocean air filled his lungs and when he breathed out, he found himself calmer than before. There was no better place for this to happen than beside the ocean. There was no place that calmed him more and he could feel the anxiety ebbing away from him even as he heard the rush of the waves pulling back and forth along the shore. Still, there was definitely moisture on his palms and he knew he wouldn't be able to shake her hand for the sweat on his hands.

He got as close as he could, thankful for the calmer sense of mind, and she walked toward him until they were a mere few feet apart from one another. She'd left her friend behind and when she stopped walking, she glanced back at her friend before looking at him. From here, he could see he'd missed much of her beauty. He'd been right about her soft features, but he didn't know about her doe eyes and her soft lips.

Those lips began to move as he looked down at them. "Did you come all the way over here to embarrass me?"

"No, ma'am," he uttered.

"Well," she smiled. "You caught me fair and square looking through the windows of the ball."

"Yes, ma'am," he returned the smile. "I sure did."

"Well, sir," her voice sweet and proper, carrying the same dancing lilt that her walk did. "What is it that I did to make you leave your friends and run all this way?"

Milton looked down at the ground, gulping the lump

that formed in his throat. He hadn't expected her to be quite this forward. When he looked back into her beautiful eyes, however, he knew just what he would say. "Well, ma'am," he murmured honestly and with a bit more confidence than before. "I saw you and that seemed to be enough for me."

"Well," she smiled wider than before. "That does seem to be a good enough reason."

The two shared a look before she extended her hand, as delicate and soft as the rest of her was.

"My name is Marjorie Wilson."

Milton was quick to wipe his palm on his pant leg, ridding it of the nervous moisture, and held it out to her. "I'm Milton Weatherbourne, ma'am. It's a pleasure to meet you."

And what a pleasure it was.

CHAPTER 8
THESE DAYS

It had been just over forty years since the day Milton and Marjorie first set eyes on one another. Now, alone and heartbroken, Marjorie continued to sort through the boxes that Milton left behind. It seemed impossible to her that a man with as much presence as he could be reduced to the contents of these boxes, and she found herself thinking about it again and again.

An old, Dutch-style copper kettle reached its boiling point on the stovetop, the sound of its whistle echoing throughout the walls of the old house. Marjorie hurried toward the kitchen, passing Seymour running in the opposite direction. As much as she was in a hurry to get to her kettle, her cat was in a hurry to get away from the high-pitched disturbance that radiated throughout the house.

"Seymour," Marjorie chuckled. "Where do you think you're going?"

It was as though Seymour could understand her, for the moment she removed the kettle from the hot surface to prepare a fresh cup of tea, her cat slunk cautiously back into the kitchen. As quickly as he'd arrived, however, was as quickly as he raced back out again. The sound of the doorbell rang and he was gone.

"Oh dear," Marjorie muttered to her beloved feline. "You're having a dog's day. *Rough, rough...*"

Marjorie opened the door to greet her visitor. "Hi, Mrs. Weatherbourne," the boys sang out!

Delighted by their arrival, Marjorie stepped aside to allow Will, Isaac, and Dez to enter her house. "Come in, come in."

The boys entered the family room of the house and looked around awkwardly. Marjorie couldn't exactly blame them. The house could use a good airing out; it smelled musty and there wasn't much she could do about it. That didn't stop the boys from taking interest in the inside of the house. Marjorie couldn't blame them for that either. She remembered what it was like to be a child – vaguely – and there was nothing more fascinating than a stranger's house. The back wall of the family room was dominated by a prominent red brick fireplace and on its mantel were several picture frames. Above that was the centerpiece of the room, a framed oil painting of an old clipper ship, accentuated by the piece above it, an antique steel and wood whaling harpoon.

Marjorie was quickly amused by the way the boys stared

at the old harpoon in wonder, nudging one another to look at it.

"Why don't you boys take a seat?" She gestured toward the sofa. "Would you like some lemonade?"

The boys nodded their heads enthusiastically. As Mrs. Weatherbourne walked away, she straightened her hair a bit. She had it pinned back and out of her face, but the grey locks hung loosely over her shoulders. The windows were open and her floral shirt blew slightly in the wind. In preparation for the active day ahead, she wore a pair of sneakers and leggings. Though she couldn't lift Milton's boxes on her own, she was a relatively capable and fit lady, even in her old age.

While she was gone, the boys continued to look around the room. Dez had never been inside the Weatherbourne house. Yet naturally they have an eternal fascination with the inside of other people's houses. It was ingrained into them to be curious and inquisitive. The houses of strangers offered small peeks into the lives of those who live there. For kids whose minds were still being sharpened by experience, it was an exhilarating experience.

There were piles and piles of old pictures and letters littering the coffee table in the center of the living room. Unable to resist the curiosity any longer, the boys began to finger through the pictures. It quickly became apparent that the images were a record of the adventures of Mr. and Mrs. Weatherbourne. There was a photo of Milton in the Navy, proudly wearing his uniform and sailor's cap, posing in a salute. Another showed an image of Marjorie and Milton, fishing on Bass River. Marjorie was young and beautiful, laughing into the eye of the camera.

"Hey," Isaac picked a photo up. "This one's from South Yarmouth. I went there with my mom when I was really little. Look, you can see the old windmill on Windmill Beach." He pointed to the windmill in the distance, showing his friends.

"Wow," Will whispered. "There are so many pictures."

"That's how you live a life," Dez remarked in what was a noticeably impressed tone of voice. He pointed at the mantelpiece suddenly. "Check it out!"

The other boys looked up to see yet another photo of a young Milton in his Navy uniform, but that wasn't what caught their attention. There was a framed picture of a more recent Milton sitting on a fishing boat. He had a fishing rod in his hand with hook, line, and sinker already in the depths of the ocean on which he sat. In the picture, it was clear as day that Milton had no left leg.

"I told you," Isaac murmured. "He lost his leg in a shark attack."

"I bet it got blown off in World War II while he was in the Navy," Dez whispered.

"Shhh," Will hissed. "Both of you. Mrs. Weatherbourne will hear you."

Both Will's friends fell silent, but none of the boys took their eyes off the image, speculating in their minds what had happened to Milton. In the past, they'd all seen Milton's artificial leg while he walked around town or when they mowed the lawn for the Weatherbournes, but they never knew what had happened to his leg. Over the years, Isaac's mother had cared for Milton and Marjorie, particularly when they'd been too sick to leave their house, so it was more than possible that Isaac had it right. Milton's leg *could* have been bitten off by a great white shark.

Without knowing it, all three of the boys found themselves thinking of the horror film that had been released a few years prior. Someone had been attacked by a huge shark. It was the only film they'd seen with images of a threatening, scary shark – not that any of them were old enough to be watching it in the first place.

Marjorie returned from the kitchen with a tray, consisting of one lemonade pitcher, three glasses of lemonade, and a cup of steaming hot tea. She held out the tray and each of the boys grabbed a glass. Placing the tray on the table beside her armchair, she took a seat across from the boys as they happily sipped their refreshing lemonade.

Almost as soon as Marjorie sat down in her seat, Seymour trotted into the room with his tail high in the air. He paused to survey the boys and, deciding that they were worthy of petting him, began brushing himself up against their legs. Will and Isaac welcomed the attention from Seymour, petting him with one hand while holding their glasses with the other. Dez looked on with wide eyes as if Seymour was evil. He was more of a dog person and cats reminded him too much of witchcraft. He knew Seymour wasn't about to cast a spell on him, but he remained wary nonetheless.

While they gave her cat attention, Marjorie began speaking to the boys in a polite tone. "Thank you boys for coming to help me today," she started. "Since I lost my

Milton, I've been a bit torn on what to do. I need to sort through Milton's old things to see what I should save and what I should donate. They're all stored in the attic."

The boys listened to Marjorie, but they all became rather distracted, their eyes flitting from her to the photo on the mantelpiece. Another side effect of being a kid was that they had one-track minds. Sometimes, they didn't know what was considered an appropriate or inappropriate time to ask something. All they knew was that they had a burning curiosity that needed to be satisfied.

Marjorie watched the boys expectantly, seeming to realize that they had something else on their minds. The corner of her mouth twitched with a smile at the boys' obvious distraction. They were gently nudging one another and whispering. As she watched, Will's eyes darted back to the photo on the mantelpiece and she caught the movement for the first time.

"Do you boys have something you wish to ask me?" Marjorie raised her eyebrows, trying not to laugh at the three. "You seem awfully interested in that picture of Milton."

The boys suddenly resembled a deer in the headlights, all three of them staring at her with wide eyes as they came to terms with being caught red-handed. They noticed that Mrs. Weatherbourne didn't seem to be upset with any of them.

Will nudged Isaac with his elbow, only to have Isaac nudge back. All the while, Dez watched this interaction with raised eyebrows. Eventually, he simply shook his head and turned to Mrs. Weatherbourne, deciding to tell the truth. They'd spent years wondering. Now was as good a time as any.

"We were curious about what happened to Mr. Weatherbourne's leg, ma'am." That was all it took. Dez broke the dam and the imaginative theories began flowing out of their mouths.

"I said it had to have been a great white shark," Isaac blurted out. "That's the only thing that would have taken off his entire leg. Right?"

"Theoretically," Dez calmly proclaimed, clearly proud of his use of the word, "it makes more sense that he would have lost his leg fighting in World War II."

With each one, Marjorie's smile grew wider and wider. The sudden excitement of the kids in the room brought her a sense of joy she'd not felt in some time. She loved that the boys were interested in her Milton. It wasn't as though she got the chance to speak about him much these days. She was glad for any excuse.

"What about you, Will?" She turned to Will, who hadn't said anything yet. "What do you think?"

Will looked up at Mrs. Weatherbourne. All eyes were on him, waiting for his big theory. Secretly, both Dez and Isaac were hoping that he'd agree with one of their theories.

"I don't know," Will shrugged his shoulders. "Maybe a killer whale?"

"Good grief," Dez rolled his eyes dramatically.

"Well," Marjorie smiled widely. She'd already made the decision to change the subject. Their curiosity was far too amusing to spoil and so, she would leave them guessing.

"You boys have quite the active imagination!"

Isaac seemed to have grasped that Marjorie wasn't going to give them an answer and changed direction himself. He tugged the business card his mother had given him that morning and passed it over to Mrs. Weatherbourne. "My mother asked me to give this to you."

"Thank you, Isaac. Please give your mother my thanks as well," Marjorie took the card and set it down on the tray. "So, shall we get started?"

The boys nodded their heads. Marjorie stood from her seat and the boys followed suit as she led the way toward the door to the attic staircase. It creaked open once she unlatched it. No one could see anything until she flicked a light switch on the right, illuminating the doorway before they ever entered the attic.

Marjorie grasped onto the banisters tightly. Careful to maintain a steady grip, her hands shakier than they once were, as she began climbing the steep steps upward. The wood creaked as she walked up and she could hear the boys following close behind.

Dust floated in the air, tiny particles swirling around in what little light there was. A single bulb swung from above and rays of sunlight broke through the spaces between the vents on each side of the attic. The wooden rafters were exposed, running the full length of the ceiling. The roof was sloped and its highest point, the center, was only five feet.

The boys could stand comfortably. The slope was at the perfect height. Marjorie, on the other hand, had the slightest squat to her stance, ducking her head low. They could see why she needed assistance. It was enough to give anyone a crick in the neck.

Will, Dez, and Isaac stared around the room in wonder. It offered fresh intrigue and they couldn't help but marvel at the attic. The space didn't offer much in the way of contents, a few dusty boxes were littered about the floor, holiday decorations were strewn haphazardly, and an artificial Christmas tree peeked out of a box otherwise sealed with duct tape.

"All right," Mrs. Weatherbourne began gesturing around the room as she handed out instructions. "Will and Dez, would you mind opening up these boxes so I could take a look inside?"

Will and Dez followed her direction and began unstacking several boxes from a pile on one side of the confined space. They worked together to bring the boxes closer to the center of the room and popped open the cardboard flaps for Mrs. Weatherbourne. For a while, the only sounds in the room were the shifting of the boxes across the floor.

Feeling a bit left out, Isaac decided to do some exploring of his own. There were a few less obvious items scattered here and there across the attic and he figured they were as good a distraction as any. Besides, he was rather curious about the attic. There was a brown leather trunk sitting on its own that caught his attention the moment they'd entered the small doorway. It was tattered and old, but Isaac could tell it had once been a beautiful case, with a metal frame, strong corners, and a large lockable clasp.

Unable to help himself, Isaac ventured toward the trunk

while Dez, Will, and Mrs. Weatherbourne were distracted by the cardboard boxes and their contents. In the back of his mind, he considered it a duty. It was up to him to investigate. He could imagine reporting everything he'd discovered back to Will and Dez once they were back in their treehouse. To his delight, Isaac reached down and found that the clasp was unlocked. He raised it and then, as quietly as he could, opened the trunk up. It was surprisingly heavy and took some effort to lift.

The moment it opened, Isaac gave a surprised cry and took several steps back. There, in the depths of the trunk, he could see the folded bones of a human skeleton. Glancing over his shoulder to where his friends stood, he had the horrible vision of Mrs. Weatherbourne pulling out an axe and, with a devious grin, yelling, "I've got you now, my pretties!"

Isaac's dark thoughts were interrupted as Mrs. Weatherbourne let out a decidedly *un*-devious giggle. "Isaac," she chuckled. "I see you found Einstein."

Will and Dez took in their friend's pale shade and, upon seeing how spooked he was, promptly began to laugh amongst themselves. Mrs. Weatherbourne made her way over to where Isaac stood, reached into the trunk, and carefully lifted the skeleton from within. She held it up proudly, allowing it to unfold. The bones rattled against each other and they didn't sound like bones at all. They sounded like plastic.

"It's not real," Mrs. Weatherbourne explained. "It's for educational purposes, he was very useful back in the day when I taught Biology. His name is Einstein."

Isaac took a closer look at the skeleton and it became clear to him that it definitely wasn't a real one. Besides, the bones would have fallen apart when she picked it up. It wouldn't have stayed whole. If he was totally honest, it was kind of cool. He looked over at Dez and Will. Based on their grins, he could see that his friends thought it was pretty cool too.

"Right then," Mrs. Weatherbourne sighed. She set the skeleton carefully on the ground beside the trunk before turning to the trunk itself. "What do we have here?"

The boys could tell that she wasn't speaking to any of them and instead was speaking more to herself because she turned to the trunk and began investigating its contents. She rummaged for a good few minutes before she pulled out a large manila envelope with the word "*save*" written on it in black marker pen. As the boys watched, she opened the envelope and pulled out what looked like a book, sealed in a plastic cover.

"Wow," Isaac's eyes lit up. "A comic book!"

Will and Dez were equally excited, practically twitching as they looked at the book in Mrs. Weatherbourne's hands.

Mrs. Weatherbourne looked at Isaac and asked, "Do you like comic books?"

Isaac nodded his head vigorously.

"Well, you can have this one then. Milton would like that."

Isaac took the comic book from her with the barest tips of his fingers, holding it like it was a priceless and fragile piece of art. His eyes were wide with wonder as he marveled over the gift Mrs. Weatherbourne and, in

essence, Mr. Weatherbourne had given him. Will and Dez sighed in mild disappointment.

While checking out the book, it became clear to Isaac that not only is the comic old, it is also in mint condition.

Printed with the date 1939. "Wow," he breathed again.

His friends came over to stand on either side of him, checking the book out. "Whoa, G-man," Dez gasped.

"You are super lucky. This could actually be worth some money."

"Dude," Isaac nudged him pointedly, glancing at Mrs. Weatherbourne, who didn't react at all.

"The Katzenstein Kids… I've never heard of it," Will added.

"Well, boys… If we find any more comics, you can have them too!" Mrs. Weatherbourne announced.

It was as though she'd said the magic words to motivate and encourage the boys to get back to work. As quickly as they could, Will and Dez got back to sorting through the boxes. This time, Isaac joined in, but not before carefully stuffing the comic book into his backpack. Mrs. Weatherbourne guided them, separating the boxes into two separate piles. One was to be kept and the other was to be donated.

The boys stayed and helped for several hours, but there were no other comic books to be found. By the time they left, however, Will and Dez felt too accomplished to be disappointed. They were too innocent to know it then, but one day they would recognize that the feelings they were experiencing came from doing a hard day's work.

"Okay, boys," Mrs. Weatherbourne finally sighed. "I think that's enough work for one day, don't you?"

They were relieved and tired, eager to get back to their treehouse and so, the kids eagerly nodded their heads in agreement.

"Would you mind carrying these boxes down?" She gestured to the donate pile.

Will, Dez, and Isaac wordlessly picked up a box each and began carrying them down the stairs. By the time they'd set them down in the living room and walked back to the attic stairway, Mrs. Weatherbourne was still making her way down the stairs after them. It was then that they understood why Mrs. Weatherbourne really needed assistance. It would have taken her an age to bring *one* box down as she needed both her hands to hold onto the banisters.

When she reached the bottom of the stairway, she heaved a sigh and smiled at them, ushering them back up to the attic.

"Man," Dez picked up two boxes at a time. "It sucks that we didn't find any more comics."

"Yeah, but today was kind of fun."

Isaac and Dez nodded their heads, mumbling their agreement as they picked up boxes of their own. All the donation boxes were moved to the living room in no more than two trips and the boys were ready to go. Mrs. Weatherbourne offered each of them five dollars for helping her out.

Before they left, the three of them downed what remained of their lemonade while Seymour watched from the armchair, curled up and ready to sleep. Mrs. Weatherbourne's cup of tea had long since gone cold. Once they were done, they set their glasses down on the tray and Mrs. Weatherbourne walked them toward the door.

"Thank you again, boys. I really appreciate it." After a long day of sorting through boxes, the exhaustion was beginning to set in. While Marjorie was still fit for her age, she definitely wasn't the woman she once was. There was only so much she could handle before she needed to rest and she had reached her limit for the day.

"You're welcome, Mrs. W," Dez smiled, folding his cash in half and pocketing it.

"Yeah," Isaac seconded.

"It was a pleasure, Mrs. Weatherbourne," Will added.

"I'll let your mothers know if I need anything else. You boys go have fun now!"

The three of them headed away, Isaac's backpack safely secured on his shoulders, as she shut the door behind them. While they were walking away from the house, they noticed an old black Mercedes parked across from Mrs. Weatherbourne's house. This might not have been a strange occurrence if it weren't for the man in the front seat, dressed in a black suit and dark sunglasses. As if that weren't odd enough, there was a woman in the backseat and she too wore dark clothes and dark sunglasses.

An eerie sensation came over the kids. Although the man and woman wore tinted glasses, they could tell they were being watched as they passed the car. After a pause, the engine purred to life and the car drove away.

Looking between one another, they said the same thing at the same time, "That was creepy." After they were finished helping Mrs. Weatherbourne, the boys decided to head home instead of going back to the treehouse. They'd agreed to meet the following day so that they could go to

Davenport's with their hard-earned cash. They were looking forward to buying stuff. It wasn't every day that they got to go shopping on their own.

CHAPTER 9
THE GRIMM TALES OF GORSKA MAIKA

Isaac and Dez arrived at Will's house early the next morning, excited and ready for Davenport's. The Five and Dime store is in downtown Dennis Port, so the boys hopped on their bikes and raced there. It was better than walking, although Davenport's was well worth the walk. It was the place to go for snacks, gum, pop, magazines, and comic books. Basically, it was every boy's dream.

As much as they wanted to, the boys couldn't always buy from Davenport's, but that didn't stop them from going in to look at the comic books they wished they could afford. Afterward, they'd hang out on the bench outside the store, chew gum and talk about the things they would buy if they had the money.

When they finally arrived, Will, Isaac, and Dez pulled

their bikes up to the side door. They are about to enter when Dez suddenly stopped and nudged them. Pausing, they turned to find him staring across the street at the laundromat. A girl was outside doing her chores, emptying the trash cans around the laundromat.

It's Amy Howard who lives in the house behind the laundromat in question. To the kids, it is simply known as the Howard's house. Collecting trash wasn't exactly the most glamorous of jobs, but thirteen-year-olds couldn't be picky.

As the boys stood there, a beat-up green Chevy Nova turned the corner up the street, driving way too fast for such a small area of town. The boys recognized the car instantly. It belongs to Puck – or as his birth certificate suggested, Greg Collins. The only reason he was known as Puck was because he was a rather popular hockey player in Dennis Port.

The car got closer and they noticed Jay Flynn, a boy whose parents owned the junkyard in the next town, in the passenger seat. That was typical. The two were best friends and everywhere they went they wreaked havoc. They were known as the town's troublemakers, but people let them off easy. If it weren't for the fact that Greg Collins was so good at hockey, everyone in the town would have hated him. As it was, they quite enjoyed the national competitions. When other schools came to play in Dennis Port, Puck's name would get cheered so loud that it made Will, Dez, and Isaac's ears hurt.

At the sight of the Chevy, the boys wanted to shrink and disappear into the ground. Still, some kind of morbid curiosity prevented them from looking away from the scene before them. They didn't like Puck and, worse than that, Puck didn't like them.

Of course, Puck didn't really like many people. He and his best friend came from scary families and they did whatever they could to deal with their heritage. As popular as Greg Collins was, his dad was less popular. He was an auto mechanic. In Dennis Port, the people hoped and prayed that nothing ever went wrong with their vehicles simply so that they wouldn't have to deal with Greg's dad. He was one of the scariest guys around and if one wasn't happy with his work, it wouldn't be a good idea to say anything about it. The fear of what he might do to them or their car was a strong enough deterrent.

Jay's family was no better. Although they owned the junkyard in the town over, known as Flynn's Salvage, they frequented the town of Dennis Port. The whole family was around for every one of Puck's hockey matches and Jay could be seen visiting far more often – especially during summer vacation. Since they were from another town, they acted like they could do anything they wanted without suffering the consequences. To make matters worse, this was behavior that Greg and his father encouraged.

Greg slowed the car down outside the laundromat and, simultaneously, he and Jay yelled at Amy. "What are you doing, Scabs? Are you looking for something to eat in the trash?"

The boys cringed on Amy's behalf. They knew what it was like to be the target of Greg and Jay's incessant bullying. They called Amy scabs because when she was little, she used to pick at the scabs she got during recess. The nickname never went away – no thanks to Greg and Jay. Their ugly laughter echoed out of the window as they continued driving by at their slow pace. It was only when a black Mercedes pulled up to park next to the Davenport's parking lot that the Chevy suddenly sped up and disappeared around the next corner.

At the sight of the black car, Will, Dez, and Isaac parked their bikes as quickly as they could and headed into the Five and Dime store. They didn't want to know if the same stoic occupants of the previous day were in the Mercedes. That would simply be too suspicious for them to handle.

The moment they stepped into the cool interior of Davenport's, the kids felt safe, though they were shaken by the sudden appearance of the Mercedes. Although they were sure it was nothing more than their imagination, they still wondered if there was a possibility that the black vehicle was following them around. No, that couldn't be true. They were only kids. What would anyone want to follow them around for?

None of the boys spoke their thoughts aloud, choosing instead to walk over to the wall of comics and magazines that dominated one side of the store. They instantly began grabbing books off the shelves and flipping through the pages. It seemed they were doing a good job of forgetting their suspicions.

That was until Dez pulled an issue of UFO Encounter off the shelf. Flipping through the magazine, he stopped on the very first article. It described the story of men in black being spotted directly after a sighting. With a pounding heart, Dez kept reading about the way these men dressed in black suits would appear if there was talk of an alien abduction.

Once he reached the point of the article where there was an illustration, he turned to Will. "Dude, check it out."

Will leaned over Dez' shoulder to gaze down at the picture. It depicted two men dressed in all black. The suits were bad enough, but the men in the illustration were also wearing black sunglasses. To top it all off, they were standing next to a sleek black car.

"Does this look familiar?" Dez whispered. "It looks like those freaks we saw in the black car yesterday... Doesn't it?"

There was an urgency to his voice. It was almost as though he wanted Will to notice the similarities too, as though he wanted to know he wasn't crazy. However, Will didn't get the chance to respond. They were so focused on the magazine that they didn't notice Isaac had wandered off to the other end of the wall. And he wasn't alone.

Isaac was so preoccupied with the stacks of magazines and comic books before him that he didn't notice the stranger until he'd bumped into her, only to find that it wasn't just any stranger. It was the woman in black, the one from the previous day. She sneered down at him from behind her sunglasses, seeming scarier for the fact that he couldn't see her eyes.

"Excuse me, young man," the woman spoke with a thick Russian accent. Isaac's eyes widened, bulging in disbelief. "You might try minding yourself. You're blocking the aisle."

As quickly as he could, Isaac stepped out of the way. The poor boy was so shaken that he moved too fast and ended up stumbling into the comic stand. Without thinking, he grabbed ahold of the shelf in an effort to stabilize himself before he fell. Thankfully, he managed to regain his footing and ended up face to face with a comic that made his eyes widen even more than before.

The cover depicted a picture of a woman dressed in black. She had white hair and a long blade hung from her belt. The cover title read, *"The Grimm Tales of Gorska Maika."* Dez and Will joined Isaac on the other side of the shelf, having witnessed the entire encounter. They followed Isaac's line of sight, their eyes widening at the sight of the comic book on the shelf too.

"That was creepy," Dez whispered, causing Isaac to jump. He hadn't noticed their arrival. "Do you think it was her? Gorska Maika, the Russian Boogey Woman." Dez shivered dramatically.

Isaac couldn't help himself as his eyes moved from the creepy comic cover and back up toward the woman even as she walked away from them. She had blonde hair and dark eyebrows on a pale face, what little they could see of her eyebrows above the glasses she wore. They checked out her outfit. Unlike the neat suit the man wore, and the UFO magazine portrayed, she wore tight black pants and combat boots. She had a t-shirt beneath an oversized black coat. She looked more like a punk rocker than an FBI agent.

"Look," Isaac murmured with a gulp. He pointed and quickly lowered his hand, afraid she might sense his pointing, "There, on her belt."

His friends looked on and Will gasped. There was a bulge along the line of her belt, hidden by the coat she wore. It could have been a knife or even a gun.

"Yes," Isaac murmured aloud, almost to himself instead of his friends. "She must be Gorska Maika."

Will nodded his head. "It's possible."

Dez, however, smirked. "Nah, guys. Come on. It's only a comic book and I was totally kidding."

After their run-ins with the Russian woman, the boys didn't really want to spend much more time in Davenport's. It seemed far too random for her to be there and she didn't seem to have any intention of leaving the Five and Dime store soon. They were far too uncomfortable to continue browsing while she was present.

"Do you guys wanna go to the library?" Will asked.

On occasion, the friends would go to the library because they could read comic books for free. It was right up the street and they figured they may as well pop in while they were in the area. This was one of those times.

"Sure, why not?" Dez shrugged his shoulders, setting the UFO magazine back down on the shelf, though not where he'd found it in the first place.

"Yeah," Isaac nodded excitedly. In his backpack, he'd packed his newly-found comic book. Both of his friends looked at him questioningly. "I want to do some research on The Katzenstein Kids," Isaac answered their imploring looks.

"Oh, right," Dez nodded with some understanding.

"Are you going to check if it's valuable?"

"Yeah, it might be worth something," Will repeated Dez' musings of the previous afternoon.

"I also wanna check out its history," Isaac added. "It's weird that I've never heard of it, but I guess 1939 was a really long time ago."

"Ya' think?" Dez asked, his tone laced with sarcasm.

"Let's go," Will interrupted before Isaac could respond.

Without spending their money, they exited the store and hopped onto their bicycles. They could see the Mercedes parked in the next parking lot, but they paid it no mind, though they couldn't deny they had a strong urge to check if the man from yesterday was in the car.

◆ ◆ ◆

Once at the library they parked their bikes outside, they headed into the big building. The library was huge. However, the books inside were primarily geared toward the older generations and people who needed to do research. A large percentage of its contents were the history archives of the town.

The best part about the library was the fact that it had so many books you can literally find anything about everything. That was how Isaac planned to research his comic book. In no time, he settled into the card catalog and began his search for book authors that have the word Katzenstein in them. Since it was summer vacation, the library was quiet and hardly anyone was there. The librarian, used to their visits by this point, simply gave them a curt nod of her head when they walked in.

They knew the rules well enough.

"Dude," Dez whispered when Isaac sat down at the card catalog. "Will and I are gonna check out books about the history of comics."

"Huh?" Isaac turned away from the catalog files his brows knitted together in confusion.

"Why?"

Will shrugged. "We figured it would be better to take a look at more than one avenue. Who knows what we'll find if we all work together?"

At this, Isaac beamed at his two best friends. "Okay! Let me know what you guys find!"

With that, he was left alone to do his own digging. The sound of Will and Dez' footsteps faded away on the wood floors as they walked toward the history section. Thankfully they were still in the same section since this was where students did their research. He could hear his friends moving from aisle to aisle every so often, but Isaac was engrossed in his own search.

With some catalog numbers and book locations in hand, Isaac began his search through the volumes of books he found. The deeper he dug, the more fascinated Isaac became. He discovered that the Nazis banned comic books in 1933, yet the comic book had a print date of 1939. Many comic books were printed in Poland and sold to English-speaking countries, with the exception of Germany. When the Nazis invaded Poland in September of 1939, the printing houses were subsequently shut down.

Beyond the release of his final comic book, The Katzenstein Kids and the Ditty Box Mystery, the author and illustrator didn't seem to have been written about.

Near as he could tell, Herman Katzenstein practically disappeared off the face of the earth. Isaac deduced that Herman's fate must not have been a good one, particularly based on his name.

Many of the Jewish people still in Poland after the year 1939 ended up being segregated and later imprisoned in concentration camps. Few of them were ever seen again. As much as he hated the thought, Isaac couldn't help but wonder if that's what happened to the author of his comic book.

Instead of searching any further alone, Isaac left with what little knowledge he had. He went to rejoin his friends at the other end of the library and found them sitting on the floor in the center of one of the aisles. Baffled, he decided to sit with them. They were each poring over the pages of a book and they had more to choose from. There was a stack of books beside them.

Isaac reached for the other books, looking to see what the two of them had found. Will and Dez didn't seem to notice his presence at all and continued to read through their own books. For some time, the only sound in the aisle was the flipping of their pages. It felt wrong to interrupt them, despite the fact that he really wanted to talk to them about his discoveries thus far, so Isaac joined them by paging through one of the books in their stack.

"Hey guys," Will suddenly spoke, cutting through the silence between them. "Check this out." Dez and Isaac paused their reading to listen to Will, glancing over at the page he was on and finding that the writing was too small to read from where they sat anyway. Will dragged his finger along the page as he read, following the sentences on the page with his fingertips. "The next reference to The Katzenstein Kids happened in 1942 and, get this, it wasn't by the same author and illustrator. It was some guy named Heinrich Hans. It was printed in Poland."

Isaac began to feel a pit forming in his stomach as the thought of what possibly happened hit him. There were plenty of people who were scratched from history during those dark days. There was a chance that during the Nazi purge of Jewish authors, the comic book was given to a German man instead – Heinrich Hans. Could it be that Herman Katzenstein was erased, like so many others during the holocaust?

"Is that the only picture you could find of it?" Dez asked, unable to mask his disappointment.

Isaac raised his eyebrows, surprised by the tone in his friend's voice. "Picture?"

"Yeah," Will nodded. "We haven't been able to find any pictures and we've been through like, all of these books already."

"And we don't even know if it's worth anything," Dez chimed in.

"Did you find anything?" Will turned to Isaac. "You were busy for a while."

"I couldn't find anything about the value either." Isaac shook his head. "And it's like the guy who wrote it just disappeared after 1939."

"Oh well," Will sighed and shut the book he'd been reading. "At least we tried."

Before Isaac knew what was happening, Will and Dez

stacked their books onto the pile and stood up off the floor. He looked up at them. "Where are you guys going?"

"I'm gonna go and read some comics while we're here," Dez answered. "I might sign something out."

"Yes, me too." Will nodded in agreement.

"Oh, okay," Isaac murmured. "Well, I'm gonna keep reading up on it."

"Suit yourself," Dez shrugged.

Both of his friends left him sitting in the aisle and wandered off to the teen section of the library. That was where the comic books were kept. Isaac continued to read, grateful for the pile of books his friends had collected. At least he didn't need to go looking for them on his own. He was a little upset that Will and Dez got discouraged so quickly, but he guessed they had different reasons for searching. His friends mostly cared about the value and pricing of the comic book.

Isaac admitted he felt that way too, at first. But the more he read about it, the more that began to change. Since he was of Jewish heritage himself, the history captivated him. He wanted to keep digging to find out if there was more to the story of the World War II comic book.

It didn't take Isaac long to find the book he was really interested in. In the collection of books Dez and Will had left behind, there was a huge, hardbound book titled *The History of Comics*. If there was one book that was going to give him the information he was looking for, it was that one. Rather than meander in the aisle by himself, he picked it up and went to the front of the library to sign it out.

The librarian didn't even blink as he took the book out.

She recorded it wordlessly and began penning his information into the sign out ledger. Isaac guessed she was used to him and his friends taking out comic books and it was only a matter of time until they reached this one. While he waited, Isaac wondered what Will and Dez were up to.

"I think she's checking you out, Willbo," Dez nudged Will in the ribs.

Standing on the opposite side of the section was none other than Amy Howard. It was like she'd heard Dez because at that moment, she glanced over at Will. However, as soon as she noticed that the boys were looking back in her direction, she immediately looked back down at the ground.

"I think Scabs might really like you," Dez murmured with a snicker.

Will spun around to face Dez and, in a stern tone, replied, "Don't call her that."

The moment he turned away from Dez, it was in time to see Amy walking toward them. "Hi, Will," she smiled.

"Oh," Will gasped. "Hi, Amy."

Dez watched the interaction with a goofy expression on his face, almost as though he was trying not to laugh at the scene unfolding before him. If Amy weren't standing so close, Will might have smacked his friend. He certainly wanted to.

"I saw you guys at Davenport's earlier, but I didn't think I would find you at a library," Amy continued.

"Yeah," Will mumbled. He was practically speechless. The last thing he expected was for Amy Howard to start talking to him at the library. "We come here all the time."

Dez looked over at his friend with a puzzled look on his face. "No, we don't."

On impulse, Will covered Dez' mouth with one of his hands and broke into a phony laugh. "Yes, we do, silly. We... read books all the time."

Amy smiled and glanced down at Will's hands, which were holding onto a few comic books. "I see you like comics."

"Oh, yeah," he grinned.

Isaac rejoined his friends, finding Will and Amy locked in a strange stare. He approached them and stated boldly, "Hi, Amy." Without waiting for her to greet him back, he turned to Will and Dez. "Are you guys ready to go?"

"Where are you boys going in such a rush?" Amy asked.

"We've got some guy stuff to do," Will replied.

Finally removing Will's hand from his mouth, with some effort, Dez added, "We're heading to our secret treehouse behind my house."

Surprised by this sudden reveal, Will shrugged. "Yeah," he turned to Amy, "you should stop by sometime."

Amy's eyes roved over each boy in turn. "Maybe I will."

With that, she walked away from the three of them, a smile on her face.

The boys stared after her, momentarily stunned. Will went to set the comic books on a shelf. He was the only one who had any books on him. Isaac's copy of *The History of Comics* was tucked safely into his backpack, along with the copy of The Katzenstein Kids. Once Will had finished putting away the books, they left the library.

It was while mounting their bikes that Will, Dez, and

Isaac noticed the black Mercedes. A man dressed in all black sat in the driver's seat. From where they stood, it looked like the man was watching them. In the back seat was none other than the Russian woman from Davenport's, Gorska Maika.

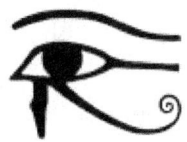

CHAPTER 10
TROUBLE IN PARADISE

Later that evening, the kids could be found hanging out in the treehouse. The sun had yet to set and they were doing more research on the comic book. Since Isaac had signed *The History of Comics* out, Will and Dez seemed to have taken more of an interest, though that could have simply been an interest in the history of comic books in general. It wasn't necessarily an interest in *his* comic book.

Still, Isaac liked to think that his friends were as intrigued by his World War II comic book as he was. He flipped through the pages, his eyes sharpened for the barest hint of The Katzenstein Kids. He'd memorized the cover by now, though he was unfamiliar with the illustrations. He hadn't even read the comic book yet!

A voice rang out from below, shocking the three of

them. "Will, are you up there?"

Will, Dez, and Isaac stared at each other, shocked by the girl's voice. Amy Howard was underneath their treehouse. None of them moved for a moment, too surprised by her sudden appearance to know what to do.

"Dude," Will whispered. "It's Amy. She's actually here."

"I know," Dez said in a soft voice. It wasn't quite a whisper because Dez had no idea how to whisper, but it was definitely an attempt at whispering. "*Say something to her.*"

Both Isaac's mouth and eyes were wide open. He pointed anxiously at the pile of dirty magazines in the corner of the treehouse, all of which were face up, their lewd images clearly visible.

"Will, Dez, Isaac…" Amy called up again. "I can hear you whispering up there, you know. I'm coming up."

An expression of alarm came over Will's face. His eyes flitted from Dez and Isaac to the confined space within the treehouse. "Hide them!" He hissed urgently.

All at once, the three boys jumped into action, hurrying to stash the magazines from plain sight. There wasn't much place to put them and so, they hid some behind a beanbag and others beneath the stack of comic books in the milk crate. They barely managed to compose themselves before Amy reached the top rung of the ladder.

Amy's head appeared at the small opening in the treehouse and she looked around before climbing into the small space. Will could barely contain himself. His nerves were all over the place at the sight of Amy. His friends were not much better at hiding their nervousness.

There was a girl in the treehouse.

"Hi, Amy," the boys spoke all at once.

Amy smiled and looked around at her three new friends. There was something about the knowing smirk on her lips that told them she knew how big a deal it was for her to be in their treehouse. She arched an eyebrow as none of the boys said or did anything more, simply staring at her like she was some kind of apparition.

"So," she started playfully. "Am I the first girl to be in your treehouse?"

Will, Dez, and Isaac looked at one another with wide eyes. What were they meant to say? Their hearts were beating too fast to think of anything else.

"You don't have to answer that," Amy shrugged, her smile growing wider. "What are you boys up to anyway?"

At first, the boys don't answer. They're not sure if they should tell her. *The History of Comics* was still open in Isaac's lap and he glanced down at it before speaking.

"We found an old comic book," he started. "Or, well, it was given to me by Mrs. Weatherbourne over on Sea Street. We were helping her move some boxes from her attic yesterday. Anyway, we found this really old comic book that none of us had ever heard of."

"We've been doing some research on it," Will added.

"The guy who wrote it was probably taken to a concentration camp by the Nazis and never heard from again," Dez said offhandedly.

Everyone else turned to look at him, shocked by how casually he made this statement.

"What?" Dez threw his hands up. "We were all thinking it."

"The comic book was written and illustrated by some guy named Herman Katzenstein in the late 1930's," Isaac continued, ignoring Dez. "He vanished soon after the Germans invaded Poland. But get this, the comic was reprinted by a German author and illustrator called Heinrich Hans."

"The copy we have is super rare." Will nodded. "There aren't many copies left under Herman's name and many of the ones written before the war were destroyed because the Germans banned comic books or something."

By this point, Amy had sat down on the floor of the treehouse and was looking between them with raised eyebrows. "Wow," she breathed. Her brows furrowed as she considered everything they'd told her so far. "Have you guys read the Diary of Anne Frank?"

The boys shook their heads no.

"I had to read it for a book review in school last year," Amy explained. "It was about a young Jewish girl who hid during the war from the Nazis. She wrote a diary of her whole experience. It's a true story."

All at once, the boys asked, "What happened to her?"

"She died. The Nazis eventually found her and she died while in captivity."

At this, Isaac's shoulders slumped and he looked back down at the book in his lap, disappointed by the answer. Dez and Will patted his back comfortingly. "Hey, it's okay," they mumble.

Amy watched on in puzzlement.

"Isaac is Jewish," Will told her.

"And his mom lost her whole family during the war," Dez added.

"Oh, I'm so sorry," Amy murmured. "I didn't know."

No one said anything for a while and the silence was not a comfortable one. Amy played with a loose thread on the hem of her t-shirt while Dez and Will sat back in their beanbags. Isaac hadn't looked up from the book.

"Why don't you tell me more about what you found?" She implored.

Isaac finally looked up and considered Amy, as though wondering if he should. Seeming to think there was no harm in it, he continued. "Well, this particular issue was printed in 1939, right? So we think it might be a rare collectible and it could be worth –"

Dez interrupted, rubbing his fingers together pointedly in a gesture they all knew well. "Mucho dollars."

The four of them laughed at this interjection, but it seemed to have put the conversation to an end. Isaac closed *The History of Comics* and tucked it back into his backpack. He opted instead for one of the comic books in the milk crate, returning to the normal order of things.

"It's a nice place you boys got here," Amy looked around the treehouse.

"Thanks," Will replied, grinning widely. "We built it ourselves."

"No way! You're kidding!"

"Nope," Dez shook his head. "We got all the wood from my garage and the scrapyard. There are loads of tools in my garage, so we used those."

"And the extension cord came from my house, but obviously it runs up to Dez' place since he's right here," Isaac added without looking up from his comic.

"That made it even cooler," Amy grinned back. She looked impressed with them, but she seemed to be done talking. She reached into the milk crate and pulled out the top comic book, oblivious to the reaction as the boys feared she might pull out or reveal one of the dirty magazines. "Do you guys mind if I read this?"

"No, no, not at all," all of them replied hurriedly. "Go for it!"

Amy raised one eyebrow, looking between them suspiciously. It was clear that she knew something was going on, but since she was unable to figure out what it was, she opened the comic and began reading. Will and Dez watched her for a few minutes, still surprised by the presence of a girl in their treehouse and even more surprised by the fact that she was reading one of their comic books, before they turned to read one as well.

The four of them hung out in the treehouse for a while, mostly reading in silence until Will put in a cassette. This time, no one sang along, but the boys approved of the occasional bob of Amy's head as she lost herself in the comic book. They bobbed their own heads as they read too.

Eventually, it began to get dark.

Isaac was the one to raise his head first. "We should probably get going before the sun goes all the way down. My mom doesn't like me riding after dark."

"Yeah, that's probably a good idea," Will nodded and

closed his comic before putting it back in the milk crate.

The other three followed suit and soon, Amy was climbing down the ladder with the boys close behind her. There wasn't much in the way of saying goodbye. The four walked toward Dez' house together and picked up their bikes. They noticed a pink bike up against the maple tree.

Amy had brought her own along. That explained how she'd gotten there.

"See ya'," she waved and climbed on, heading down the driveway before any of the boys could say a proper goodbye.

Will, Dez, and Isaac had taken a liking to Amy and they could tell that she had taken a liking to them in return. Isaac and Will climbed onto their bikes. Dez waved awkwardly as they began riding down the driveway.

"See ya'," Will called back.

"See ya'!" Isaac repeated.

Dez could only grin as his friends cycled away. "Amanha."

As the night passed by, in the early hours of the morning, a mysterious stranger found their way into Mrs. Weatherbourne home. Moving under the cover of night, a dark shadow snuck in through one of the windows. What Mrs. Weatherbourne didn't know was that the stranger had visited before. The last time they were there, they didn't get what they'd come for, but they'd made sure to leave one of the windows unlocked.

Mrs. Weatherbourne would never notice the unlocked window. In her old age, it wasn't a priority to walk through every room of the house. While sorting through Milton's old things, she'd been taking it room by room. The attic had the most boxes and so, that was where she started. Until she finished, she didn't have any intention of moving on to the next one. Besides, Seymour liked having alternative entrances and exits to get in and out of the house. He came and went as he pleased.

The stranger tiptoed through the kitchen and into the living room, squinting into the darkness. It wasn't until she walked further into the room that her eyes began to adjust to the darkness and she noticed the pictures and letters scattered all over the coffee table, illuminated by the sudden light as the clouds shifted. Moonlight shone through the open curtains, revealing the identity of the stranger, not that anyone was around to see it.

Gorska Maika went over to the coffee table, looking over the mess there. Several empty cardboard boxes were strewn across the floor, but many of them still had their contents. She got down on her haunches and began rummaging through them as quietly as she could.

"Dammit," the woman cursed beneath her breath.

She was annoyed by the darkness of the house. If she could have brought a flashlight or switched on the light, she would have. As it was, the stranger couldn't afford to wake Mrs. Weatherbourne. Operating in darkness was the only way to go. That didn't make it any less frustrating, though.

After searching through two boxes without any luck, Gorska Maika moved on. She couldn't search through them forever. Besides, the boxes had the word *donate* scrawled along the sides and she had a feeling Mrs. Weatherbourne wouldn't be donating what she was looking for.

The mantelpiece caught her attention and Gorska Maika walked toward it. The photos of Milton from the Navy were the only things she'd seen relating to the war so far. Up until this moment, she hasn't come across any other clues. Surely Milton had left behind something.

"Perhaps those boys found it," Gorska Maika muttered to herself.

"Who are you?" Mrs. Weatherbourne's voice suddenly rang out.

Gorska Maika froze, her eyes widening at being caught. She turned around to find Mrs. Weatherbourne standing in the doorway of the kitchen. The old woman was holding an umbrella over her head, ready to use it like some sort of makeshift weapon.

"I said… Who are you?" Mrs. Weatherbourne repeated loudly, but she couldn't hide the slight tremble in her voice.

Rather than answer her, the stranger suddenly ran toward her at full speed, knocking her to the ground. The force was such that Mrs. Weatherbourne made no sound. Her head hit the ground and she was knocked unconscious. The stranger leaned over her, checking to see if she was really out. Satisfied that Mrs. Weatherbourne really was unconscious, Gorska Maika raised her wrist and checked that the old woman still had a pulse. Only once she'd confirmed that Mrs. Weatherbourne was still alive did the stranger turn away.

There didn't seem to be any more clues in the house

and the stranger wanted to get out of there before Mrs. Weatherbourne woke up. She made her way toward the door. There, Seymour stood in front of it. Every little hair on the cat's body stood on end and he did not look happy to see Gorska Maika. He hissed as she neared him.

"Go away, you stupid cat," the stranger muttered.

Seymour attempted to swipe at Gorska Maika and narrowly missed. The woman ignored the cat and grabbed at the door, quietly slipping out. Once she was outside, she broke into a run and jumped into the Mercedes that was waiting for her across the street.

The car started up and drove off into the night, its purring engine waking no one as it disappeared from the neighborhood.

When Marjorie eventually woke up the morning sun was shining. She felt her aching head and a sore arm. Making her way to the phone she made the call for help.

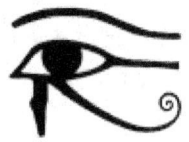

CHAPTER 11
A DAY AT THE BEACH

Since it was their summer vacation, Will, Dez, and Isaac planned on spending as much time together as they could. Before they knew it, they would be back at school and the holiday would be replaced by curfews and homework. They weren't going to waste a single second of it. That's why they made an effort to have at least one adventure every single day of the summer – save for those first few days when it rained.

On this day, they were going to the beach. They'd been so busy in town the previous day, what with their visit to the library and Davenport's, that there had been no time left for a trip to the beach. The cool thing about their town was that they could cycle everywhere, so they never had to ask their parents to take them to places. They were perfectly capable of getting there on their own.

"It was pretty cool hanging out with Amy yesterday," Dez called as they rode through the town. The wind blew against their shirts as they raced each other down the narrow back roads.

Isaac, barely able to breathe due to how hard he had to pedal in order to keep up with Dez, simply nodded his head vigorously in response.

"Yeah," Will agreed. "I didn't expect her to actually come 'round!"

Dez grinned knowingly, looking sideways at Will. "Nah, I knew she would."

A puzzled expression came over both Will and Isaac's face and they looked at their friend questioningly. Dez either didn't notice their bafflement or had no intention of explaining things to them. He continued racing as fast as he could, the muscles in his caramel legs stinging with the effort of how fast he rode. Will and Isaac hurried to catch up with him, determined not to lose a race they had already lost.

Dez only slowed his bike, with some effort, when the boys came to Mrs. Weatherbourne house. They had arrived right in time to witness a police car pulling out of her driveway. All three slowed down and pulled up to the curb outside her house, their brows knitted together in confusion as they watched the police car drive away. The police officer in the driver's seat looked them over before disappearing, leaving them without any explanation.

"What do you think happened?" Dez asked. "Should we go and find out?"

"No way," Isaac shook his head. "My mom would kill me if she found out we did that. She would say it's none of our business."

"Actually," Will gestured. He looked over at Mrs. Weatherbourne's house, curiosity merging with worry and burning the pit of his stomach. "My mom would want to know what happened."

"Why don't we ask that guy?" Isaac pointed to a landscaper working in the neighboring yard, using a trimmer to edge along the sidewalk. He looked like he'd been working a while. "He might know something."

"Good eye, G-man," Dez nodded and rolled up to the landscaper. "Hey!"

At first the landscaper seemed taken aback by the boys' sudden appearance. His eyes narrowed. "Hey, kids. Can I help ya'?"

"We uh… We saw a police car driving away from here," Dez stammered, suddenly nervous to ask about Mrs. Weatherbourne. His friends might be right about it being none of their business, but his mom wouldn't have bothered telling him off at this point. So, he plowed ahead. "Do you know what happened?"

The landscaper's eyes narrowed even more than before. "What's it to you?"

"Hey," Isaac interjected. "There's no need to be rude. We're friends of Mrs. Weatherbourne's. We were helping her move boxes from the attic the other day."

Some form of recognition lit up the man's face and he became decidedly less suspicious of them. "You're the boys who helped with Milton's things?"

The kids nodded their heads.

"She mentioned ya' when she was talking to the police, said you were good kids." He nodded solemnly. "Someone broke into her house last night and ransacked the place, including some of those boxes you boys helped with."

"Whoa," Dez muttered, his eyes widening. "Is she okay?"

"She was injured in the scuffle and she's been taken to the Cape Cod hospital."

The boys looked at one another in a mixture of shock and panic. They had no time to ask any further questions because, at that moment, Mike Kelly arrived in a van with his news station's name written on the side. The Cape Cod Daily was the local news outlet and Mike Kelly was its number one reporter. Everyone in the town knew him, not only because of his channel and radio station, but because he was one of the most eccentric men around. He was definitely the most eccentric in their little town of Dennis Port as well as all the surrounding towns.

Mike Kelly's hair was slicked back with an inordinate amount of hair gel and he wore a baby blue suit, complete with a pin that had his company logo on the breast pocket. He had a grin on his face that brought out the dimples in his cheeks. At the sight of him, Will, Dez, and Isaac grimaced. Most of the women in Dennis Port and beyond had a thing for Mike Kelly, but they thought he was pretentious and arrogant. He winked at the end of every news report and they thought it was the most embarrassing thing they'd ever seen.

"Well, well, well," Mike grinned as he stepped out of

the van. Close behind him was a teenager holding a massive video camera on his shoulders, panning it over the landscaper and the boys. "What do we have here?"

"What's it to you?" The landscaper repeated, his expression even more deterring than it had been when the boys turned up.

"I'm here to do a news story on the break-in at the Weatherbourne house," Mike stated proudly, standing straighter than before. "Things like this don't happen often around here, you know."

There was something about the way he spoke that made it seem as though he was excited about the break-in. The boys shook their heads in irritation. They liked Mrs. Weatherbourne and they didn't think this guy had any right to be outside her house.

Nevertheless, they couldn't say or do anything to stop him as he turned and walked up the driveway. The teenager with the camera followed him. Their entourage was joined by a woman in her early twenties who jumped out of the van and followed after them. She had some kind of electric box in one hand and a long wire connected it to the microphone in her other hand. As they watched, the woman and the teenager got ready in front of Mike Kelly where he stood posing in front of the old house.

From where they stood, the landscaper and the boys could still hear Mike Kelly as he spoke into the microphone. They were getting front row seats to the latest news report. As they watched, Mike Kelly introduced his news story the same way he always did.

"Welcome back to the Cape Cod Daily. I'm Mike Kelly,

here with the latest news in the little town of Dennis Port."

Mike Kelly began walking further up the driveway and the camera and microphone smoothly followed. One could tell they did this on a regular basis. There were no rehearsals involved because the competitive industry meant that the news reporters had to rush for the latest scoop – not that there was much competition in Dennis Port.

"Today, something happened in our friendly little town of Dennis Port that well, to be frank, just doesn't happen here. Things like this don't happen here," Mike repeated what he'd said to the boys and the landscaper for the viewers, shaking his head in disbelief. "Behind me, you can see the house that we here in Dennis Port fondly refer to as the old Weatherbourne house. It's one of the oldest houses in this humble town, built long before I was born, but we're not here to talk about the history of the house." Mike paused for effect. "Today we're here to talk about its sole occupant, Marjorie Weatherbourne. Some of us know Mrs. Weatherbourne well and most of us knew her husband Milton Weatherbourne even better."

Mike Kelly shook his head solemnly, his voice suddenly taking on a somber tone. "Milton Weatherbourne passed away recently. Some of you may have known him. If you did, you were lucky. He was an influential part of our community, having served in both the Navy and World War II. We thank him for his service."

"He was a hell of a man," the landscaper murmured, enrapt by the news show.

"Now, if that wasn't enough, Milton did a lot for us. He

was always there to offer a helping hand, wasn't he? Did you know that Milton had a secret though? There's a rumor that years ago, Milton brought a treasure back with him from World War II." Mike raised his eyebrows. "It seems that the rumor may be true as last night, sources say someone came to the Weatherbourne house looking for Milton's Treasure."

Will, Dez, and Isaac could scarcely believe what they were hearing. Was it true? Did Milton really have a treasure? And if so, what was it?

They waited with bated breath, watching Mike continue with the story. They were taking in every word as Amy Howard joined them, riding up on her bike like she was a part of the group all along. All three boys noticed her in their peripheral vision and turned to face her.

Will was the first to turn away. He barely had his eyes on her for a second when he felt the heat rising in his cheeks and prayed that he didn't look as red as he felt. The warmth rushed all the way to the tips of his ears. She grinned at him and he knew that if he continued to stare, he would get lost in her big blue eyes.

It was much safer to turn away before that happened.

Although he was no longer looking at her, Will could still feel Amy's eyes on him. He took a deep breath in through his nose and exhaled through his mouth, hoping that he wasn't being too obvious. Above all, he had another hope on his mind; he hoped that Amy's thoughts about him were good ones.

"Hi, Will," she said in a singsong voice.

The blush deepened and Will turned to look at her once

again. "Hi."

Amy's smile grew wider, but thankfully she didn't torment Will for much longer. She turned to the scene before them, taking in the Cape Cod Daily van and Mike Kelly standing in front of Mrs. Weatherbourne's house.

"What happened here?" Amy asked.

Mike Kelly had already finished reporting about Mrs. Weatherbourne's injury. The boys had missed it because of Amy's arrival. It didn't matter though, because they could tell Mike didn't know much more than they did.

"Someone broke into Mrs. Weatherbourne's house," Dez answered. "They hurt her and now she's in the hospital."

"Oh, my goodness," Amy gasped, covering her mouth. "Is she okay?"

"We don't know," Isaac responded with a shrug. "I guess she must be since Mike Kelly didn't mention anything serious about it."

"Yeah," Will murmured. "He wouldn't have looked so happy, right?"

Dez and Isaac nodded their heads, but Will could tell they were hoping they were right just as much as he hoped for the same thing. The truth was that the boys had no idea what had happened, and they didn't know if Mrs. Weatherbourne would be okay. All they had was hope.

That train of thought was far too gloomy for a clear summer's day.

As if agreeing that they should probably head out, the landscaper suddenly spoke. "Well, I'd better get on with my day. I have lots of trimming to do." He turned to the kids and nodded his head. "You kids have a good day now, you hear?"

The boys and Amy nodded their heads, smiling awkwardly as the landscaper turned to continue down the sidewalk. Behind him, Mike Kelly and his news crew were already packing up the van. They paid the kids no mind.

"Do you guys wanna get going?"

"Where are you going?" Amy asked. She added, with a grin, "You guys are always running off to be somewhere else when I show up."

Will ran a hand through his hair, ducking his head nervously. "No, it's not like that at all."

"Oh, Will. I'm just joking."

Glancing over at her, Will saw that Amy was smiling. She definitely didn't look like they'd offended her. "Oh," he said simply.

Beside him, Dez snickered. "We're going to the beach if you wanna come."

"Sure! That sounds like fun!"

Will didn't look back at Amy, but he couldn't help but smile at her willingness to join them for the day. Dez didn't wait for anyone to say anything else. Amy's confirmation was all he needed to start riding once more, allowing everyone else to speed off after him toward Sea Street Beach, the wind blowing through their shirts and Amy's long hair.

♦ ♦ ♦

Sea Street Beach rested high along the eroded shore. The only sound louder than the crashing of waves against one another was that of the squawking seagulls flying overhead. The greedy birds could be heard squawking for miles around, hovering in the hopes that a tourist at the local restaurant might leave their fries behind. Such was their nature.

The sandy beach stretched on in both directions, kissing the edge of the ocean, long enough that the end of either side couldn't be seen from where the kids entered. Over the previous summer, the boys had walked all the way to the end of one side, only to find jagged cliff sides that they couldn't climb. They'd walked back feeling accomplished but exhausted, their feet and muscles aching for days afterward. Nonetheless, the pain had been well worth it. Their venture had been an adventure, and they were glad that they'd made the trek because they would always know what was at the end of the grainy, tan path. They didn't have to spend any time wondering anymore.

A set of weathered wooden stairs led down to the beach, a muted golden hue that seemed to glow beneath the sunlight. The sky was mostly clear. The few lone wisps of clouds that floated across the cobalt expanse were too weak to dream of blocking out the sunshine. It was a beautiful day and the kids had been smart enough to apply sunscreen before they left the house, though each of them already had the barest hint of a tan to their skin, Dez being the darkest of all.

Amy and the boys parked their bikes near the stairs and ditched their shoes before hurrying down the stairs to the beach. The sand was soft and warm between their toes and Amy sighed at the feeling of the grains against her feet. The boys watched on as she tilted her head backward and threw her arms out, closing her eyes and basking in the sun as it shone down on her face. They were surprised by this behavior and even more surprised when she returned to normal and burst into a run toward the ocean.

After a shocked exchange of glances, the boys chased after her, following her lead toward the tumultuous ocean and its turquoise depths. They didn't run for long, losing themselves only briefly to the feel of the cool breeze against their skin, the scent of salt in their noses, and the feel of sunshine on their faces. Before long, they were breathless and laughing.

Amy was the first to tumble to the ground, giggling wildly as she rolled around in the sand. The boys dived after her until all of the kids were on the beach. Adrenaline rushed through their systems and they panted at the sudden exhilaration Amy had elicited.

In the silence that followed, with the exception of the whispering waves, they were left to their thoughts and they were all thinking about the same thing. After the morning they'd had, it was no surprise. What else would they be concerned about?

There hadn't been much chatter on the bikes since they were too busy racing toward the beach trying to get there as soon as they could. Keeping up with Dez exhausted all three of the other kids. It was clear he spent a lot of time riding his bike. Then again, it helped that he was much taller than the other kids his age.

"Do you guys think the story about Milton's treasure is true?" Isaac suddenly asked. He didn't look at his friends, staring instead at the sky above them.

"I don't know," Will murmured. "It all seems so weird. Maybe Mike Kelly was making it up to sound more exciting."

Dez snorted derisively. "More exciting than an old lady getting attacked? C'mon. This is Dennis Port. You heard the man. Stuff like this doesn't happen here."

"I wouldn't call Mrs. Weatherbourne going to the hospital an exciting piece of news," Amy admonished him.

"You know what I mean!" Dez exclaimed. "If you think about it, when last did you hear about someone's house getting broken into?"

The other three were silent for a moment before Will muttered, "Never."

"Exactly," Dez sat up in the sand. "I mean, what if it is true?"

Isaac also sat up at this question. He'd been concerned that the others might make fun of him for asking the question in the first place. "Well, I've been thinking," he started, adding to Dez' account. "What if Gorska Maika had something to do with it?"

At this, Will sat up too, spraying sand in every direction due to how fast he moved.

"Hey!" Amy yelled, sitting up and dusting the sand off herself. "Who is *Gorska Maika*?"

"Uh…" Will looked at his friends for help, but they simply raised their eyebrows at him.

"She's this Russian lady Isaac bumped into at Davenport's."

"A Russian lady?"

"And she always travels around in a black Mercedes,"

Will added.

By this point, Amy was staring at him like he was crazy, but for once he wasn't blushing. I don't understand."

The boys exchanged a glance. They hadn't told Amy about the events of the previous morning. She only knew about the comic and its history.

"Yesterday, when we were in Davenport's," Isaac began. "I bumped into this scary Russian lady who was dressed like some kind of punk rocker spy."

Amy arched an eyebrow. "A punk rocker spy?"

"She was really scary," Will offered. "But the thing is, it wasn't the first time we'd seen her. There was this black Mercedes outside of Mrs. Weatherbourne's house when we helped with Milton's boxes. And she was in the car."

"Yeah, her and some creepy man in black," Dez added with a shiver. "I found a magazine about UFO encounters and the picture on the cover looked just like those two. The magazine said these people show up after alien abductions or whatever."

"Alien… abductions…" Amy said slowly, testing each syllable.

"We're not crazy," Isaac sighed. "Forget about the UFO thing. This same car was outside Davenport's when we went there and then again when we left the library. It was like they were…" Isaac couldn't seem to finish his sentence.

"…*following us.*" Will finished it for him.

None of the kids had spoken about it, but they'd all seen the Mercedes too many times for it to be a coincidence. Could it be possible that they were being followed? Should they be worried? Were the man and woman dressed in black to blame for Mrs. Weatherbourne's injuries? They didn't know.

"Okay, well, that's really creepy. Why do you call her Gorska Maika?" Amy asked.

"Isaac found a comic book, *The Grimm Tales of Gorska Maika,* the Russian boogey woman, who looked kind of like her right after they bumped into each other," Dez shrugged.

Amy looked between them as if trying to deduce whether or not they were making up some elaborate story to trick her. Her eyebrows were raised and she looked at Will for a second too long, longer than the other boys. Finally, she seemed to decide that they weren't messing with her and released a low whistle.

"You boys have been having an adventurous summer, haven't you?"

Dez grinned widely. "Every day is an adventure, baby."

He received a stare from Isaac, Will, *and* Amy. The longer they looked at him, the redder Dez grew. Suddenly, all four of them burst into a fit of laughter that lasted for minutes.

By the time Amy stopped, she had to wipe tears away from her cheeks. "You're a funny guy, Dez."

"You have no idea," Will grinned.

"Yeah, Dez is a special kid," Isaac smiled widely. "You should hear about this one story about the hand grenades."

"Oh, no," Dez murmured, covering his face with his hands.

"Hand grenades?" Amy asked.

"So, you see, Dez used to dress up in his Dads clothes and play army when he was younger," Will started, looking over at his friend fondly. "One of these days, he was all dressed up in army clothes and he'd found something in his house that he could use as part of the roleplay."

"*Why* must you tell this story?" Dez cried out with a short chuckle.

"Anyway," Isaac continued Will's story. "When Dez' mom came home, she saw him from the car. He was jumping around in the front yard, dodging these strange white things and making explosion sounds with his mouth."

"Dez' mom wasn't the only one to notice, of course. She was shocked by what she saw, sure, but so were like half the neighbors who watched the fiasco." As he spoke, Will's smile grew and grew. For once, he didn't seem to have an issue with looking at Amy when he spoke. This was one of his and Isaac's favorite stories about their best friend.

"And our Dez loves putting on a show," Isaac laughed.

"He sure does," Will nodded.

"What happened next?" Amy asked, clearly enthralled by the story. "Why was everyone so shocked?"

"Well, Dez' mom got out of her car and ran up to Dez. She starts hurrying to pick up all these small white things that he's been throwing all over the yard. And she asks him what he's doing with them while holding onto one of them." Will glanced over at Dez, building the anticipation, and Dez finally removed his hands from his face. There was a tinge of pink to his chubby cheeks. "Dez was confused by the question. I mean, it should have been obvious that they were hand grenades. He pulled the string, he threw them into the air, and they exploded."

"Except," Dez finally joined in on the story. "That was when my mom was like, *hand grenades?! These are my tampons!*"

The kids all started cracking up, including Dez. He was embarrassed, but there was no denying that the story was amusing. Will laughed so hard that he clutched his belly in pain and Amy could hardly breathe.

"I can't believe you did that," Amy finally said through her giggles. "All this laughing is making me need to use the bathroom. I'll be right back!"

Amy wandered off back to the stairs. Despite the run, the kids were actually still pretty close to the stairs. The beach restrooms were right near them and Amy stopped at the bikes to put her shoes back on before heading into the bathroom building.

On her way out, Amy stopped to fix her hair in the bathroom mirror. As she was walking out, Amy's throat tightened at the sight of the two brutes walking down the sidewalk nearby. She tried backing up into the bathroom, but it was too late. Greg Collins and Jay Flynn had seen her and they sped up at the sight of her.

"Well, well, if it isn't Scabs," Greg grinned menacingly revealing his missing front teeth, knocked out by a slap shot to the face during a hockey game. "Whatcha doing here?"

"Using the bathroom?" Amy snapped, rolling her eyes.

"I wouldn't take that tone if I were you," Jay said, taking

a step toward her.

"Well, it's a good thing you're not me, isn't it?" Amy knew Jay was nothing more than Greg's lazy eyed side-kick. Using his slightly smaller and slightly closed lazy eye as an excuse for not being a great hockey player as well. Amy was trying to put on a brave face even though she could barely breathe for the fear. Her heart was racing too fast. "Why don't you two just go away?"

Greg and Jay exchanged a glance and at the same moment, turned to laugh in her face. "Maybe we should take you into the bathroom and clean you up?" They added.

Amy looked past them. She could see her and her friends' bicycles and they weren't that far away. Right beyond that was the set of stairs. She briefly considered making a break for it, wondering if it was possible for her to get past Greg and Jay. They were older and bigger than she was, taller and wider. Still, there was a space between them that she might fit into if she ducked down.

It would be a tight fit, but it could work.

Long before she had the chance to run for it, she caught sight of Will in the tiny gap. He walked up the stairs, looking around and Amy realized he'd come looking for her. How long had she been gone? It didn't matter because he noticed Greg and Jay. He couldn't see Amy, but he put two and two together and came sprinting toward them.

"Hey!" Will called. At the sight of Greg and Jay cornering Amy, Will felt moisture beginning to form in his palms. His heart was racing. "Get away from her!"

The bullies turned around to face Will. Jay spoke first.

"How about you mind your own business and piss off?"

All logical thoughts faded away, replaced by the adrenaline coursing through his body. His instincts told Will that he should either run or beat the living daylights out of the bigger boys. Amy could barely breathe as she watched Will, praying that he wouldn't do anything stupid even as he took another step forward. He was toe to toe with Greg, who towered above him.

"Leave her alone," he breathed.

"Oh-ho," Greg chuckled. It didn't last long before Greg pulled his arm back. It was obvious that he was preparing to take a swing at Will.

Before Greg got the chance, Amy could hear the sound of Isaac and Dez' footsteps as they charged up the sidewalk, joining Will.

Greg lowered his arm and snorted at the sight of the three boys. "What are you dickweeds gonna do about it, huh?"

"Why don't you try us and find out?" Dez snapped, standing taller than ever before. He was the only one who reached the heights of Greg and Jay and the bullies seemed to shrink back the slightest bit.

Greg and Jay looked over the boys and after a moment's deliberation, they stepped away. They shoved past Will, Dez, and Isaac. Greg was sure to bash his shoulder into Will's shoulder on his way past. They were already walking away from the four kids when Greg turned and looked over his shoulder. Greg held up his hand and Jay automatically gave him a high-five.

"Whatever, losers," he said.

"Yeah," Jay added. "We don't have time for you anyway."

Amy and the boys watched them until Greg and Jay were far enough away that they knew the bullies had no intention of returning. All of them seemed to relax. Will's shoulders, which had been tense, loosened up and he released a heavy sigh.

"Thank you," Amy suddenly broke the silence, her voice soft. "All of you."

Though she added the last part, Amy didn't take her eyes off Will. He'd come to defend her all on his own, against two of the biggest and meanest boys in the town. She was incredibly grateful to him.

Dez grinned. "That was awesome."

"Anyone hungry?" Will changed the topic. He couldn't stop staring at Amy either.

"Yeah!" The other three cheered.

They went to the nearest restaurant, which was a burger and seafood joint that they have been too many times before. Will, Dez, and Isaac had yet to spend the money Mrs. Weatherbourne had given them, so they ordered the most affordable burger, chips, and drinks on the menu. Plus, they had a little extra for Amy as well. By the time the food arrived, and they ate the kids were restless and tired of the beach.

Besides, none of them wanted to hang around when there was a chance that Greg and Jay might return.

"Do you guys wanna go back to my house?" Dez asked.

The group rumbled in agreement. They hopped back onto their bikes and rode off.

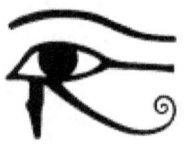

CHAPTER 12
SWEET WONDERFUL YOU

By the time they finally arrived at Dez' house they decided to gather some snacks and hangout in the treehouse.

"Maybe we can ask my grandma for some snacks," Dez shrugged, parking his bike up against the maple tree. "Come on."

The others followed his lead. They heard the sound of the Pomeranian while they were still walking up the driveway, bouncing up and barking at the door wildly. Amy seemed to have shrunk somewhat and none of the boys realized why until the front door of the main house opened and Dez' grandmother appeared.

"Hey, Grandma Ruth," Isaac and Will greeted her.

"Hey, Grams," Dez hugged the old lady. Cocoa calmed down at the sight of Dez, running in circles around his feet until Will leaned down to pet her. "We were wondering if we could have some snacks for the treehouse."

Grandma Ruth looked at the four of them, raising her eyebrows. "Aren't you going to introduce me to your new friend?" She turned to face Amy. "You're a pretty little thing."

"Oh," Dez blinked. He and the boys looked down at their feet, feeling mildly embarrassed. This was the first time any of them had introduced a girl to any of the adults who cared for them and their families were one and the same. "Uh, this is Amy Howard. She lives downtown, behind the laundromat."

"Hi," Amy mumbled in a small voice. She grew even smaller once everyone's attention was on her. "It's nice to meet you."

"I'm Grandma Ruth, darling. It's a pleasure to meet you too." She looked between her grandson, Will, and Isaac. "Welcome to the Fernandez house. Can I get you something to eat?"

Dez couldn't hold back the eye-roll. His grandmother loved feeding new people. It was one of her favorite parts of their culture.

"*Grams*," Dez whined. We just ate, we just want snacks!"

"Don't you be rude now, Emilio," Grandma Ruth's tone was stern. She made her way over to the kitchen counter and came back with a tray in her hands. There was a steaming bowl of soup and a teapot on its surface. "You take your mama her tea now. I'll get you kids some snacks."

"Thanks, Grams," Dez mumbled, chagrined at being

told off. He took the tray from her wrinkled hands and began walking into the back of the house, taking slow steps so as not to spill a drop.

Grandma Ruth turned to the other three kids in her living room with a warm smile on her face. She didn't seem to notice that they were mortified for both themselves and their friends. All three of them had gotten down on their haunches and were giving Cocoa affection, rubbing her belly and that special spot behind her ears, in an attempt to distract themselves from the situation with Dez.

"I'll make you kids some Cape Cod popcorn, eh? Grandma's special recipe," she winked and walked into the kitchen. "You can go on up to the treehouse. I'll send Dez with the snacks."

"Thanks, Grandma Ruth!" Will and Isaac stood, both going into the kitchen to give the elderly woman a hug. She chuckled as she wrapped her arms around both boys. When she released them, she waved her hand at Amy, gesturing her over.

Amy's nervousness dissipated at the sight of Grandma Ruth offering her a hug. This woman was a total stranger, but she had a sense of homeliness about her. Grandma Ruth was the type of grandmother that one often thought about making soup during a cold winter's day and making Christmas jumpers. At the same time, however, she seemed a strong and capable woman that no one should ever cross or underestimate.

Grandma Ruth's hugs were much the same. Amy had gone into the kitchen and, wrapped up in Grandma Ruth's arms, she thought that they were the best hugs in the world.

Ruth's arms were strong and firm, but they were also gentle and warm. Amy could have stayed in them forever, but eventually, Grandma Ruth pulled away. She tucked Amy's hair behind her shoulders and gave her a smile.

"There now," she clapped her hands. "You run along with the boys to the treehouse. I'll see you around, Amy."

"Thank you, Grandma Ruth," Amy smiled back before making her way over to the boys, who were waiting for her at the door.

"No, Cocoa," Will pushed the Pomeranian back from the door with his foot. "You can't come with us."

Once the door was finally closed, they walked across the yard and headed toward the woods outside Dez' house. It was as though they did this all the time. Though they'd only been hanging out with Amy for a short while, she already felt like she was a part of their group and had been all along. Grandma Ruth's hug made her feel more welcomed than anything.

"Grandma Ruth seems nice," Amy mentioned as they walked.

"We love her," Isaac nodded.

"She likes you," Will added, looking over at Amy. He was pleased to see a smile appear on her face.

They climbed into the treehouse and Isaac flopped into his beanbag straight away. Will and Amy lingered near the tiny entryway until Will walked over to the box of cassettes and put one into the radio. Unaware of their awkward predicament, Isaac had already switched the lamp on, taken a magazine out of the milk crate, and happily flipped through its pages.

"Uh," Will mumbled, shifting from foot to foot. "You can share my beanbag if you want."

"Sure," Amy nodded.

With that, Will sat down on one side of the beanbag and Amy sat on the other. It took some shifting to get properly balanced, but by the time Dez returned, they had it. They were bobbing their heads to the music and Will had taken out the Superman 1938 comic Dez had said wasn't worth much. He was flipping through the pages and Amy read over his shoulder. He didn't move on to the next page until she nodded her head, confirming that she was finished reading.

"Hey guys," Dez called up the ladder. "Could someone help get the popcorn?"

It was only when Isaac raised his eyes from his magazine that he saw how Amy and Will were seated. He raised his eyebrows slightly and set the magazine aside before slowly getting up and sticking his head through the hole in the floor of the treehouse.

"What is that?" Isaac called.

"Take the bowl, bonehead," Dez responded.

Isaac leaned through the hole, half his body hanging out of the treehouse, and he reemerged a moment later with a bowl of something blue in his hands.

"What is that?" Amy and Will repeated Isaac's question at the same time.

"I think it's popcorn," Isaac murmured, staring into the bowl. "Didn't Grandma Ruth say she was going to make popcorn?"

"She said she was going to make her special Cape Cod

popcorn," Dez answered the question, climbing into the treehouse. "She used blue food coloring to make it look like the ocean since we went to the beach today. Isn't it great?"

The other three were skeptical and they looked it. Dez didn't seem to notice though. He grabbed the bowl from Isaac's hand, set it down atop his lap and flopped into his beanbag.

"So, what did I miss?" He was grinning at the sight of Amy and Will in the beanbag before him. "Anything interesting?"

"Shut up and eat the popcorn," Will rolled his eyes, knowing all too well that his best friend was looking for a rise.

Dez gave a snicker and began eating the popcorn. He hummed along to the song that was playing. Amy, Will, and Isaac returned to what they'd been doing before Dez arrived. Suddenly the sound of a new song resonated from the radio.

"*Sweet wonderful you...You make me happy with the things you do...*" Dez sang in a low voice.

Will could feel his heart rate rise at the sound of the Fleetwood Mac song. He looked at Amy out of the corner of his eye. Despite how shy he felt, he wanted to sing the next line, but didn't.

"*Oh, can it be so,*" Isaac continued.

The boys weren't doing it intentionally. It simply happened.

"You can turn," Amy whispered to Will, looking over at Dez and Isaac.

Both boys were watching Will expectantly. Will didn't move. He was staring at the page without taking in anything on it. Amy had finished the page already.

"*I never did believe in miracles,*" Will sang the next line along with the song.

"*But I've a feeling it's time to try!*" Isaac and Dez sang the rest of the line as loudly as they could.

Together, the three of them sang the rest of the verse. Will no longer cared that Amy was there, but the last thing he expected was for Amy to start singing with them when the chorus started. She had a pretty voice and Will found himself smiling. They sang the whole song together and by the time it was done, they were all grinning widely.

Will felt kind of breathless. He never expected singing one of his favorite songs to be so exhilarating. It took him a while to be himself around Amy and now that he had, he felt free. The best part was that she sang with them as though it was totally normal.

No sooner had he had the thought did Amy start giggling. Dez and Will stared at her. The only difference between their two expressions was that Dez' had a mouthful of popcorn and it was slightly agape, revealing the blue of the Cape Cod ocean colored popcorn within. Isaac joined in with Amy's giggling and Will realized they were both looking at Dez.

"What's…?" Will didn't get the chance to finish his question because Dez had finished eating the mouthful and the sight of him had Will chortling too.

"What?" Dez asked, looking around at all of them. "What's so funny?"

"Dude, your mouth is blue," Will finally managed to utter between laughs.

Dez' eyes went wide and he didn't move for a moment. His hand was still in the bowl of popcorn. He looked down to see that the tips of his fingers were blue. Suddenly, he laughed too. "Well," he snickered and set the bowl down on the floor of the treehouse. "I think that's enough ocean popcorn for me."

"Grandma Ruth is pretty cool," Amy finally murmured, beaming at the three boys.

"Yeah, Grams is awesome," Dez nodded.

"Is your mom sick?"

The room fell silent quite abruptly. The only sound was that of the music playing. Amy looked between the boys, a confused expression on her face.

"It's just…" Amy spoke quietly, afraid that she may have said something wrong. "I saw the soup on the tray. My dad always makes me soup when I'm sick."

Dez took in a breath. "Yeah, my mom's sick. But she's not like, normal sick. There's no getting better for her."

"What do you mean?"

"She's dying. She has cancer."

"Oh, Dez," Amy breathed. "I'm so sorry. I didn't know."

"Of course you didn't," Dez shrugged. "How would you? It's okay though."

Amy, of course, had the feeling that it was very much not okay, but she didn't really know what to say that would make it better. "I guess, at least you get the chance to say goodbye to her."

At this, all eyes were on Amy. It seemed as though she wasn't going to elaborate at first. Her mouth opened and closed like she wanted to say something, multiple times. "My mom left," she shrugged her shoulders. "She didn't say goodbye or anything like that. She just... *left*. Me and my dad, we haven't heard from her since. She hasn't written or visited."

Will was the first to say, "I'm sorry."

Isaac and Dez' quiet apologies followed soon afterward.

"It's okay," she murmured.

"I still have my mom," Isaac stated. "But there's something wrong with her. I don't know. It seems like she's always really sad."

"Sad?" Amy shifted in the beanbag slightly.

"Yeah. She doesn't have anyone but me, you see. Since she lost her family in the war and everything, I'm the only one she has. It's almost like there's something broken inside her."

"That's why she's so overprotective of Isaac," Will added.

"I'm all she has," Isaac repeated.

"Seems like we all have problems with our moms," Will muttered, easing back into the beanbag. He closed the comic book. Things were too serious to have it open at that moment.

Behind them, the cassette had finished playing. Will reached into the box beside him and he was about to rummage through the tapes, but Amy interrupted him by reaching toward it.

"May I?" She offered.

"Sure," he passed the box over to her and she began rifling through the different artists.

"What's wrong with yours?" She finally asked him, not looking up from the box. She'd chosen an artist and she was in the process of removing the other tape and replacing it with her choice when Will began speaking.

"Well, it's more what's wrong with my dad," Will muttered. "I don't really know what to do about it though. He's been drinking a lot lately. It never used to be like this."

Amy flopped back down next to him as the music began to play, the sound of a guitar solo filling the treehouse. "But why did you say that there's something wrong with your mom then?"

"I said it was a problem," Will corrected. He looked over at the boys before he spoke. This wasn't something that they'd heard yet. "Since he started drinking, he's gotten angrier. And well, it's scary. It's gotten physical once or twice."

"Physical?" Amy's voice was soft.

Will had told his friends that things had gotten worse, even told him that part, but he'd refrained from going into detail. "The last time it happened, he hit my mom."

A pit formed in Amy's stomach. She hadn't thought that the conversation would turn this dark and she didn't know how to react to this bit of information.

"Dude," Dez sat forward. "You never told us that."

Will shrugged. "I guess I didn't know how."

"You know you can tell us anything, man," Isaac said.

"Yeah, you heard the G-man." Dez nodded his head. "That's what friends are for."

"G-man?" Amy looked at Isaac.

"It's his nickname," Will explained. "You know, 'cause his last name is Goffman, we call him G-man."

"That's such a cool nickname."

"Why, thank you, ma'am." Isaac tipped his head and gave a wink. Rather than looking suave, however, he ended up looking like there was something wrong with his eye and Amy giggled. Isaac wasn't offended, smiling at the fact that he'd made her laugh.

All at once, the treehouse felt light again. The four kids had moved on from the dark topics, but they weren't forgotten. On the contrary, they felt closer to one another and after what Dez and Isaac had said; they knew that they could always count on one another. After all, that was indeed what friends were for.

"I should probably go and wash my mouth," Dez stood up from his beanbag and began climbing down the ladder. "Can someone pass me the bowl when I reach the bottom?"

"Sure," Isaac stood too. "I should probably get going too. It's getting late and my mom will be worried."

"Cool." Dez began climbing down the ladder.

When he reached the bottom, Isaac grabbed the bowl of popcorn and leaned down into the hole to pass it on. He climbed down the ladder afterward. Taking their cue, Will turned the radio and the light off and climbed down next, with Amy close behind him.

Dez and Isaac were waiting for them at the end of the ladder.

"Is this where we say goodbye?" Dez asked, raising his

eyebrows. "I have a feeling Grams isn't gonna let me back out after I bring the bowl back."

Will laughed. "Yeah, considering it usually takes us a week to take dishes back from the treehouse."

"Which is why," Dez turned to Amy. "I'm glad you're here. We aren't allowed to have snacks anymore, but Grams couldn't resist our new friend, it seems."

Amy grinned and gave a faux curtsy, wearing shorts and all. "Well, I'm happy to be of service."

"Even if Dez was the only one to eat ocean popcorn," Isaac pointed out.

The four of them laughed at that, though Dez ran an embarrassed, blue-fingered hand over his face.

"Well…" Dez started. "See ya'!"

He couldn't take after Amy and ride away on his bicycle after making such a statement, so instead, he broke into a sudden run and raced across his backyard. He held the bowl with both hands and the few pieces of popcorn that were left flew out and landed on the dewy green grass. The other three could hear his maniacal chuckling all the way to the main house and they joined in with it.

"Dez really is a funny guy," Amy remarked, still giggling.

"He is," Isaac nodded. "I guess I better follow the lead. See ya'."

Decidedly less comically, Isaac broke into a run toward the gate. Once there, he turned and gave Will and Amy a wave. They waved back and watched him head to the old maple tree for his bike. And then they were all alone.

Neither of them seemed to know what to do until Amy

glanced up at the sky. It was already near dark. In the confines of the treehouse, the kids had let the sunset slip by them and they were well past the grey tinges of twilight. The night sky didn't have a single cloud in sight. Every twinkling star was visible, shining brightly down on them.

Will found himself gazing up at the sky too, uncertain of what else to do. The only sound for miles around was the persistent chirping of crickets in the woods and the occasional rustle of leaves as an imperceptible breeze blew through the trees behind them. It didn't feel like it was Will's moment of silence to break.

"I love the stars. They make me feel peaceful in a way nothing else ever has," Amy whispered. "My mom and I used to look at them. Two years ago, when my mother left me and my father, we looked up at the stars together. My mom pointed to the north star, the brightest one above us," Amy pointed to what was indeed the brightest star in the sky, which faced the end of a compass. Will looked over at it. "That one."

Will looked from the star to Amy and back again, following her finger, and waited for her to continue the story. At her attention, the star seemed to glow brighter than before. Perhaps it was Will's imagination, but it seemed almost as if the star knew it was being spoken about, knew the story, and knew it was being retold.

"That night, she told me that if we're ever apart and I look up at the bright sky above, she'll be looking up at the north star at the very same time somewhere in the world." Amy looked down at the ground sadly. "We made a pinky promise never to forget it. That was the last night we looked at the stars together. I haven't seen or heard from her since."

Will didn't know what to say. What could he possibly say that would make that better? There was nothing. Amy seemed to know that there weren't any words that could ease the pain of losing her mother because she did something else, something Will never expected in his wildest dreams. She slipped her hand into his, linking their fingers through one another. Will felt a smile, accompanied by a certain familiar warmth, come to his face. Looking up at Amy, he could see she was smiling too and he squeezed her hand gently.

"All these stars and it's just us," she murmured.

"If it's just us," Will recited a quote he'd once read in science class. Amy had been in that class. "That seems like an awful waste of space."

"Carl Sagan," Amy answered at the same time as Will.

They stared at one another in wonder and then laughed. It was as if time slowed down and sped up at the same time. Will knew what was happening, but he still couldn't bring himself to react as Amy leaned in, her hair touching his shoulder as she got closer than any girl had ever been before. Without thinking, he closed his eyes and found himself wondering if Amy had closed hers too. Every part of him felt warm as her lips touched his, and he couldn't help but marvel at how soft a girl's lips were as they kissed. His heart was beating so erratically he thought it might break through his chest and fly away.

The kiss only lasted a few seconds, but it seemed so much longer to both of them. When Amy pulled away, her cheeks were warm and every inch of her skin tingled. She didn't know that Will felt much the same way. Butterflies were swirling in her stomach, doing somersaults at her expense.

That felt good, she thought to herself.

For some time, neither of them said anything. They simply held hands and looked up at the sky. There was nothing *to* say, if they really thought about it. In that moment, Will understood what Amy meant by feeling at peace. They were as content as could be and their hands were the warmest thing in the world.

Eventually, the night grew colder and Amy gave a shiver. Will looked over at her. "We should probably head home. It's cold and you live further away."

"Yeah," Amy agreed. "I think that's a good idea."

They walked to the maple tree, hand in hand. They were reluctant to let go, but they couldn't help smiling when Amy said their new catchphrase. Only, this time she added a new word that made Will's stomach do a backflip.

"See ya' tomorrow," Amy smiled as she hopped onto her bike.

Amy rode away without waiting for his response, but that didn't stop Will from whispering, "See ya' tomorrow."

Will was on top of the world as he rode home. He couldn't recall ever feeling as happy as he did right then. The tips of his ears were warm and he couldn't bring himself to wipe the smile off his face as he peddled up the street. That was until he saw a familiar sight.

Up the street from Dez' house, barely visible in the pale streetlights, was none other than the black Mercedes. It blended into the night and Will paused to take it in, squinting to make sure that he wasn't seeing things. The occupants must have noticed him because the car suddenly purred to life, the lights flickering on as it zoomed forward. He had to pedal out of the way of the street as the car sped away, nearly running him over. His heart raced as he watched the taillights disappear into the distance.

When Will finally parked his bike in the driveway outside his house, he could already hear the cacophony of fighting coming from within. His stomach felt hollow as he tiptoed around the back of the house and snuck in through the backdoor. He headed straight to his room without greeting anyone, the sound of his father's anger echoing through the walls of the old house long after he was able to fall asleep.

◆ ◆ ◆

Late that evening, well after everyone in Dennis Port should have been asleep, Greg Collins – otherwise known as Puck – could be found wandering through the parking lot of a hotel. During the summer, the hotels were rather packed and tourists were unfamiliar with the etiquette of the little town. If they had been, they might have known to be more careful.

As it was, Greg moved silently from car to car. His well-practiced eyes could tell if they were unlocked without having to get too close.

Greg came across a beautiful black Mercedes and the corners of his mouth curled into a triumphant smirk. "Jackpot," he whispered as he made his way toward the fancy car.

The driver's door opened without a hitch and, looking around to make sure no one was witness to his actions, Greg climbed in to look for valuables. He started with the glove box and there, he found a newspaper clipping of Milton Weatherbourne's obituary, a passport, and a few Russian and American bills.

Greg had no interest in the passport or obituary, so he discarded them onto the passenger seat and shoved the cash into his back pocket. He couldn't see anything else of value in the otherwise empty car, so he climbed out. Closing the door, Greg turned and found himself face to face with Gorska Maika.

The woman in black did not look impressed. In fact, as she stared down Greg, she looked furious. The sharp, dark stare intimidated him and Greg took a reflexive step back. Instead of gathering some distance, he walked backward into a man dressed equally in black and built as big and hard as a wall.

Gorska Maika looked into Greg's eyes as the man in black grabbed him from behind. He lifted the school bully off of the ground and forced him into a chokehold with his forearm wrapped around Greg's neck before Greg could try to call for help. Gorska Maika didn't break eye contact as the life left Greg's eyes and he faded out of consciousness.

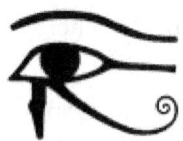

CHAPTER 13
SCHATZGRABER
Alexandra Land, Arctic Sea – 1943

Darkness fills my eyes, he thought to himself.

Through the rambling thoughts, he realized that things may be better off this way. It was better to see darkness than to see what might be waiting for him on the other side of his closed eyelids. Sometimes darkness was the only place he could use as an escape from the truth of his reality.

Herman Katzenstein had gone from a quiet and rewarding life in Berlin, to a train car, to a crate, and finally to a cell. It was in the cell that he found himself waking from a fetal position on the cold, hard concrete floor. The dim glow of light drifted through the steel bars of his cell, coming in from the concrete hallway just beyond.

The loud clicking of hard, leather-soled boots approached from the right. These were sounds Herman had grown accustomed to in his time there. The shadow of a figure cascaded down the hall. It was the only thing to break the dim light, though it did little for Herman's eyes. It was nothing more than another form of darkness in his vision. Finally, however, he knew he had to open his eyes and face what was coming. There was nowhere he could hide.

He could hear the words, spoken in native German. The voice of the strictly disciplined Nazi Officer resounded out abruptly, stern and as cold as the hard concrete Herman was surrounded by. "Is he here?"

"Yes, sir," a uniformed guard responded.

Herman unraveled his stiff body, feeling every ache in his bones and joints as he stretched his limbs out and forced them to rise to the moment. Slowly, he eased himself into a standing position. He'd only just managed when the Nazi Officer approached the bars.

The officer was well dressed, wearing his uniform and clean-shaven. It was clear from the double piston ring insignias on both his cuffs that he was one of the higher-ranking officers. He was one of the Waffen-SS.

"Can you walk?" The Nazi Officer spoke English in a deep German accent.

Herman nodded his head to answer that he could walk.

"Good," the officer sneered. "You wouldn't be of much use to me if you couldn't."

The Nazi Officer called on the uniformed guard and, speaking in German once more, ordered him to clean Herman Katzenstein up and escort him from the cell up to the Nazi Officer's quarters.

◆ ◆ ◆

A clock with tiny black numbers hung from a wall, overlooking a small office, made of a mesh of cold concrete floors and walls of wooden panels. The small hand moved past the numeral twelve, while the bigger hand slowly eased over to the six. The subtle motion of the clock's inner mechanical movements could scarcely be heard by the trained ear, each tick passing by without much notice unless one was watching out for a certain moment in time.

Below the clock, the Nazi Officer reached for a picture on the polished wooden chest of drawers. The glass was polished and shiny, regularly cleaned, and the pewter-frame surrounded a black and white photograph of a beautiful woman holding a young boy. She wore a floral dress and smiled into the lens of the camera, as did the boy, who looked to be around five years old.

The Nazi Officer's moment of reflection was interrupted by the sound of footsteps down the hall, followed by a knock on the door. The officer sat the picture back down on the cool wooden surface as the uniformed guard arrived with his escorted prisoner, Herman Katzenstein.

"Enter," the officer murmured.

The door opened and, upon having escorted Herman, the uniformed officer gave a curt nod and made his way back out of the quarters, closing the door behind him.

"Come in," the Nazi Officer spoke to Herman as he sat down behind a big wooden desk littered with papers and ledgers. He gestured to the chair across from him. "Have a seat."

The unchained prisoner did as he was told and sat down across from the Nazi Officer. He remained still and upright, but not without a bit of a lean to his stance. He couldn't help it after all those hours without any form of comfort. His body had felt better days, but he could no longer remember them. They were nothing more than dreams from a distant past he didn't think he would ever get back.

Herman knew what he was: a Jew. Due to this fact, he had watched the world he once knew get turned upside down. He knew that the lives of Jews were being taken every minute of every day, without cause or reason. Inside, he felt hollowed by the knowledge. At the same time, his body wanted him to feel what he was feeling. There was an undeniable twinge of painful hunger in what had become the literal pit of his stomach, quiet now that it had given up on growling, somehow aware that there was no point in asking for a meal it would never receive. His joints and what was left of his muscles were weak and sore, stiff and uncertain of how to move or what it felt like to be free of pain. Deep in his bones, he could feel the subtle chill of the trauma he'd endured at the hands of Germans, slithering up his spine and making his blood forget that it was meant to be warm.

As though Herman's thoughts of food could be heard, a soldier dressed in a grey uniform entered the room. In his hands, he carried a plate of bread and cheese. Without a word, he sat the plate down on the desk and returned moments later with a cup and a kettle steaming with the scent of tea before departing again.

Herman stared dead ahead, determined not to look toward the plate of food or tea, no matter how much he wanted to. There was a possibility that it could be a test, some kind of excuse to do him harm or otherwise cause him mental anguish. He was not going to give in for the pleasures of the moment. He wouldn't give them the satisfaction.

"Are you a good Jew?" the officer asked.

Herman nodded his head.

"Good. You would not be much use to me if you weren't," the officer repeated his words from before. "Have you ever seen the opera *Der Schatzgräber*?"

Herman nodded his head again, recalling that the first performance of *Der Schatzgräber* played at the Vienna State Opera on the 18th of October in 1922. It was composed by Franz Shreker. He could hardly remember the tiny details. They'd been scorched out of him. He'd been made to understand, under hours of torture inflicted upon him, that he was nothing.

He wasn't even a human as far as his captors were concerned.

The people Herman had once shared a seat within the Vienna State Opera House when he first saw *Der Schatzgräber* in 1932, ten years after its very first opening, were no longer around. There were people who he had once entertained with comic strips full of humor and hand-drawn characters that were no longer around too. They were all gone.

Now, Herman sat alone, nothing more than a hungry mouse who could smell cheese but knew he could not reach it because there was a cat who would rather play than let him eat.

"You know," the officer murmured, bringing Herman

crashing back down into the office and dragging away all thoughts of the glorious house of the Vienna State Opera, only to replace them with an altogether harsh reality. "They call this place Schatzgraber, like the opera."

Herman did not respond, nor did he move.

"And would you believe my name is Franz, like the composer?" The officer, who Herman now knew to be Franz, spoke with a tinge of humor in his voice. "I guess you could say that this is my performance to compose." He looked at Herman's face, the muscles in his jaw twitching as he clenched it. "I know who you were before the war. You're a writer, though of nothing classical. Comic strips... Isn't that right?"

Herman nodded his head once more.

"Anyway," Franz continued. "*Der Schatzgäber* means *the Treasure Hunter*. The opera has four acts and the premise, which I'm going to remind you of, is simple. The queen loses her gems and with them, her beauty and fertility. The king then seeks out the advice of his lowly fool and after this, the king offers that same fool a reward if he can hunt down the gems and return them. The reward the king offers is love, the love of the innkeeper's daughter, Elis." The officer paused and tilted his head, looking at Herman. "Do you remember this?"

Herman nodded.

"Good," Franz murmured, nodding his own head. "Are you hungry?" Before Herman had the chance to nod again, however, Franz waved his hand dismissively. "Of course you are."

Franz called out to the uniformed guard, who entered

the vicinity almost immediately, as though he'd been waiting to be called upon. In German, the officer instructed the guard to wrap up some of the bread and cheese in paper for Herman. In spite of himself, Herman felt his stomach lurch hopefully as the guard followed Franz' instructions.

"Do you have a wife and children?" Franz asked once the guard had exited.

"Yes," Herman spoke softly, his voice cracking from lack of use as he tested it, "a wife and a daughter."

"Do you know where they are?"

Herman was reluctant to respond, but he did anyway. "Poland."

"Hmmm," Franz hummed. "No, I don't think so. Poland is for the Polish. Don't you mean Auschwitz?"

"Auschwitz is for Jews," Herman nodded his head absently, gulping down the lump in his throat at the thought of his wife and daughter locked up somewhere and out of his reach.

"Terrible place," Franz agreed with Herman's unspoken thoughts. "Perhaps I could find them and bring them here."

Herman's eyes flitted toward Franz' face, but he remained wary. He had no choice, after all. The only way to survive was to be cautious of the gameplay within this facility.

Franz stood and, taking his cue, Herman followed suit. The Nazi Officer began to walk with Herman and the guard, who'd joined them as they left Franz' quarters, close in tow. They made their way down a long hallway lined with lights that hung off ropes and wire, trademarks of a temporary location. The climate beyond the walls must have been cold because the air was ventilated in such a way that it couldn't have been an air-conditioner. The cold air drifting through the concrete was natural.

The Nazi Officer led Herman toward a steel door with a heavy-duty locking mechanism. It was massive and stank of fresh paint, the color of battleship-grey. Herman realized that wherever they were, it was a new facility.

As they arrived, the guard rushed forward and opened the heavy metal door. It was not without some effort. Franz gestured for Herman to enter as it swung open and so, the Jewish man did.

Herman's skin was clammy and his heart was pounding wildly in his chest. It was clear that there were plans for him, but he wasn't sure what they were. He didn't know where he was being taken, nor did he know for what purpose, and both facts terrified him immensely.

The room they entered was large and it resembled some kind of office, laboratory, or surveillance unit. It could have been a combination of all three. There were desks and chairs, lab equipment, cameras, and video devices. A large object standing upright at one end of the room drew the attention, covered by a black sheet that would make anyone curious to know what lay beneath. The back wall of the room was made of two dark glass windows, with the exception of a lonely door between them as if they were there for the people within to peer into an observatory of some kind.

Franz led Herman toward the door located between the

two observation windows and opened it to reveal yet another hallway, shorter than the previous one. Each side of the hallway had a steel, barred cell door. Franz opened one of the doors and offered his hand, signaling for Herman to enter the enclosed space.

Inside, Herman was faced with a room. Before him, lay the sight of a cot and a locker containing a few pieces of one-piece clothing. A low-walled partition separated a shower, toilet, and sink to the left. Pushed up against the opposite wall was a writing desk and chair, complete with a table lamp sitting on the desk. He could see the window and realized that his new quarters were to be behind one of the observation windows from the previous room.

The Nazi Officer turned to Herman questioningly, as if seeking his approval. "Good?"

Herman nodded.

"Speak," Franz spat in frustration. "You can speak out loud."

Without meeting the officer's eyes, Herman spoke his confirmation. "Yes… Good."

At this, Franz leaned in, his mouth so close to Herman's ear that the Jewish man could feel his breath, hot and sour. "My fool," he spoke quietly. "You love your daughter, yes? I will reward you with love… if you find me my gem." Pulling back, Franz laughed boisterously, his belly rumbling with his chortles. "Like the opera, remember?"

The officer did not wait for a response from Herman. He turned and walked out of the room, closing the steel-barred door behind him. His footsteps echoed in the small space as he made his way back out, leaving Herman alone once more.

Herman began familiarizing himself with his new quarters. He was still locked in a cell, but he knew that matters could be much worse for him. Only three weeks earlier he'd been on a train to Auschwitz, a death camp in Poland. Now, he was faced with luxuries he never dreamed he'd have again.

Sitting on the cot, it occurred to Herman that it was the first time that he'd sat on something soft in months. It was surreal and for one moment, he wondered if he was dreaming. He lay back on the cot and stretched his body - which still ached and probably would continue doing so for quite some time, if not forever – and sank into the comfort of the springy, albeit thin, mattress. The squeaky structure willingly gave way to the weight of his tired body.

In his right hand, Herman still held the package the guard had wrapped up for him. He'd taken it off the table, at Franz' indication, and hadn't let go of it since. As he slowly unfolded the paper, he realized that he'd squashed the bread somewhat, but that didn't matter. He began taking small bites of the cheese and bread, noticing that his stomach didn't respond immediately. Slowly, however, the ache Herman had gotten used to feeling began to fade away.

For this moment, Herman was okay, but he still had no idea what had brought him to this place of unfamiliar comforts and whether or not Franz was serious about finding his daughter. What role was he to play in Franz' so-called performance?

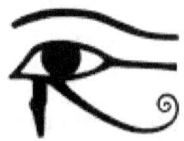

CHAPTER 14
HERMAN KATZENSTEIN

The sodium bulbs ignited and the flickering light illuminated the lab beyond the observation window of Herman's quarters. The man was already awake and the lamp on his desk lit his new cell up enough for him to prepare for the day that awaited him, though he knew not what it might bring. The first thing he did was wash his face; a pale callused hand didn't look like his as he reached for the bar of soap by the sink, lathered soap, and began washing his hands and face, surprised that he remembered how to start the day at all.

Peering from behind the privacy partition in his room, Herman could see three to four suited men and two uniformed guards moving around in the lab beyond the observation window. No one seemed to take note of him though. They were gathering out of his sight, more focused on whatever lay behind the observation quarters on the opposite side of the hallway outside his room.

Herman dried his hands and face. He was already dressed in the clean, grey jumpsuit provided by his captors, having showered the previous evening before falling asleep. There was no way he wasn't going to test the shower while he had the chance to wash away months of dirt and anguish from his tired body and the water ran dark when he did.

The curiosity was too much for him to bear, so Herman, barefoot, walked over to the barred cell door and peered across the hallway in the hopes that he might catch a glimpse of whatever it was that was so interesting in the other room. Even though his eyes had already adjusted to the dim light, as he stared densely into the adjacent quarters, he could see nothing. It was too dark.

Assuming that it must be empty and that the suited people in the lab were distracted by something outside of his vision, he diverted his attention to the observation window. He had a wide view of most of the lab room. The only thing that lay beyond his sight was the other observation window.

If I'm in here, he thought to himself. *Who was being observed? Was it him? Or was it whoever lay across the hallway?*

Herman pressed his face to the glass and looked to the right, trying with all his might to see if he could see the suited men that had gathered on the other side, outside of his view. Out of the corners of his eyes, he could just make them out. They seemed to be transfixed on some kind of standing object, large and well out of his line of sight.

Through the glass, Herman could hear voices, though they were low and he had to strain his ears. He thought he heard something about an inexplicably cold object. Someone read out that it indicated minus thirty degrees Celsius.

Suddenly, the voices got closer and Herman stepped away from the glass in time to notice an intercom system at the base of the glass.

"Herman Katzenstein is here, as you requested," one of the suited men stated and Herman realized that he was the observee.

The suited men began to disperse from the opposite window, spreading out in the lab and coming into sight once more. Herman took yet another step back from the glass. As he did, one of the suited men approached his window.

This one was tall and thin, with light, tan-colored hair that was kept short and neatly combed. Herman took him in. The man wore a German officer's uniform, without the coat and extra trimmings, yet there was something unique on his shirt. It was a lapel depicting a gold falcon with its talons extended.

Stopping at Herman's observation window, the man pressed the intercom button on the other side of the glass and the speaker on the inside of Herman's quarters emitted an articulate and soft voice with a clear German accent, made slightly staticky by the intercom.

"Herman Katzenstein?"

Yes," Herman replied, remembering Franz' annoyance

when he'd simply nodded his head the previous day.

"I take it you are comfortable," the man stated.

"Yes," Herman repeated.

"My name is Lieutenant Edmund Himmel," the man introduced himself. "I am the lead researcher at this facility and I will not harm you."

Herman knew these words meant nothing in such terrible times. In fact, sometimes, the worst nightmares ever to come to life began with those very words. He chose not to respond.

As though he knew what Herman was thinking, the lieutenant continued, "I understand that it may take you some time to trust me, but time is not on our side." Himmel paused, taking his hand off the intercom to take a breath. When he pressed down, static transmitted once more. "If you cooperate, I will keep you as safe as I possibly can. But understand something, Herman Katzenstein. Cooperation and progress will determine how you are treated in here."

It occurred to Herman that survival was an ever-changing thing. It came with no guarantees. He still didn't know what his purpose here was. He was an artist, an illustrator and a writer before the war. What purpose could he possibly serve in a place such as this?

"Herman," Himmel interrupted his thoughts. "I understand that you attended the University of Vienna."

"Yes," Herman answered.

"You studied Linguistics, Literatures, and Cultures?"

"Yes," again.

"Your records show that you worked under Dr.

Wilhelm Alzinger, the Egyptologist. Is this correct?"

"Yes," Herman nodded, his brows knitting closer and closer together as each question confused him further.

Beneath the observation window was a space. It was sealed by a metal barrier, which could be lifted and opened from the outside. It clattered and squeaked open, allowing Himmel to slip a black and white photograph through this opening before sliding the barrier shut again. It was a picture of a surface covered in hieroglyphs.

"Can you translate these images, these hieroglyphs?" Himmel asked him.

Herman stepped forward to take a closer look at the photograph, wondering why these were so important to the Germans. "Yes," he nodded. "I believe I can."

"Use the notepad and paper we have supplied you with. They can be found on your desk. If it helps, I have offered some reference books, but bear in mind that they were published in 1908 and they do not seem to include these particular hieroglyphs... at least not in their entirety."

Herman nodded and, at the lieutenant's guidance, made his way over to the desk. He opened the single drawer and removed a clean sheet of lined paper, alongside a sharpened wooden pencil. Behind him, he heard the clatter of metal and turned to find that the metal door had been reopened and a tray was being passed through the opening.

Walking back over to the glass, Herman blinked at the sight in shock. On the tray was a small plate of buttered toast, a roll brushed with honey, and a steaming cup of coffee. His eyes widened as he took in this delivery. He hadn't expected food, and he couldn't believe his good fortune.

The Jewish man recalled stories of the Jews, commonly known as kapos, being used to serve the needs of the German war efforts. They were prisoner functionaries, assigned to supervise labor or otherwise carry out administrative tasks. Back then, he hadn't considered the stories to be true, failing to understand what purpose those of his religion might offer the Germans. At this moment, however, he began to realize that the stories might have been true, which meant that he was one of the kapos and he supposed that this was his administrative duty.

Herman was being offered a minor reprieve from the pain and agony of the past few years and he grasped onto it with both hands in the recognition that he might have a chance at survival, if only as the cat's toy. He could only hope that the cat wouldn't be through with him any time soon.

◆ ◆ ◆

Weeks passed by and continued to pass until they turned into months. The routine remained the same. Herman Katzenstein sat at his desk and did all that he could to translate the patterns in the photographs provided, puzzling through the many combinations of possible solutions to the unfamiliar hieroglyphs. He'd managed to establish at least sixteen possible alphabetic matches from symbols to letters. He worked and did whatever Lieutenant Edmund Himmel asked of him and, in return, Himmel remained true to his word in ensuring that Herman was not harmed.

Whilst in captivity, it was impossible for Herman not to

hear the bits and pieces of activity whirring outside his new room. Most of it meant little to him, but that didn't stop it from eliciting a morbid sense of curiosity. They often performed tests and discussed results, though Herman was none the wiser to what it was that they were testing. The only thing he knew, which was more of a hunch than anything else, was that the tests and the hieroglyphs were related. Nothing had been confirmed.

On one such occasion, the test results were being discussed by Lieutenant Himmel and none other than the Nazi Officer who'd brought Herman to this facility, Franz.

"It's fascinating," Himmel murmured as he read the results on the piece of paper in his hands. "It's not made of silver after all, but zinc." He turned to Franz, seemingly excited by what he was saying. "It has always been thought that Ancient Egyptians unintentionally used zinc, combined into the mined copper ores they used. There is no historical evidence that the zinc they used was actually separated and forged as its own element. This is a significant finding."

Franz always seemed less interested in the details of their findings and more interested in some kind of power whatever the object was supposedly created, not that Himmel seemed to take notice of that fact. The nights were the worst for Herman. Despite the new living situation that he found himself in, he didn't know how long it would last. He thought about how quickly the tides could turn and about the possibility of being discarded once he had fulfilled his purpose for the Germans. The worst was that he had already suffered so much that he couldn't stop himself from reliving the awful memories of the torture he'd so far endured. They came to him when he least expected, creeping into the recesses of his mind like snakes rustling in through the long blades of grass. He often woke from terrible dreams. They were almost always filled with the sound of his daughter, Sofia, crying. At other times, he couldn't sleep at all.

One evening, Herman awoke to the eerie feeling that someone was watching him. A tingle along the back of his neck alerted him to the eyes that stared through the bars of his cell door. At first, Herman couldn't bring himself to move for the fear that his instinct was correct and that someone or something was indeed staring at him. Worse than that, he didn't want to open his eyes.

This was not an unusual instance. Herman feared waking more often than not. Deep within, he worried that he would wake to the cold hard concrete of his previous cell and that, with it, he would feel the discomfort and pain in his bones and hunger that he had grown so accustomed to. It was only the feel of the unmistakably soft mattress beneath his body that gave him the strength to open his eyes. When he did, he heard the gentle clasp of a cell door closing – only, it was not his own.

Inquisitive, he sat up in bed. Through the observation window, he could see the German soldier who'd been assigned to keep guard in a chair near the main door of the laboratory. He was fast asleep; his arms were crossed over his chest, his head was bent forward, and his chin rested against his chest as he dozed away.

Herman wondered what could have made the sound.

Had he dreamed it or was someone taken into the neighboring cell? He decided to take the risk of garnering a peek through the steel bars of his cell door.

There, in the darkness, he saw a figure standing in the adjacent cell. His heart skipped a beat at the sight of the silhouette and for the briefest second, he thought that he might be imagining things. Squinting, he quietly pressed himself against the door.

"Stranger," he whispered. "Stranger... Can you hear me?"

The figure moved, proving that Herman wasn't seeing things, moving out of the dark shadows of the cell and approaching the door. The hallway had no lighting, so the newcomer was not visible. His face was shadowed by the steel bars.

"My name is Herman Katzenstein," Herman hazarded an introduction.

The stranger hesitated and turned his head. Herman could see that he was looking over at the observation window in his own room and wondered if the stranger would speak at all. He craved the voice of someone other than himself, Himmel, and Franz – if only to prove that the stranger in the next cell was not some kind of apparition of his imagination.

Herman was ready to turn away from the door and return to his bed, even as desperation coursed through his veins and caused sweat to form on his brow, when the stranger finally spoke.

"My name is Rashid."

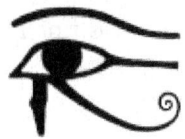

CHAPTER 15
THE HALL OF TWO TRUTHS

A calendar hung on the wall in the laboratory. Herman watched as the pages flipped with each month that passed them by. He never saw the person who flipped them, assuming that it happened while he was still asleep, but this was his only way of measuring the time that had passed. Apart from the observation windows, there were no windows that told them what time of day it was and no form of sunshine or moonlight to guide him in the orbit of the earth. His body simply adjusted and reacted to the movements of the Germans, telling him when it was time to wake and when it was time to sleep the way a clock once would have.

The only silver lining in this new life he led, aside from the luxuries that he didn't have in his previous cell, was the fact that he had a new friend – to an extent.

By this time, Herman had told Rashid his story and how he had come to be there. He'd also told him what it was that he was doing for the Germans. He wasn't sure if it was a good idea to reveal this much to Rashid until it proved to be the thing that made Rashid finally open up to him.

Herman could not blame Rashid for keeping to himself. The reason he'd been hesitant to tell Rashid of the role that he played was because he didn't know if it was a test of some kind. For all he knew, Rashid was some kind of German spy, put in the adjacent cell for the purpose of making Herman let his guard down. The moment he did, he feared that the Germans would harm him for it. If Rashid was indeed a real prisoner in the same boat, would he not have the same fears about Herman?

Eventually, Rashid shared with him that he was an Egyptian philosopher that had been brought here to aid the Nazis with their efforts in the war. He revealed that the Nazis were getting desperate, enough that they considered looking for some kind of mystical greater power. Apparently, they believed that they had discovered a way to tap into that of the Ancient Egyptian deities.

The conversations Herman had with Rashid were hushed and hurried. They took place in the late hours of the evening and the early hours of the morning in the only breaks they got from their assigned tasks for the day. The assigned guard usually fell asleep around the same hour each night and when he did, Herman and Rashid would be ready to resume their conversations. They were few and far between, frequently ending abruptly.

Above all, their time together was short enough that Herman and Rashid still had many more questions than answers even after the many days that had already passed.

◆ ◆ ◆

As time went on, Herman continued to update Himmel through his progress. Each time he thought he might be done, Himmel would slide yet another portion of the hieroglyphs through the small opening in the observation window. Herman wondered why he didn't simply pass them all through, but it occurred to him that the Germans might want to keep their plans a secret.

Herman couldn't remember everything he translated, but he held onto a fair amount of knowledge. He'd begun to unravel some of what it was that the Germans were dealing with. However, the more Herman uncovered, the more he hoped it wasn't real. If it was, he couldn't help but think that the world was doomed. The last person who should have that kind of information was Adolf Hitler, and Herman feared he was feeding the wrong people the information that could destroy them all.

He never gave all the information away at once because it wasn't given to him that way. Instead, the story was uncovered bit by bit. It was intriguing enough that, even without the potential threat it brought, Herman could remember the tales long after he shared them. The hieroglyphs had begun to haunt his dreams, filling them with the images of Ancient Egyptian Gods and rituals of death and blood.

Sometimes, the translations would take days. Other times, they would take weeks. Herman noticed the meals he was served tasted better the quicker he translated, but it was not always up to him. He worked as fast as he could.

"How are you doing today, Herman?" Himmel's voice would echo from the intercom.

"I have made little progress, Lt. Himmel," Herman would find himself saying too often for either of their likings. Nevertheless, he would give what little information he had. "These hieroglyphs tell me about the death of Horus."

"What do they say?" Each time Himmel heard the familiar Egyptian terminology, he grew excited. Herman could almost see the disgust of his colleague, Franz. "Tell me everything."

Of course, Himmel never let Herman tell him everything. He would be too anxious, desperate to know more. With that in mind, he'd stop Herman from whatever he was in the middle of saying.

"No, never mind," Himmel would say. "Continue with the translations and make haste."

The hieroglyphs spoke of one of the Egyptian deities, Horus, being killed by another called Set. Some of Herman's translations included certain spells that could be found in the Book of the Dead, a collection of spells the Egyptians used to navigate through the afterlife. The beliefs of the Egyptians began to scare Herman the more he translated. One of the spells, number seventeen in particular, depicted a human head rising from a coffin that was guarded by the four sons of Horus.

They also mentioned the four sons of Horus in more detail, not that Herman knew who or what they were before he read the Egyptian reference book provided by Himmel. In its pages, Herman learned that the four sons were a group of four gods in the Egyptian religion. Their names were Imsety, Hapi, Duamutef, and Qebehsenuef. They were thought to be personifications of the four canopic jars. It was in this same book that Herman learned the four canopic jars were actual jars used for the safekeeping of human organs, in particular, those that were believed to be necessary to the Egyptians in the afterlife. They were the stomach, intestines, lungs, and liver. At first, Herman found it confusing that the heart was not considered an important organ, but he discovered the heart had no jar at all. The heart was said to embody the human soul – known as the seat of the soul – and therefore, it was left inside the body.

The only thing that made life in the base tolerable were the late-night conversations with Rashid. The evenings remained the safest time for them to speak. It was a reprieve from the never-ending translations Herman was forced to complete. They were quiet conversations and they couldn't risk speaking about the work they did for the Germans, but that didn't matter. It was a welcome distraction.

Afterward, when Herman finally climbed into bed, his dreams were troublesome. Egyptians dominated his thoughts and one of the things that often visited him was an ancient ritual referred to as the weighing of the heart ceremony. It was yet another thing that he'd read about.

"Herman," Himmel stated, breaking through the silence of his quarters. His voice came through the intercom as a whisper.

Herman, who had been sitting at his desk as usual, turned to see the lieutenant standing at the observation window. For a change, there were no other suited scientists or guards with him. Herman's eyes narrowed as he noticed Franz standing off to one side, somewhere near the mysterious object that Herman could not see from his quarters. Cautiously, he stood and went over to the window. He had a feeling that Himmel didn't want anyone else to hear this conversation, though he didn't yet know why.

"Yes, Lieutenant?" Herman asked.

"Are you all right in here?"

Herman blinked. Was he all right?

"I've been watching you these past few days. You seem slower than usual. I note that," he looked down at Herman's face and clothes. He'd not shaved that morning and the grey jumpsuit was wrinkled as he'd slept in it the previous evening. "You have not been grooming as well as you usually do. There are bags under your eyes."

Although the lieutenant was waiting for a response, Herman didn't know how to respond. He simply stared at the German. Why did Himmel care?

"Are you sleeping well?" Himmel finally asked when it became apparent that Herman was not going to respond. "If your sleep is affecting your productivity, we need to know."

Oh, of course. They didn't really care about me, Herman thought. *Only about the project.*

Herman considered telling Himmel about the dreams,

opening his mouth and closing it again. He didn't know how they were pertinent. It seemed like another thing the Nazis could use to torture him if they really wanted to.

"Herman?" Himmel repeated. Himmel looked around the laboratory and Herman realized he was checking that no one was watching them. As he waited for a response, he looked down at a clipboard in his hands and pretended to be reading or writing something down, as if it were pertinent to his work that he stood at the observation window. "We don't have much time."

It was Rashid who finally convinced Herman to speak. Out of the corner of his eye, Herman saw his neighbor moving between the steel bars that separated him. It had been nothing more than a shadow, but shadows often had the ability to scare grown men. The fact of the matter was that Herman had mentioned the dreams to Rashid. If the two ever did end up in a concrete cell, the Germans would likely find out about these dreams one way or another.

Herman thought it better that he be the one to voluntarily share the information.

"I've been having dreams," Herman admitted. "They are strange dreams, plagued with hieroglyphs and Ancient Egyptians."

Himmel arched an eyebrow. "Tell me about these dreams."

"I…" Herman paused. Where did he start? This time, he could tell Himmel really was writing down what he said. "I find myself in the Hall of Two Truths."

"The Hall of Two Truths?" Himmel repeated. "The passage before the Afterlife?"

Herman nodded. "Yes. I meet with Maat, the Goddess of Truth and Justice, and she performs the weighing of the heart ritual."

At some point, Himmel had moved closer to the glass and Herman could tell he was fascinated and hanging on to every word. "Go on," Himmel whispered.

"At first, I didn't know what to do. I would arrive and there she would be, a beautiful woman wearing a single ostrich feather, and she would wait for me. Neither of us would say anything. One day, I got the courage to ask her what she wanted from me."

Herman furrowed his brows, recalling the strange dream and the strange place. It had been a visit to another world. The floor was the whitest marble there ever was, so white that it sometimes felt as though Herman were walking on air. Around them, he could see space. The night sky, bathed in a sea of stars, surrounded them from every angle. It wasn't quite the same as the night sky, however. There were hues of color splashed across it – ribbons of purples and blues and reds – that seemed to dance each time he looked at them and stop each time he looked away.

"She told me she wanted the truth," Herman continued quietly. Both he and Himmel glanced around once more, checking that no one was listening to or watching their conversation. "Eventually, I had to tell her everything. I had to explain to her why I was innocent or why I was guilty." The truth shook Herman and he shuddered at the many times he'd been forced to repeat every reason why he should pass on to the Afterlife and every reason why he shouldn't go to the Underworld. It was a grueling process to have to go through again and again. "And once I was done, she would perform the ceremony."

"Incredible," Himmel murmured. "Tell me about the ceremony."

Herman knew that Himmel knew how the ceremony worked. A man with such extensive knowledge, as far as the Egyptians were concerned, would not be unaware. Nevertheless, Herman had come this far and he knew Himmel could make things much worse for him if he did not cooperate.

"There is a scale," Herman explains. "I didn't see it when I first entered the hall. It only came into sight after I told the Truth. Maat would walk to it, gesturing for me to follow, and only then do I realize how massive it is." Herman used his hands to show Himmel how much taller than him it was, spanning four or five feet above his head. "And then Maat would undress, removing the single feather she wore and setting it down on one side of the scale. The scale wouldn't move at all. It would be perfectly balanced."

"And then?" Himmel asked breathlessly, his face practically pressed up against the glass. "What would happen to your heart?"

"Maat approaches me and rips it out of my chest. It still pulses, covered in my blood." Herman recalled the way it dripped on the white floor. "And I wake before she sets it down on the other scale. I never find out if it tips or not."

Himmel sighed and Herman could tell that the lieutenant was disappointed. "I see," he murmured. "Very well. Herman, I want you to tell me if this dream changes.

If anything new happens, I want to know. Do you understand?"

"Yes," Herman nodded.

"Good. I'll see what I can do to help you. Perhaps if you finish the dream, it will no longer plague you."

Herman wasn't so sure about that, but he didn't know how to respond and so he simply nodded yet again.

"Return to your translations," Himmel dismissed him, taking his clipboard and making his way back to the other side of the laboratory where the others were.

Herman noticed Franz look from Himmel to the observation room, meeting his eyes suspiciously. Herman stepped back away from the glass to break away from Franz's stare, *If only the Hall of Two Truths awaited all who deserved judgment,* Herman thought.

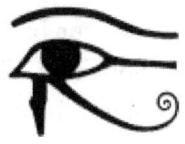

CHAPTER 16
MOUSE TRAP

In another part of the base, somewhere beyond the grey walls of the laboratory, an eight-year-old girl was in a locked room with a cell door, steel bars blocking her from the world. For many days, she has not seen the sun, nor has she seen anyone but the Nazi and German officers who walk up and down the hallways in their crisp uniforms. Her name was Sofia Katzenstein.

As Sofia sat in wait for whatever the dreaded new day might bring her, she heard the clang of the lock on the door being released. She scuffled back hurriedly, dragging her body along the ground. An officer in a grey uniform wasn't there for her. He had with him a young girl and at the sight of her, Sofia's eyes lit up. She dare not risk moving forward while he was in the room though.

The officer sneered down at Sofia before shoving the other girl forward with a push of his hand against the center of her spine. She stumbled and Sofia hopped up from the ground instinctively, ready to catch her if she fell forward. With that, the officer took a step back out of the room and the door swung shut behind him, the slam of steel falling into the doorframe echoing off the cold concrete walls. The two girls were left alone.

Sofia thought that the other girl looked older; she was taller and her features were sharper. Her long blonde hair hung loosely around her face, the curls cascading over her shoulders. She was dressed in a white dress that looked as if it came from home, with a pocket in the front. The girl's hands were tucked into that pocket.

"Hello," Sofia spoke, her voice high-pitched and soft.

"Hello," the other girl answered and her voice was thick with a German accent.

Sofia was taken aback. She half-expected that the other girl wouldn't speak at all and she was so unused to the voices of anyone but the guttural Germans who held her captive. "Who are you?"

"Margrit Himmel," the other girl spoke just as quietly. "Who are you?"

"My name is Sofia Katzenstein. I was brought here from Auschwitz."

"I was brought here by my father because my mother was killed," Margit stated frankly. "The Soviets bombed and liberated Kirlenes in Norway, where we had been staying."

"I have not seen my mother since we were first taken

to Auschwitz. They separated us."

"Then you are a Jew," Margrit looked her up and down.

"Yes," Sofia nodded. "And you are a German."

"Yes," Margrit nodded.

There was silence between the two girls. They had reached a standstill and neither of them knew how to move forward from there. The Jewish girl and the German girl were both young and both aware that they were supposed to hate one another. Yet, the war between the adults around them was not to do with them. They were mere innocents.

Margrit moved over to the cot behind Sofia and sat down on the mattress. She looked at the younger girl through narrowed eyes. "Would you like some cheese?"

At the mention of food, Sofia's ears perked up. She was being fed by the Germans, but it was not often and it was never much. Still, she couldn't complain. The treatment here was far better than it had been at Auschwitz. "Yes, please."

"Come, sit with me," Margrit patted the space beside her. "Tell me about yourself."

Sofia hesitated. There was something about the other girl that set her off. She wasn't sure that she trusted the other girl. Perhaps it was the fact that Margrit was a German or perhaps it was simply her instincts telling her that something was wrong.

Nevertheless, Sofia walked over and sat down on the bed, keeping a wider space between them than was necessary. She could tell that this bothered Margrit, based on the way her lips thinned, but the older girl didn't say anything. On the contrary, she forced a smile that resembled more of a grimace than anything else.

"There," Margrit nodded. "Good. Now, how old are you?"

"I'm eight. What about you?"

"I'm ten." Margrit reached into her pocket and pulled out a small paper package. She carefully unwrapped it, revealing the pale orange cubes of cheese. She popped one into her mouth. "You know, I heard that all the Jews will be gone soon."

Sofia flinched at the statement, holding her tongue. She was afraid to respond because she didn't know *how* to respond. The truth was that she was sure Margrit was right. Her people were dying all around her and she had not seen her mother for many months. Deep within, Sofia had the fear that her mother may already be dead, but she hoped that she was wrong.

There was no point dwelling on it. Sofia would lose her mind if she had to think about all the things she had already lost. All of her friends, her things, her home, and her parents were lost to her. The only hope she had left was that her mother might still be alive out there and that Sofia might one day see her again, however unrealistic that hope might be.

What else was an eight-year-old to do?

"Where is your mother?" Margrit asked, seemingly annoyed that Sofia had not responded to her jibe.

"I do not know," Sofia shrugged. "I last saw her on the train, before we were separated at Auschwitz."

"She could be dead, you know," Margrit spoke Sofia's

fears. Before the younger girl could respond, she continued. "She could be like my mother. This would mean that we are both orphans. And we can blame the same people for killing our mothers."

"What do you mean?" Sofia hazarded a glance at the cheese cubes in Margrit's hand, her stomach squirming uncomfortably.

"The allies killed mine, after all," Margrit popped another cube into her mouth and then extended her hand to Sofia, offering her the cheese at last. As Sofia reached out to take a piece, Margrit snatched her hand back. "I have decided that since you do not have anyone left, I will be your friend."

Some friend, Sofia thought. All she wanted was one cube of cheese. Why had Margrit offered it if she wasn't going to let Sofia have any? It made no sense and she was beginning to get irritated with the German.

"I'm not allowed to share my food with you. You're a prisoner. My father is a lieutenant. We are not the same."

Sofia shook her head. She decided that she didn't like Margit and she didn't want to be her friend either. The other girl was cruel and bitter, much like the other Germans she had met along the way in this war. It might have been something in their blood. Sofia did not know. However, she knew that if she ever made it out of this war alive, she would not see Germans the same ever again.

That was a big *if*.

For the rest of the first evening, Sofia did not speak to Margrit. Soon, it grew dark and they fell asleep together on the small cot. There was enough room for both of them, but Sofia wished that she'd never complained about the lack of comfort in her room before. Now that she had to share, things were so much worse and she wished that they would put Margrit in a different room.

Over the next few weeks, Margrit continued to goad Sofia. At every opportunity she got, she told Sofia that she would soon be the last Jew alive and that the Germans would win the war. As if she was doing Sofia a favor, Margrit told Sofia that if she was a good friend to her, Margrit would ask her father if they could keep her around. Once the war was over, she would take Sofia home with her and she could be something resembling a maid-in-waiting.

These stories annoyed Sofia, but she was deathly afraid that if she wasn't kind to Margrit, she might never be safe again. If the only way that she survived the war was to become friends with the German girl, then that was what she would have to do – at least until another opportunity presented itself to her. Sofia didn't think that it would any time soon. And so, she began to behave in a more polite manner around Margrit.

In the mornings and evenings, the officers brought food for the girls. Sofia had grown used to her meals; they were simple, a slice of bread and a cup of water. She was lucky if the bread was still soft. On the other hand, Margrit ate like a princess; she was sometimes brought warm tea with a roll slathered in honey. The first few times, Sofia would look on in envy, but she stopped after a while. It seemed to make Margrit eat slower than usual, as if to tease her and remind her that Margrit was not allowed to share her food. Sofia wasn't so sure that Margrit was telling the truth when she said this.

One day, after weeks of sharing the room, Margrit asked Sofia about her father. "Who is he? Where is he?"

"I do not know," Sofia answered, which was true. She'd given up hope that her father might still be alive long before her mother, for the simple fact that she had seen her mother at Auschwitz. They'd been on the same train to the concentration camps and her father was separated when they arrived.

"Was he a soldier? Is he fighting in the war?" Margrit prodded.

"No," Sofia shook her head. "He used to write comic books for me. He illustrated them and told me stories about the adventures of the Katzenstein Kids."

Margrit wouldn't respond further than pursing her lips and Sofia was convinced that she looked down on her father's choice of profession. She supposed that to someone such as Margrit, whose father was a lieutenant and a man of great importance, it would be.

That was until Margrit returned from one of her visits with her father. Every so often, though not every day, a guard would come collect Margrit. She would be removed from the cell and taken to visit her father somewhere else in the base. As much as she disliked Margrit, Sofia had to admit that she was rather lonely in these moments. Sometimes they would be short and other times they would last for hours. It all depended on how busy Margrit's father was, as she often reminded Sofia upon returning.

On this particular occasion, Margrit was gone for mere

moments and she reentered the room with her hands behind her back, concealing something from Sofia's sight.

"What do you have there?" Sofia asked, peering around Margrit curiously.

"It is a present," Margrit responded. "It's for you."

"You brought me a present?" Sofia furrowed her brow skeptically. She didn't trust Margrit, but she felt her heart skip a beat and hoped that it was food. At the same time, she hoped that it wouldn't be like the first day when Margrit offered Sofia some cheese only to say that she wasn't allowed to share her food.

The older girl brought the present out from behind her back, revealing the present, and Sofia instantly recognized the illustrations depicted on the cover. She knew the artist well. The gift was far better than any meal Sofia could have dreamed of eating.

Margrit had brought her one of The Katzenstein Kids comic books and her father's name was emblazoned across the front.

It turned out that Margrit didn't actually have to share a room with Sofia at all. She'd only been sleeping in the same room to annoy Sofia and it had worked. However, Margrit got tired of the situation and began sleeping in her own room. She would only visit Sofia when she felt like it, which was most days, unfortunately. Still, Sofia was glad she had the cot to herself again.

With Margrit's disappearance, feeding times grew less frequent. The guards didn't bring her food as often as they once did. Sofia couldn't help but wonder if Margrit had something to do with this new arrangement. Her belly grumbled and ached each morning.

"I know you're hungry," Margrit stated the moment she arrived Sofia's cell door.

Margrit was right; she was hungry. Sofia looked up and saw that Margrit had returned. "Do you know what this is?" From behind her back, Margrit brought forth a small box.

"It looks to be a dybbuk box," Sofia murmured, examining the small wooden box. It was small and it had Hebrew engravings carved into the sides and top. The mere sight of the thing sent a chill down her spine and Sofia took a step backward.

Dybbuk boxes were said to be haunted by a dybbuk, an evil and malicious spirit. In Jewish folklore, it was believed that these malevolent spirits could possess and inhabit one's body. The only way to remove the spirit was to perform an exorcism. They were thought to be the dislocated soul of a person.

Growing up, Sofia had heard many horror stories about dybbuks and those who messed with the boxes in which they lived. These boxes were often sealed using a substance such as wax, to prevent the cursed thing from escaping. If the boxes were ever burned – though they took a long time to burn – the spirit would be free and would never be able to be returned to the box.

At her reaction, Margrit lips curled into a nasty smile. She stepped closer, holding the box out to Sofia. "If you're hungry, I put some cheese inside the box. You can just open it and get it."

Sofia's heart began to race and she thought her suspicions must be correct. Margrit had told the guards to stop feeding her so that she could tease her with this box. Well, Sofia was not going to fall for it.

"No," Sofia stated. She moved away from Margrit and went over to her cot.

As Sofia lay back, staring at the ceiling, Margrit approached and set the box down beside the small cot. Sofia didn't look at the older girl, but she could tell that Margrit was annoyed. She was the cat in this equation and Sofia was the mouse. She wanted Sofia to play along with her little game and it made her angry that Sofia refused.

In spite of it all, Sofia found herself looking down at the box often throughout the night. With the growing ache in the pit of her belly, she struggled to find solace in sleep. It hurt to know there was something that could end her suffering, but she was too afraid to touch the box. Dybbuks were the stuff of a Jewish child's nightmares. It wasn't worth the risk of allowing some kind of evil entity to possess her body – not for a cube of cheese.

The following morning, Margrit returned to the room while Sofia slept. She immediately made her way over to the box and noticed that it was unopened. The thin seal she'd placed along the rim of the lid was unbroken. Sofia hadn't touched the box. She pursed her lips and stood to look down at the sleeping girl.

Suddenly, she slammed her fists down on the cot, causing the metal to creak loudly and Sofia to wake abruptly with a cry of surprise.

Sofia stared up at Margrit. "Have you gone mad?"

"You didn't open the box," Margrit responded. "Why not?"

Sofia looked down at the box, biting her lip. If she weren't so scared of it, she might have moved it further away from her bed. As it was, she didn't want to touch it at all if she could help it.

"Dybbuks aren't real, Sofia," Margrit rolled her eyes. "There is no such thing as a dybbuk. If you're hungry, just open it."

At that moment, Sofia's stomach grumbled loudly, humiliating her so much that her cheeks reddened.

"Ha! I knew it! I knew you were hungry!" With that, Margrit bent to pick up the box and shoved it onto the bed.

The box landed on Sofia's lap and she screeched, jumping back from the thing like it had burned her. "I'd rather starve than release the evil spirit!" She screamed at Margrit.

Margrit took pleasure in scaring the younger girl, laughing at her screams.

"Why are you doing this?" Sofia asked. "I'm hungry! Why do you have to make me suffer for it?"

The giggles stopped and Margrit simply grinned mischievously down at Sofia. "When I was staying in Norway, we lived in a small apartment in the city," Margrit began telling her a story. "In the evenings when I was meant to be in bed, I would lay my head on the pillow and stare across the dark room. We had a heating pipe in the corner and by the radiator, I saw a small mouse pop her little head out of the hole." At the mention of the mouse, Margrit's eyes seemed to dance. "The mouse mostly came out at night, when all the lights were out. So, one night I snuck a small piece of cheese to bed with me and after the lights went out, I put it on the floor near the hole. As I watched, the mouse creeped out so slowly and carefully, and began to eat the cheese."

Margrit paused and sat down on the end of the bed, looking at Sofia out of the corner of her eye. "I was alone in the apartment and that mouse was like a little friend to me. For many weeks, I would leave it a small bite of cheese. One night, I woke up to a loud bang and I found my mother standing in the room. On the floor, in her shadow, was the mouse. It was dead, squashed."

At this, Sofia's hands flew up to cover her mouth as she stared at the other girl.

"My mother looked at me and told me, *Margrit, you must never do that.*" Margrit waved her index finger sternly for effect. "*You cannot feed or touch such creatures. They are filthy little beasts. They have no place in this world.*" Margrit heaved a sigh and there was silence between the two girls. Eventually, she spoke again. "I was sad and angry. And at that moment, I remembered that my mother had used those words once before." She looked over at Sofia. "She caught me playing with a little Jewish girl in a park back in Germany."

Sofia didn't know how to respond. She was too shocked to do anything but stare at the German girl. Margrit looked kind of sad as she recalled the memory of being told off by her mother for playing with the mouse.

"Do you understand it now?" Margrit finally broke the awkward moment, turning to face Sofia. "You remind me of that little mouse and all mice like cheese, do they not?

So, go ahead. Open the box and eat the cheese… Or are you afraid the dybbuk will come and squash you too?"

Margrit didn't wait for a response. She had said all that she needed to and with that, she got up and walked toward the door. She knocked firmly on the door and from outside, the girls heard the clang of metal as someone unlocked it for her to exit. Margrit looked back at Sofia one last time before she departed.

The following morning, Margrit returned. This time, Sofia was sitting up on the bed with a small smile on her face. She was more awake than Margrit had seen her in days. Margrit's eyes drop to the box, which had shifted slightly.

"Sofia," she murmured. "You look better today. Did you finally open the box and eat the cheese?"

Sofia didn't respond.

This was enough for Margrit. She felt a small burst of triumph in her chest and walked over to the Jewish girl's cot. She'd won. Sofia had opened the box, in spite of her fears. She leaned down and turned the box so that it faced her and opened the lid.

Margrit gasped and jumped back from the box, horrified and shocked by the sight before her. The cheese was still inside the box, but it wasn't as she left it. It had turned black and moldy and there were small bugs crawling over its once fresh surface. She didn't understand.

"You little trickster!" She screamed at Sofia, her high-pitched voice bouncing off the walls. "You let me think you opened the box! You let me think you ate the cheese! You did this!" She spat harshly. "My mother was right. You have no place in this world. You are nothing but a filthy little beast."

Sofia didn't move. She didn't say or do anything. She simply watched as Margrit threw her tantrum. The Jewish girl knew that it was mean to trick the German girl, but she knew that she had to do something. Margrit's story had resonated with her and once she realized that her suspicions were correct – that Margrit really did consider herself the cat and Sofia the mouse – she knew there was only one thing to do. The only way for a mouse to survive was for the mouse to outsmart the cat. After all, it wasn't really a fair fight. The cat was faster, bigger, and had sharper claws. All the mouse had was its wits.

Margrit picked the box up and stormed off, slamming her fist down on the door for the guards to release her. "This means nothing," she hissed at Sofia as she waited, clutching the box tightly. "You will pay for this soon enough."

The words worried her, but Sofia continued to look on in silence. She accepted what she had done. If a dybbuk truly had been in the box, its malicious possessive spirit surely clung onto Margrit.

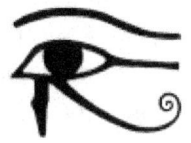

CHAPTER 17
THE EYE OF HORUS

Alone once again, Herman and Rashid fell back into their pattern of dialog. Rashid's words fell from his lips almost too quickly for Herman to understand them. His tone was hushed. "The Nazis do not understand what they are doing. They will release a great evil upon this earth." He told Herman, looking through the bars of their cells. "Have you been translating the hieroglyphics? Do you know what they mean?"

"Yes," Herman muttered. "They seem to relate to some kind of dark entity."

"They found something evil out there, Herman Katzenstein. It is a sarcophagus; one which can harness the power of Ra for the purpose of resurrecting evil from the Underworld." Rashid paused, looking to see that they were still alone. "They want to use it as a war machine."

"This seems an awful lot like Sacred Drama", Rashid continued. "All the stories of the birth of mankind and the tales of the deities have been inscribed on the walls of the Temple of Horus at Edfu. It's located along the west bank of the Nile. These inscriptions tell the Sacred Drama. You can read about the age-old conflict between Horus and Set. I feel these tales are enough warning to stay away from whatever this evil power is, yet the Nazis do not heed it."

"When I was a boy, my father told me one of the tales about the Sacred Drama. Would you like to hear it?"

Herman nodded his head before remembering that Rashid couldn't see him well. "Yes, please."

"One day, a traveler entered the town of Quseir. It is near the Red Sea. He was a one-eyed old man. With him, he brought a small puppet theater and he set it up in the town square," Rashid began. "For a day or two, he performed a show, but most of the villagers did not pay attention to him. They walked on by. Soon, however, the children would stop. They wanted to see the show and, in turn, their parents would watch as well."

As Rashid spoke, Herman could almost see it all in his mind's eye. He could see the sandy Egyptian town and the dark-skinned locals meandering through the village. The children would have been excited by a puppet show.

"A new puppet appeared in the show, one that had the body of a man and the head of a falcon. The children loved the puppet. He was colorful and strong, and his name was Horus. The story unfolded and the audience was introduced to the four sons of Horus: Imsety, Duamutef,

Hapi, and Qebehsenuef." Rashid looked at Herman. "You know these names, do you not?"

"Yes," Herman replied. "They are in the hieroglyphs."

Good," Rashid nodded, continuing his tale. "Horus was proud of his four sons, but he was troubled. He would have dreams that showed visions of death and he grew concerned for them. To ease his mind and rid himself of his fears, Horus pleaded with Ra, the Sun God, to protect them from harm. By the third show, Horus looked upward and asked a question of Ra."

Rashid stopped, so Herman asked, "What did he ask?"

"He asked, what must he sacrifice to protect his sons from harm?" Rashid answered. "Suddenly, a voice descended down from the top of the stage and the audience was surprised as the voice seemed as if it had come from the sky above." He used his hands to tell the story, making it more dramatic, shadows moving through the air, not unlike the puppets on the stage. "*I am in need of an eye,* Ra said. *If you give me yours, I will grant you the protection you seek.*"

Herman's heart began to race as he listened to the story. He fidgeted, checking through the observation windows every five seconds to make sure that the guard was still asleep. The atmosphere was tense and he could only imagine what it must have felt like to be there.

"Though the storytelling was dark, the villagers kept coming and the crowd grew with each day that passed. The people had been talking about the show and by the final one, most of the town had gathered to watch his dark tale unfold. The show began with the puppet of Horus watching his four sons sleep. It is then that he makes his decision." Rashid changed his voice, deepening it to match the voice of Horus. "*I will sacrifice my left eye, the stronger of my two eyes which symbolizes protection, power, health, and prophecy, if it will protect my sons from harm.*" Rashid threw his hands down so suddenly that Herman jumped. "All of a sudden, a puppet of a half-man, half-beast that resembled no known creature appeared, dropping down onto the stage from the sky. It extended its muscular arm and opened its hand, its fingers tipped with long, sharp claws." Rashid took hold of the bars, pushing his face up against them so that Herman could see aged features. "Do you know what Horus' eye looks like, Herman?"

"Yes," Herman breathed, moving closer to the bars so that Rashid could see him too.

"Tell me."

Herman recalled the eye. It was a green gemstone. "In the center of the green gem," he whispered, "there is a star with four points."

"Yes," Rashid nodded approvingly. He continued. "The half-man, half-beast plucked the left eye from the head of Horus and then, he turned and began to devour the four sons while they slept. Horus, shocked by the horror unfolding before him, grabbed his silver Was-Scepter and drew his arms back to plunge the point through the half-man, half-beast's back."

Suddenly, Rashid let out a howl. It was low, but it still made Herman gasp. Both men paused to look toward the guard and, upon seeing that he was still asleep, Rashid continued eagerly. Herman was hooked on every word.

"The half-man, half-beast let out a howl and fell to the ground. Horus took his eye back from its opened palm. He realized that he had not called on Ra, as he thought, but had instead succumbed to his deceptive brother. Set was injured, but dangerous. Horus knew that he had to stop Set and cast his dark soul to the Underworld." Rashid's voice grew higher as he put on the voice of Set. "The God of Chaos and War cried out; *give me the eye of Horus and all its power or I will devour the children of men!*"

Rashid took a deep breath after that.

"Are you all right?" Herman asked.

His neighbor continued, ignoring the question. "Horus knew that he must do something to protect the children of men. He no longer had his four sons and he'd been weakened by the attack. He raised his left eye into the sky and called out; *I cast your dark soul to the Underworld.*" Rashid reached up into the air of his cell. "A black void opened beneath Set and his soul was sucked from his body, cast into the Underworld. The curtains fell and the audience gasped."

"What happened to Horus and his eye?"

"It's believed that Horus entombed the body of Set and, using the Was-Scepter, broke the eye open at the center. It broke into four separate gemstones."

"And what about the one-eyed elderly man?"

"My father told me that the next day the one-eyed man had vanished. All the children in our village had awaken with a birthmark on the palm of their hand shaped like the Eye of Horus, the symbol for protection. It is believed the one-eyed elderly man came to warn us of a great evil. It is said that the dark soul of Set continues to roam the world and will one day return to devour the children. But not as long as he is separated from his body and unable to be resurrected or reborn." Rashid sighed. "His son, Anubis, is the ruler of the Underworld. He rejects Set's soul from entering the realm of death and allows the dark soul to wander the earth, creating chaos and war among mankind." Rashid waved his hand around the room. "Look around. Thousands upon thousands of children have been killed since the start of this world war, including the children of the Israelites. Perhaps there is some truth to this story?"

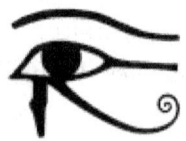

CHAPTER 18
RETURN OF THE DEITY

It was the anniversary since the Nazi Officer removed Herman Katzenstein from his previous cell. He'd been translating the hieroglyphics one piece at a time for twelve months to the day. The Germans had been growing angrier and the pain of hunger in Herman's belly reminded him of it with each day that passed without a meal delivered to his quarters.

"Katzenstein," Lieutenant Himmel hissed into the intercom, waking Herman. The Jewish man rolled over and blinked the sleep out of his eyes, looking over at the observation windows. "I need more answers. We need to solve this puzzle."

Herman could tell that Himmel was bothered. "I've been making progress on the translation," he murmured, his voice cracking. "We're close to solving it."

"That's not good enough, Katzenstein. Franz has just returned from a meeting with his superiors and he is not happy. In fact, he is furious. He will be returning for results." Himmel shook his head, looking at Herman with pleading eyes. "I can only do so much for you, Herman. I told you that your treatment here depends on your progress and cooperation. If they cannot tap into the power of the Red Ruby soon, I cannot tell you what Franz will do. These are not men to be crossed."

Standing from the bed, Herman moved toward the glass. His hands were sweaty with nerves. This early in the morning, his heart was already pounding. "I'm doing the best that I can, Lieutenant. I'm only able to solve portions from the pictures that you give me." He was panicking. He feared the Nazis and what they might do if they thought he was intentionally hindering their mission. "It might help if I could see the whole thing."

Suddenly, Himmel slammed one of his fists against the glass. It didn't break – it was too thick – but the glass vibrated in its frame, making Herman jump backward. Out of the corner of his eye, Herman saw Rashid's shadow. The noise must have woken him.

"Fine," Himmel finally snapped into the intercom. "I will be back to open the cell in five minutes. Be ready."

Himmel walked away, heading back to the door of the laboratory. The guard, who'd been standing nearby, made no movement. He didn't look at either Himmel or Herman.

Realizing that he didn't have much time, Herman

rushed into action. He changed into a fresh jumpsuit and hurried to wash his face. When he heard the clang of his cell door opening, he'd only just managed to dry his face off.

"Come," Himmel ordered.

Herman did, moving toward the door and following Himmel into the main laboratory. On his left, he could see the observation window, but it was too dark to see into the opposite cell. Rashid had not turned his light on. All Herman could see was his own reflection, his unkempt facial hair and the curls that framed his face unlike he'd ever worn his hair by choice. The hooked nose stood out against the center of his face and his olive-toned skin was stretched tight over his cheekbones, gaunt with exhaustion.

In an effort not to draw attention to the fact that he and Rashid had been communicating, Herman kept his eyes straight ahead. He'd thought that he might get to see the actual object, but the sight before him didn't detract from the magnificence. The scientists had been gathering around a table. Its surface was covered with photographs.

The hieroglyphics Herman had been translating came from an engraved sarcophagus. They had taken photos of every inch of the thing and arranged them in order on the table. At the sight of them, Herman began piecing together everything he'd translated thus far. Now that he'd seen them laid out in order, they began to make more sense. He had done enough work that it became easier to read them.

Leaning forward, Herman looked closely, blown away by what he was seeing. It was the sarcophagus Rashid had told him about. It was skinned in zinc, as he'd recalled

Franz and Himmel discussing, and larger than he'd expected. Herman began translating the hieroglyphs that prominently surrounded the Eye of Horus symbol on top, pointing and using his hands to keep track of his translations. Behind him, Himmel and the other scientists were waiting with bated breath. Herman knew their patience was thin and growing thinner the longer he took.

He began reading;

> *"Hidden from the eyes of Ra*
> *Sealed inside the body of Set*
> *Separate from his dark soul*
> *Upon the world, he will bring chaos and war*
> *A dark soul holds the key to resurrect he…"*

Suddenly a thunderous blast could be heard in the distance. It resounded the moment Herman finished reading the inscription. Herman concerned; *was it related to what he had just spoke aloud?* Everyone froze at the sound of it, but it didn't stop at one. The noise broke through the silence of the room for a second time and then a third. The scientists, the lieutenant, and Herman looked up at the ceiling as it rattled and the lights flickered with each crash. Dust came off the surface of the ceiling, spraying from the edges and cracks above them as if breaking through each tiny connection.

Yelling could be heard from the hallway, and Herman jumped as the door flew open, revealing Franz and several guards dressed in grey uniforms.

"We are out of time!" Franz shouted, his German

accent more pronounced than ever. "The Furor needs his Red Ruby now or we will fail."

"But sir, we cannot deliver what we do not fully understand!" Himmel cried out.

"We don't need to understand raw power," Franz hissed. A vein in his forehead twitched. "We only need to wield it against our enemies. Anything short of that will be our destruction."

In the distance, they heard more of the loud booms ringing out. The whole base seemed to rattle with them. The scientists glanced around, their fear transparent, they fled the room leaving Himmel to explain.

"Do you hear that?" Franz pointed to the ceiling. "That is our end. The Allied forces descend upon us as we bicker over this nonsense! You have had a year and you haven't even got the thing opened yet!"

Franz had not paid Herman any attention and his eyes fell on the Jewish man now. The vein in his forehead throbbed again and he stormed toward Herman. Grabbing the collar of Herman's jumpsuit, Franz pulled him closer until they were nose to nose.

"Give me my Red Ruby," he breathed into Herman's face. "What do all these symbols mean and how do I open it? Tell me!"

"I've shared all I know!" Herman yelled, throwing his hands up in surrender.

Franz released Herman with such vigor that he stumbled back several steps. The Nazi Officer turned to the guards. "Bring the girl!" He turned back, sneering at Herman and pacing through the room as he waited for the guard to return. "I should have done this months ago. Perhaps her life will motivate your cooperation, eh?"

Moments later, the guard returned, dragging a young girl by her arm. The girl's eyes were downcast, staring at the ground as they walked.

"My Jew," Franz spoke to Herman. "Was I not clear to you when we first met? I will reward you with love... *if you find me my gem.*"

Franz grabbed the young girl away from the guard, gripping onto the scruff of her neck. The girl cried out in pain and raised her head. Her eyes landed on Herman.

She grew more animated than before. "Papa! Papa!"

Herman dropped to his knees, clasping his hands together ecstatically at the sight of his daughter. "Sofia... My Sofia! You are alive!"

One of the guards moved at the hand signal of Franz. He trained his rifle onto Herman, keeping him at bay.

"Yes, my Jew," Franz murmured. "Your daughter is alive. I kept my promise. Now it's your turn. How long she stays alive is up to you."

A second girl had arrived, it is Margrit, but no one had noticed her yet. She peered curiously into the room, witness to the events unfolding within. As Franz removed his pistol from the holster on his belt and pressed the cold barrel against the back of Sofia's head, the corners of Margrit's lips curled into a malicious grin.

"No, please!" Herman pleaded. "I beg you, sir! She is all I have..."

"I am not a monster, Katzenstein, but she will die if you fail me again. Give me my gem and I will reward you with your love."

"Stop," Himmel interjected. "This is not necessary."

Franz swung his arm, training his pistol instead on the lieutenant. "Shut up. You failed me too." He tightened his grip on the pistol as the lieutenant stepped back. He brought it back to the head of the young girl and spoke to Herman once again. "I will give you to the count of three."

"Please… I beg you!"

"One…" Franz began his count. "Two…"

"Okay!" Herman cried out. "Okay!"

The room came to a standstill. Everyone's eyes were locked on Herman. They'd been privy to his reading only moments before Franz and the other officers had arrived.

Herman took a deep breath;

> *"Hidden from the eyes of Ra*
> *Sealed inside the body of Set*
> *Separate from his dark soul*
> *Upon the world, he will bring chaos and war*
> *A dark soul holds the key to resurrect he…"*

Franz released Sofia and the little girl raced for her father's arms. "Papa, papa," she whispers, her voice shaky as they hold one another.

"You are a good Jew after all," Franz nodded. "Now, tell me what that means. How do I open it? Where is the great power it rains down from the sky?"

"I don't know," Herman murmured. "Maybe Rashid can tell you."

Franz looked over at the lieutenant with a puzzled

expression on his face and then back at Herman. "Who is Rashid?"

Herman furrowed his brows in confusion. Was Franz serious? "The man in the neighboring cell, the Egyptian philosopher that I speak to at night…"

"Guards," Franz snapped, pointing toward the hallway between the two observation quarters. "With me."

The guards moved toward the door, opened it, and stormed in with their guns drawn. Herman heard the familiar metal clang of the heavy lock and then the steel creaking as they threw the door open. They stormed the cell and Franz followed close behind, only to find that the cell was empty.

He stormed back into the laboratory, his face red with fury. "It's empty! You've been talking to a ghost, you crazy Jew." He spat on the ground in front of them. "What does the translation mean? Or do I really need to shoot your daughter to get my answer?"

The ceiling rattled yet again. Dust rained down and the lights flickered. The explosions were getting louder with each one that rang out, sounding closer than before.

With the fresh reminder that his daughter was actually present, Herman replied with trepidation. "A *dark* soul holds the key to resurrect he… The hieroglyphs seem to indicate that a *dark* soul needs to touch it. Only that will activate its power."

Franz moved toward the large object covered by the black sheet and ripped it off, revealing the shimmering sarcophagus. The scientists must have covered it from Herman's sight, making him believe that only the photos existed. The real thing was far more astounding in its entirety and Herman gasped at the sight of it. All eyes were trained on the box, mystified by it.

The Nazi Officer raised his hand over the eye of Horus symbol, the dark eye engraved into its center on the top of the box. He repeated the translation quietly;

> *"Hidden from the eyes of Ra*
> *Sealed inside the body of Set*
> *Separate from his dark soul*
> *Upon the world, he will bring chaos and war*
> *A* dark *soul holds the key to resurrect he…"*

Everyone else in the lab looked on, including the two young girls. No one warned Franz that there was a possibility of harm coming to him if he touched the object with his bare hands, simply standing by and watching as he brought his palm down over the symbol, making contact.

The moment his hand touched the sarcophagus, Franz was jolted with a sudden flashback. He was thrown back in time to a moment in his past. He glanced around at the buildings that surrounded him, remembering what had occurred in this place. They were in one of the worst neighborhoods around.

He was a few years younger, but he was no less cruel than the man he had become since. He ushered Jewish families out of an abandoned house in the ghettos, lining them up in the public street of the town. He made them kneel down on the ground with their hands locked behind their heads to await their fate.

There were several officers behind him and at his command, they moved. Franz didn't need to use words. He simply used the hand signals they'd practiced in the army. He didn't flinch, didn't even blink as he ordered the men to pull their triggers, killing each Jewish person in front of him at once.

In the lab, a black smoky light appeared, creating a strange mist that changed the saturation of everything. It reached out, spreading outward over the entire sarcophagus. With each area the dark cloud touched, the hieroglyphs began to emit a red glow and soon, the entire object was glowing.

A seam appeared around its perimeter, revealing to everyone where the sarcophagus and its lid separated. The lid had risen slightly. It was opening.

"I can feel its power," Franz cried out into the air, throwing his head back and looking into the bright light that shone from above. "I can feel its dark soul coming to life!"

It was as Franz uttered those words that a shadow appeared from the opposite side of the laboratory. He didn't appear to be the same, but Herman recognized him immediately. He walked – or rather, *floated* – through the concrete wall and looked down on them all. His feet didn't touch the ground and his head was tilted to the right side in an eerie fashion. This drew attention to his missing eye, the socket empty.

For the first time, Herman got a good look at Rashid. He could see the man he'd been speaking to for who he really was: a one-eyed elderly man, much like the one from the story. Rashid threw his left hand into the air, holding up four green, glowing gemstones.

"I am Horus, son of Osiris and Isis," Rashid spoke, revealing his true identity as all in the room took note of his presence. "I am the Protector of the North, South, East, and West; the Holder of the Eye of Horus; and the Keeper of the Tomb of Set."

As the words fell from his lips in a deep, booming voice, his form began to change shape. He took the form of a half-man, half-falcon. His left eye was still missing, but he wore the white and gold clothes of a deity and his head was adorned by the Pschent double crown.

Franz hissed in pain as he was forced backward, his hand breaking contact with the surface of the sarcophagus. The glowing receded and the red perimeter where the lid met with the box grew dark once more. It had returned to its normal state.

The Nazi Officer screamed out in anger and raised his opposite hand. His fingers were still curled around the handle of his pistol and he pointed it at Horus. Two guards turned their rifles onto Horus too, following the lead of their superior officer. Every visible gun in the room was drawn all at once.

It seemed as though they would all fire at Horus and end things, but that didn't happen. Instead, Franz began turning toward one of his soldiers as the soldier turned toward him. The two guards turned to face one another too. Their movements were hitched, as if they were fighting for control over their own bodies. It was clear that they had lost the battle when the sound of four gunshots struck through the room, echoing off the concrete and making the onlookers flinch in shock.

With the German officers out of the way, Horus crossed the room, walking on his own invisible platform toward Lieutenant Himmel. At that moment, Margrit pushed past the door and raced toward her father, wrapping her arms around his waist and holding on tightly.

"The Falcon Sky," Horus reached out to gently press the back of his right hand to Himmel's cheek. "Dig deep into your soul. There, you will see the truth. The prophecy gem does not lie and it has foretold your destiny."

Horus' right hand was clenched into a fist and within his curled fingers he held the gemstones. They began to glow, green beams emerging from between Horus fingers and making his hand glow in the same way. Himmel's eyes began to water, tears threatening to spill over his waterline. The lieutenant felt an ache in his chest and his throat tightened with emotion.

"Ahhh... You can see it, the scale awaits you in the Hall of Two Truths," Horus sighed. "Did you think your journey to Egypt was an accident? Did you think your role in all this was mere coincidence?"

Himmel's voice quivered as he answered, "N... n... no..."

"Your fate does not end on this day," Horus' voice boomed. "Take your seed and leave this place."

Himmel didn't need to be told twice. He reached down and grabbed his daughter's hand. Together, they ran, fleeing the deity and the awful powers that be. Their footsteps echoed as they slapped out of the room.

Turning to the last two people in the room, Horus found Herman and Sofia holding onto one another on the floor. He knelt before them and opened his hands, baring his palms to their eyes. None of the three notice that Margrit is lagging behind her father, that she looked back at the last moment, right in time to see that Horus was revealing something to Sofia and her father.

"You have found your love," Horus looked at Herman.

"Yes," Herman nodded, pulling Sofia closer to his side.

"You have found your father," Horus looked at Sofia this time.

"Yes," she whispered.

"You must now leave this place," Horus stated.

"But we'll never get out of here alive," Herman muttered.

Horus leaned forward and unfolded Herman and Sofia's arms, making them stretch their hands out. With their palms up, the deity reached into his garments and pulled out a burlap sack. He placed the four green gemstones, the pieces of the eye of Horus, inside the sack and passed it to Herman. With his hands free, Horus traced his fingertips over the tattoos on the inside of Herman and Sofia's wrists, the serial numbers they'd been branded with when they were sent to the concentration camps.

The voice rang out on the inside of Herman's skull the next time Horus spoke. "You are both joined in love and pain, marked for death, and yet you continue to live. Your destiny is to save your daughter and fulfill the deed I ask of you. For that, Sofia will live a full life."

Rather than speak the deed to Herman, Horus passed

the message on within his mind, giving him the key to his daughter's future.

When Horus spoke again, his words came from his own mouth, ringing out loud and clear for both of the Katzenstein's to hear. "Now go. My destiny follows another path. The Tomb of Set must never be found again. I must stay here and keep him from rebirth, out of sight of his brother Ra..." His voice trailed off and his head snapped down as he locked eyes on the two before him. "Go!"

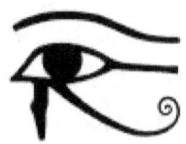

CHAPTER 19
THE GREAT ESCAPE

Herman and Sofia stood as Horus yelled down at them, hurrying to their feet. Herman shoved the sack into one of his jumpsuit pockets before grabbing his daughter's hand and gripping it firmly. They ran out of the room, fleeing in the same way that Himmel and his daughter had before them.

It was clear that they were heading toward the base as the awful thunderous explosions could be heard clearer than they were in the laboratory. They were coming out of the depths of the operation. With each blast, their situation grew more urgent. The ceiling rattled and dust fell freely now. It was as though something in the foundations had broken and the lights flickered almost constantly, adding to the air of urgency.

From outside, they could hear the immeasurable ruckus of gunfire. It wasn't far off, coming from somewhere up ahead. They turned down a hallway and Sofia suddenly pulled her hand free of her father's.

"Wait!" She knew this hall well. She'd memorized each trip in and out of her room.

The only thing that had gotten her through the past months, though she hated to admit it, was a gift from Margrit. She didn't want to leave it behind and so, she ran toward the door that she knew was hers. Herman followed close behind, baffled by his daughter's actions until they were in her room. He barely had a chance to take in the dismal, cramped space with its lack of furniture and its identical cot.

Sofia grabbed the copy of The Katzenstein Kids comic and hurried back to where her father stood in the doorway. With her free hand, she took his and they were off once more. She held on tightly to both of the things her fingers were wrapped around, the comic book and her father's hand.

They neared a door at the end of the hall and Herman threw it open. They'd had no idea what time it was deep in the base. There were no clocks to measure the day by. From the doorway, they could see darkness beyond the door and felt the bitter bite of the cold February night. In the distance, there was a loading dock. They were near the sea.

The entire facility shook with the force of another explosion. It was easy to identify the sounds of bombs when they were this close. The deafening, short bang of gunshots rang out in the night sky as the battle raged on outside. In the darkness, Herman spotted a soldier running through the rocky terrain and burning orange sparks of gunfire broke through the darkness as he fired off his gun. Further along, the answering gunshots could be seen bursting forth from the Allied forces.

Tracer rounds burst through the air, brighter than anything Herman and Sofia had witnessed thus far. The white glow of the bullets flying through the air like flairs was blinding. They broke apart, exploding in midair and raining down miniature explosions near the loading docks.

Herman watched all of this with a pounding heart and sweat dripping down the back of his neck and into his collar. His eyes flitted back and forth as he tried to navigate the best escape route for him and his daughter. He had an idea and he wasn't sure if it would work, but he supposed there was only one way to find out. He turned and looked back down the hallway, into the open doors of the soldiers' quarters. In one of them, Herman could see a storage closet and went to open it.

There was a large bag – similar to laundry bags – that was filled with cans of water and wool blankets. Herman had a feeling it was for this very purpose. He tugged it out and threw it over his shoulder, making his way back to the door.

"Stay close," he told Sofia.

"Wait for us!" Margrit's voice rang down the hallway behind them.

As Herman and Sofia turned to face her, Margrit noticed two things at once; the first was that Sofia had the comic book in her hand and the second was that the green glow of Horus' eye could be seen in Herman's pocket. The next thing she knew, there was another explosion and the roof between them fell inward. The cave-in brought about a cloud of dust and the debris trapped Himmel and Margrit inside.

Through the dust, Margrit could see Sofia turn away and escape with her father from the base.

The father and daughter duo raced toward the boats, running across the cold ground with their hands locked together. They knew only one thing; they had to get as far away as possible. Horus had been clear in his instruction and they could not let anything distract them from their goal. They ran past barrels, small buildings, and Germans and the Allied forces locked in ferocious battle.

Herman ignored the chaos swirling around him, absently thinking that this was exactly what Set would bring about, in the hopes that they might not take note of him and Sofia if he didn't pay any attention to them. It became clear that his plan was not going to work as a small patrol boat came into sight at the dock. They heard the bullets rather than saw the people who fired them, the bang echoing through the night sky far closer than any other battle noise they'd heard thus far.

"Papa!" Sofia screamed as her father cried out in pain.

Though a bullet had struck him, Herman continued to run. Agony stemmed from the wound, burning and spreading through the area where the bullet grazed his skin as he and his daughter climbed onto one of the boats. Herman dropped the bag on the seat and grabbed a knife off the floor of the boat, cutting them loose from the dock. The boat drifted slightly and Herman moved to get the thing started.

By now, the Germans had taken note of their captives making an attempt to escape, and the soldiers in the small patrol boat began firing at them.

"Get down!" Herman yelled to his daughter. "And stay down!"

He released a cry of pain as yet another bullet pierced his skin, forcing him to heed his own advice and duck low. His plan had been to outwait the soldiers as they would need to eventually reload their guns, but he and his daughter didn't need to wait for as long as they thought. Another bomb went off, so close that Herman and Sofia's ears rang with the sound. It ricocheted off the insides of their heads like a gong, making them shut their eyes with its force.

When the ringing finally stopped, Herman hazarded a glance over the edge of the boat. The German patrol boat was hit by an explosion. The sight of blood and what Herman thought to be a severed limb greeted him. His stomach lurched and he forced himself to look away before he threw up at the repulsive spectacle. Standing, he went back to the engine of the boat and began tugging at the chain that pumped fuel into the carburetor manually.

"Come on," Herman muttered, well aware that he was pleading with an inanimate object. "Please start."

His arm stung with the effort of pulling the chain, the wound in his shoulder bleeding into the jumpsuit he wore, but he gave one final powerful tug and the boat cranked to life as he released the choke. He got behind the wheel and the boat sped away from the dock, drifting further out onto the sea, the moonlight glistening off the surface of the water as they made their great escape.

Behind them, moments after they'd pulled away from the dock, they could see the bombing of the base from the air. The explosions whistled through the air as they fell and bright sparks flew in every direction as they broke through the rubble and landed on the ground with a gigantic crash. Sofia and Herman turned away from the sight, trying to block out the thunderous noise as they settled in on the boat.

Eventually, Herman could allow the boat to drift freely on the water. He moved toward his daughter and pulled her into his arms before reaching into the bag he'd brought along and wrapping both their bodies in the wool blankets. They shivered as they held each other, vainly trying to stay warm in the freezing evening. All too soon, the gas ran out and the engines came to a stop with a spluttering metallic cough. They were miles away from any landmass, drifting out on the open sea with no way to get home.

In the silence, Sofia finally glanced up at her papa. Her eyes widened as she spotted the blood on his shoulder. "Papa," she whispered. "You were shot."

"I know, sweetheart," Herman murmured, smoothing her hair with his hand. "I'll be all right."

Sofia didn't believe her father, but she didn't think that arguing with him was going to help anything. She decided instead to hold him as closely as he held her, showing him how much he meant to her in the love that she offered. "I love you, papa," she whispered.

"And I love you, my Sofia," her father leaned forward and pressed a gentle kiss to the top of his daughter's head.

They did not drift to land that night, nor the night after that. The days passed them by as they floated along the water, lulled by the sound of splashing against the hull of their small boat. They had no food, but at least they were not dehydrated. The water beneath their vehicle was far too salty and the mere thought of it touching their dry, cracked lips, made Herman wince. The bag he'd grabbed from the storage closet had enough water to keep them going, though he could do nothing about the red tinge to their pale skin. The sun baked them during the day, as harsh as the evening chill that seeped into their bones and wracked their bodies with tremors.

While Sofia slept, Herman knew he grew weaker with each moment. He looked down on his daughter, hoping that he would be able to save her the way Horus had said. The sight of her brought out his paternal instinct and he tucked the edges of the heavy blankets in around them, holding her close as he closed his own eyes and allowed himself to glide into a dreamless sleep.

♦ ♦ ♦

Sofia and Herman were startled into wakefulness by a loud horn at daybreak. The USS Mason loomed over them. It was an Evart-Class Destroyer Escort that had been commissioned out of Boston.

When the US ship found the Jewish father and his daughter, Herman was at his weakest. Over the course of the past two days, he had lost an awful lot of blood. His pale skin had a tinge of yellow to it and he could hardly say two words. Soldiers brought the two onboard, rescuing them.

"Welcome aboard," Commander Milton Weatherbourne greeted them with a straight back. "How long were you…?"

The commander didn't finish his question because he noticed there was something wrong with the man before him. The man could hardly focus two eyes on him, let alone stand straight. If the commanding officer didn't know any better, he would say that the little girl was the only reason he was standing, as his hand rested on her shoulder.

"Medic!" The commander called.

A medical officer had been in wait and, upon seeing how badly wounded Herman was, ordered that both their new arrivals be taken to the sickbay. However, the officers wanted to separate the two and Sofia's high-pitched screech rang in everyone's ears. She refused to let go of her father, clutching the arm of his jumpsuit desperately.

"Sofia," Herman spoke, looking down at his daughter weakly. She had no idea of the way she danced in his vision or that he saw double if he moved too fast. "Go with the crew. They'll look after you, clean you up, and feed you. I will be okay."

"But papa," Sofia stared up at her father with pleading eyes.

"No buts, Sofia. Go."

Sofia held her tongue and nodded her head curtly. She allowed one of the officers to lead her away, watching as her father went in the opposite direction with the medical officer and the man who had first welcomed them onto his ship. The last thing the little girl wanted was to watch her father be removed from her sight ever again, but she had to listen to him.

◆ ◆ ◆

"Who are you?" Commander Milton Weatherbourne stood over Herman's bed as he was treated for his wound. The fact that it wasn't the best of times to ask such questions didn't seem to occur to the Navy officer.

"My name is Herman Katzenstein. My daughter and I were kept in captivity by the German Nazi's on a base they called Schatzgraber."

"How did you and your daughter get here? How did you escape?"

Herman hissed in pain as the medical officer dug through the hole in his shoulder. His jumpsuit had been pulled down to his waist. "The Allied forces," Herman grunted in pain, "were attacking the base. We found our way to the boats under the cover of gunfire and explosions and were able to escape."

Anything the commander was going to say next was cut off as Herman screamed out in pain again. The medical officer suddenly stopped what he was doing and cleaned the wound with an antibacterial swab. Herman lay back against the hospital bed, breathing heavily as his shoulder was bandaged.

The medical officer turned to the commander. "I've done all that I can, but I cannot remove the bullet. We're too far away from port to transfer him. We need a hospital ship at this point."

The commander looked back over at their patient, his lips tightened into a grim line.

Herman could read the mood of the room well enough. He may have been exhausted and the officers may have been speaking too low for him to hear, but that didn't matter. Instincts had kept him alive thus far and now, he knew that he was going to die soon.

"Please," he murmured to the officers. "I'd like a pen and paper, as well as the belongings my daughter and I brought with us."

Knowing that he had little time left, the commander nodded his head. He walked away from the bed, toward another Navy officer, and whispered the orders. Herman relaxed against the pillow, wincing as a sharp pain rang out in his shoulder. He wondered if it would be the blood loss or the lead poisoning that killed him first.

Minutes later, the officer returned with everything that Herman had requested. The Katzenstein Kids comic book that his daughter had rescued was brought along with the pen and paper, as well as the burlap sack with the four gems of Horus.

Upon receiving his items, Herman sat up in bed with some effort, ignoring the hushed admonishments of the medical officer, and began to write a letter on the lined piece of paper with the ink pen he'd been given. His scrawl was slanting and thin and it flew across the page, filling each line. He quickly covered the majority of the page with tiny words written in his handwriting.

The medical bay was silent but for the scrawls of the

pen's point against the page. All the officers in the room wondered what it was that the man wrote, but no one interrupted. They let him carry out what they believed to be his dying actions with furrowed brows and narrowed eyes. It was an unusual occurrence if ever there was one. This was a mission that would go into the record books.

When he was done writing his letter, Herman folded the piece of paper in half and grabbed the copy of The Katzenstein Kids comic. He scribbled something onto the cover as quickly as he could, though he allowed no one to see it. By the time he was done, Herman was exhausted. The actions had been small, and they should not have taken as much as they had out of him, but the wound in his shoulder dominated all sense of feeling. The weaker he felt, the closer death came.

"Commander Weatherbourne," Herman mumbled, breaking the silence of the sickbay, and garnering the attention of everyone within it.

"How are you doing, Mr. Katzenstein?" Milton asked, approaching the bed.

"I need to speak with you alone," Herman murmured, glancing at the other Navy officer and the medical officer in the bay.

Milton hesitated, looking from Herman to the other officers. He wasn't actually allowed to ask the other officers to leave them alone – it wasn't protocol – but he found himself nodding. On one hand, he knew that the man on the sickbed could not be fully trusted. They had no idea if what he'd told them thus far was true and he could be out to deceive them. However, Milton thought that Herman was far too weak to try anything. Besides, he was curious about what it was that Herman wanted to discuss with him. Up until this point, he'd said more with the pen than with his mouth.

At his signal, the other two officers quietly walked out of the room.

"Thank you," Herman nodded tiredly. "I need you to make me a promise."

"What is it?" Milton asked, leaning in close.

Herman passed the letter, the comic book, and the burlap sack to Milton. Then, he tugged the man close by the lapels on his shoulders and whispered into his ear. Milton hung on to every weak word that fell off Herman's lips and when the Jewish man pulled back, resting against his pillow, Milton was hesitant.

"Please," Herman pleaded.

Clenching his jaw, Milton finally nodded his head, reluctantly agreeing to fulfill the promise of a dying man.

"It is no accident... that you found us..." Herman murmured.

With that, Herman's eyes fell shut and he drifted into unconsciousness. Milton's jaw twitched as he turned away from the bed and left the bay. On his way out, he ordered the medical officer to return to the sickbay and take care of Milton. Meanwhile, he made his way toward his quarters, feeling tense and anxious about the promise.

Once in his cabin, Milton pulled a medium-sized wooden storage box, known as a Ditty Box, from beneath his bunk. He opened the lid, revealing the interior. It was packed with pictures and letters from home, as well as a few small knick-knacks that were of no consequence to anyone except Milton. He carefully placed the comic book and the letter inside the box, shifting some of the photographs so that they concealed the book from view.

The burlap sack concerned Milton more and he looked down at it, squeezing it between his fingers. It was full of something hard, almost like rocks. He had a feeling that they were valuable, though he knew not what they were. A large part of Milton *didn't* want to know what was inside and to look would violate his promise. The commander glanced around his room and noticed something that he could use to conceal it.

Milton put the burlap sack inside the container to help hide it and then added the container to the Ditty Box before sliding the wooden storage box back under the bunk.

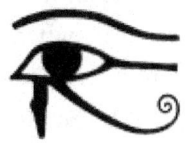

CHAPTER 20
THE FIRST CLUE
Dennis Port, Massachusetts – 1979

Isaac sat at the kitchen table as his mother moved around the kitchen, preparing breakfast for them. It was pancakes once again, and the enticing smell wafted around the room and into Isaac's nose, making his belly grumble. For once, he wasn't in a hurry. He and his friends had spent the last few days together and nothing would stand in the way of them doing so again.

It was when she served the plate, setting it down on the table in front of Isaac, that he took note of her tattoo. He had seen it many times before, but he and his mother never talked about it. They don't speak about her past, about the serial number on the underside of her arm, about the concentration camps, about the holocaust, and about her dreadful childhood. All he knew was that it haunted her and with each year that he aged, they learned more and more about the war in school. The lessons were the only reason he knew anything about his mother's past at all.

In the afternoons, Isaac would arrive home from school, abuzz with questions about what they'd learned. It was only during these sessions when they spoke about the war that his mother would reveal more about herself, bit by bit, until finally, Isaac began to understand why his mother was so sad all the time. He had yet to reach the age where he fully grasped the horror of World War II, but he was old enough that he understood the gist of it. He was old enough to respect his mother's wishes that he come home before dark and keep safe. He was old enough to realize that there was a reason behind her overprotectiveness.

Most times, if Isaac saw the serial number, he averted his eyes as quickly as he could. He didn't want to draw attention to it, afraid of upsetting his mother further than she already was. On this particular morning, however, something about it looked extremely familiar. It wasn't the familiarity bred by the fact that he'd seen it many times before. It was the kind of familiarity that came from having seen it somewhere else before.

Isaac narrowed his eyes, squinting down at the tattoo, but his mother pulled her arm away before he could identify it. He cursed under his breath, trying to remember it without looking at it. His mother dished some pancakes up for herself as he wolfed down the first two bites of his meal, desperately trying to link the memories.

It came to him quite suddenly. He dropped the fork on

the plate with a clatter and, with his mouth still full of pancakes and warm butter, Isaac raced up the passage toward his bedroom. His footsteps were loud in the small house.

"Isaac?" His mother called after him. "Where did you go?"

In his bedroom, Isaac dived for the top drawer of his bedside table where he kept his precious comic book. He pulled it open, the recollection of something he'd seen on the cover of The Katzenstein Kids coming back to him. The drawer was empty and Isaac was filled with panic, his heart racing even faster. He was still breathless from the run up the hallway.

"Where is it?" Isaac breathed.

His eyes roved over the room and he caught sight of his backpack, lying on the ground near the door. Had he not taken it out the previous day? Isaac couldn't recall. He'd been reading the comic book in bed for the last few nights, but he must have been too tired to do so the previous night.

Isaac unzipped the backpack and held his breath as he pulled the comic book out to confirm his suspicions. He almost wanted to close his eyes. The anticipation coursed through him and goosebumps rose on his skin as he laid eyes on the cover of the comic.

With the same urgency as before, Isaac ran back down the hallway. His mom peered out of the kitchen doorway with a baffled expression on her face right in time to see Isaac stop at the phone. Before she could ask him what on earth had gotten into him, Isaac had already picked the phone up off the wall and was dialing Will's house number. He knew it by heart. He knew all of his friend's numbers by heart – including Amy's.

He told Will and Amy to meet him at Dez' house as soon as possible and called on Dez to tell him that they would be there shortly. Dez could hear the excitement in Isaac's voice, but Isaac couldn't afford to say anything in front of his mother. Instead, he cut his friend off.

"I'll tell you all about it when we get there!" Isaac hung the phone back up, slamming it down, and hurried to get ready.

◆◆◆

Once the four were gathered at Dez' house, Dez ushered them all into the garage. It was the quickest place to talk without anyone hearing them and Isaac's excitement was palpable. Isaac practically trembled with the level of his urgency. Once they were in the garage, Dez shut the door so that they were sheltered from prying ears.

Will and Amy had both arrived before Isaac because Isaac's mother had insisted that he finished his breakfast first. The pit of his belly still burned with the heat of the pancakes he'd wolfed down. He'd barely chewed, virtually inhaling his meal as his mother watched on. It seemed as though she was too shocked to say or do anything more when Isaac hugged her goodbye and raced out of the house. She only found the sudden energy to go after him when he was already turning off the driveway, peddling away from the house on his bike.

It had been no use and she didn't know that her son had seen her as she came out of the house. He knew she wanted him to stop, even if she didn't call out for him, but there was no way he would have. It was the lack of a desire to hurt his mother that kept him from looking back at her. Instead, he pretended as though he hadn't noticed her at all. A pang of guilt hit him square in the chest as he made his way toward Dez' house.

"All right, G-man," he turned to Isaac. "What is it? What's so urgent that you called us all here before we'd even finished our breakfast."

"I discovered something about The Katzenstein Kids," Isaac told them. He tugged his backpack off his shoulders, unzipped it, and pulled the comic book out. "I might have figured out a possible clue to all of this. If my hunch is correct, it's a clue to Milton's treasure. Remember the one Mike Kelly was talking about?"

The others watched and listened intently. At the sight of the comic, they grew excited too. They hadn't done as much research on the comic book as Isaac had, particularly since he had signed out *The History of Comics* from the library, but that didn't stop them from showing interest. The whole mystery behind Milton, Gorska Maika, and the comic book filled each of the kids with great intrigue. It was the most interesting summer adventure that they had ever had.

"Look at this," Isaac finally ordered.

He set the comic book down on the makeshift workbench and his friends edged closer, glancing over his shoulder at the numbers he pointed to. The cover had two cartoon characters, both boys, illustrated on the cover. On their arms were two six-digit numbers, much like the tattooed holocaust serial number on the inside of his mother's arm.

The four kids squinted down at the cover before Dez stood up.

"Wait," he murmured.

Dez crossed the garage and on the other side, began rummaging through one of several toolboxes on the floor. The others watched him in confusion as he dug around, looking for something. After a moment, Dez returned to the workbench with a magnifying glass in his hand.

"This should help," he nodded and passed it over to Isaac.

"Thanks, dude," Isaac took the magnifying glass and moved it over the comic book, making the numbers look ten times bigger than before. There was no mistaking them. They were two sets of six-digit serial numbers, much like the one on his mother's arm. "They're similar to the tattoo on my mother's arm, the holocaust serial number."

Isaac sat back and his words were dropped like bombs, leaving the others speechless. No one knew what it might mean. They could understand Isaac's excitement, but they didn't know where they were going to go from this point.

"Wait," Amy murmured.

The blue-eyed girl was still staring down at the cover of The Katzenstein Kids. Isaac had released the handle of the magnifying glass and it was resting on top of the comic book. As she squinted down at the comic book, Amy reached over and grabbed ahold of the magnifying glass. The boys shifted to allow her better access.

"Look," she repeated Isaac's first words. "Is it just me

or does it look like these numbers weren't a part of the comic book to begin with?"

The boys moved forward all at once, staring at the cover, and they realized that Amy was correct. The six-digit numbers hadn't been printed out on the cover. Instead, they had been inked onto it. Someone had written the numbers so well that they blended with the cover, but they definitely weren't a part of it. They didn't belong there.

"I wonder why someone would add those numbers to the cover," Amy whispered. Something about raising her voice in the garage felt wrong. It was almost as though someone was watching them, but she knew that was impossible. "Are you sure that they're similar, Isaac?"

"I'm sure. I saw it this morning when she was making breakfast. I've seen it hundreds of times before, but this time I remembered it from the cover." Isaac glanced down at the comic book. "They are similar."

At that moment, they heard a scuffle somewhere outside the garage, making all of them jump. The kids froze, looking toward the side door of the garage. They were worried that the door would burst open, and it was becoming clear to them that they had stumbled onto a dangerous secret. They didn't know what was so special about this particular comic book, but they got the feeling that someone else did.

"We should go back to the treehouse," Dez eventually whispered, breaking the silence in the garage. "I think we can talk there."

The others nodded their heads eagerly, following him to the door. Dez being taller than they were, and he only had to stand on his toes to see out of the window on the garage door. Will, Isaac, and Amy would have had to stand on something in order to reach. Dez peeked through the glass, looking from left to right for the source of the sound and back again. When he decided that the coast was clear, he pulled the door open and the kids tumbled out of the garage. Isaac held the comic book in one hand and the magnifying glass in the other as they made their way across Dez' grassy backyard.

It was a clear day and the sun shone down happily. The blue sky was free of clouds, making the sense of foreboding that hung over the kid's heads worse. It seemed wrong that the kids should be feeling as scared as they were. The pounding hearts and sweaty hands seemed like symptoms they should have suffered in stormy weather, with flashes of lightning breaking through a dark, angry sky, and a nip in the air that bit into the skin of their faces.

Instead, the day was perfectly ordinary. The circumstances would have been fantastic for any other summer day. As it was, however, it only made the kids more antsy as they hurried across the backyard.

One at a time, the kids climbed the rungs up to their secret spot. Amy went first, followed by Dez, then Will, and Isaac brought up the rear after passing The Katzenstein Kids and the magnifying glass up to the others. No one made a sound when they first entered the small entryway into the treehouse.

Isaac arrived to see the others standing near the hole in the floor, surveying the treehouse in shock. He, too, could scarcely move. His blood ran cold and every hair on his body stood up with fear as he looked around at his, Will, Dez', and now Amy's secret spot.

"Whoa," Dez murmured. "Dude…"

"Who could have done this?" Amy asked.

No one needed to ask what she was referring to. The small space had been trashed by someone. The bean bags were overturned and unzipped, their stuffing scattered all over the floor as if someone had opened them up and rummaged through them in search of something. Will's cardboard box of cassettes was emptied out onto one side of the treehouse and discarded haphazardly. The lamp had been ripped free from the extension cord and knocked off the milk crate, its bulb shattered, while the milk crate itself had been emptied. Magazines and comic books were strewn all over the floor and what was left of the beanbags, some of them with pages torn from their bindings. The entire place was overturned. The only thing that remained untouched was the radio hanging on the wall of the treehouse.

"I'll give you three guesses," Isaac whispered.

"I only need one," Dez responded. "Gorska Maika."

"She must be looking for the comic book. She knows that we have it," Will stated. "What are we going to do?"

"We could tell our parents," Isaac offered, though he didn't seem keen on the idea.

"I don't think that's going to help," Will shook his head at the thought of his parents. "They'll never believe us."

"Nah," Dez shook his head. "Will's right. Besides, the only person I can tell is Grams and she'll think I'm making it up to play some kind of game with you guys. I can already see it now."

"Yeah, I don't really want to make my mom any more worried about me than she already is," Isaac admitted. "I could only imagine how she would react to the serial numbers."

"Okay, so, we might have something really valuable here, right?" Will asked.

The others nodded their heads.

"Does anyone else think that the police will react the same way as our parents?"

"C'mon, dude," Dez shook his head again, his voice laced with disbelief. "You know we can't take this to the cops."

"Okay, okay," Will held his hands up in surrender. "Well... What about the person who told us about Milton's treasure in the first place?"

"You mean Mike Kelly?" Isaac asked. His brows knitted together as he thought of telling the news reporter. Finally, he shrugged. "I can't think of anything else we can do."

"Anyone else have any arguments?" Will looked pointedly at Dez.

Amy and Dez shook their heads.

"Okay," Will nodded. "Then let's get going. The Cape Cod Daily is about three miles away."

Will didn't wait for the others to respond before climbing back down the ladder. At the bottom, he couldn't shake the feeling that someone was watching him. He looked around, his eyes focusing on the woods as if he would be able to see someone in the cover of the trees, but no one came into sight. He shook it off, blaming the uneasiness on the excitement of the day.

Soon, he was joined by Amy, Dez, and Isaac. Isaac had tucked the comic book and the magnifying glass back into his backpack, which was securely strapped to his shoulders.

The four ran across the yard toward their bikes, hopping on and making their way toward the Cape Cod Daily to see Mike Kelly. They all knew where it was located because of its prominent location on Old Main Street just over the Bass River Bridge in South Yarmouth. In fact, the bridge was a regular fishing spot for the boys when they ventured that way.

There was no speaking on the way to the Cape Cod Daily. The kids peddled as fast as they could and Dez, with his long legs, ended up far ahead of them. Unlike most days, they didn't call after him to slow down. They simply worked as hard as they could to keep up.

By the time the four of them arrived on Old Main Street, they were breathless and sweaty. They parked their bikes up against the side of the station and walked into the building. A bell on the top of the door rang out, announcing their arrival as they entered. At the sound of the chime, Mike Kelly stood up from behind a partition. His eyes widened at the sight of the kids and he came around to greet them.

"Hello," Mike Kelly smiled. "I remember you four. You were at the Weatherbourne's house when I did the break-in story, right?"

The kids nodded, still too breathless to speak.

"What can I do for you? What brings you down here?"

He looked over their faces. "You seem to have come in quite a hurry."

Dez nodded his head vigorously. "We have, sir. We have to tell you something. It's about Milton's treasure."

Mike raised his eyebrows. He seemed torn between wanting to laugh and wanting to take the kids seriously. The corners of his mouth twitched as he tried to decide. It was the serious expressions on their faces that made Mike gesture toward the chairs in the waiting room at the front of the building.

"Get some water for these kids, will you?" He spoke to the receptionist behind the desk.

She was quick to move and follow his orders. The kids recognized her as they caught their breath. It was the same woman who'd carried the camera when he filmed outside Mrs. Weatherbourne's house.

Will, Dez, Isaac, and Amy each took a seat and Mike swung one around so that he could sit in front of them. "Now," he started with the familiar twinkle of a new story in his eye. "What's this about Milton's treasure?"

None of the kids knew what to say now that they were face to face with Mike. They exchanged glances, as if hoping to find the answer written on one another's faces but were left empty-handed. Mike seemed to grow suspicious of them the longer they stayed silent.

"It all started with Gorska Maika," Isaac finally spoke.

"Who is Gorska Maika?" Mike asked.

The receptionist walked into the waiting room with a tray in her hands at that moment. She stopped in front of the kids and each of them grabbed a cup off of it, eagerly gulping down the cool water. It refreshed them and quenched their thirsty throats. On the tray, the receptionist had also brought the same notepad they'd seen Mike write on outside Mrs. Weatherbourne's house. He took it and the pen from the tray, licking the point and poising his hand over the first lined page of the notepad, waiting for Isaac to continue.

Isaac downed his entire glass, but the receptionist had already left the room, taking the tray with her. He was forced to hold onto the empty cup while speaking to Mike. "She's a woman who dresses in all black and drives around Dennis Port in a black Mercedes. Only, she isn't the one driving. There is a man who drives her around."

"I don't suppose you happen to have a plate on that black Mercedes, do you?" Mike arched an eyebrow.

"No, sir," Will answered, shaking his head.

"Come to think of it, kids, I have seen a black Mercedes driving around here over the summer holiday." Mike looked between them and wrote something down on the notepad. "Okay, so tell me about this woman. What is she to you? How do you know her name?"

"We don't know her name," Amy interrupted. "It's just what we call her. But that isn't important."

Mike's expression grew incredulous, but he said nothing. "It isn't important. Okay…"

"What's important is that we think she's following us," Isaac stated. "We think that she might have been following Mrs. Weatherbourne too. For all we know, she's the one who broke into the house and ransacked the place. And now, she's done it to our treehouse too."

"I'm sorry," Mike interjected. "Did you just say your treehouse?"

"Yeah, we got to our treehouse and it had been turned upside down," Isaac confirmed. "Someone was looking for something in there. They probably think that we have the treasure because we helped Mrs. Weatherbourne sort through Milton's boxes."

Mike gave an exasperated sigh. He couldn't believe he'd been so interested. "Did it ever occur to you that perhaps another kid went through your treehouse? Do you kids know anyone who would want to freak you out? A bully, perhaps?"

"It wasn't a bully," Amy snapped at Mike, annoyed that he wasn't taking them seriously.

"Yeah, Gorska Maika is trying to find the treasure. We think that it was real." Dez added anxiously. "Weren't loads of people interested in it when Milton came back to town after the war?"

"Perhaps," Mike nodded, "It was before my time. It could just be an urban legend, kids. There was no truth behind the rumors."

"Well, what if there was?" Isaac insisted. "What if there was and Gorska Maika really is trying to search for it? If she's the one who broke into Mrs. Weatherbourne's, then she's already hurt one person. What's to stop her from hurting someone else?"

"And she had a Russian accent," Will told Mike. "She might be a commie or a KGB agent from the Soviet Union."

"Kids will be kids," Mike snickered under his breath, shaking his head. "Look, I'll investigate it, all right? But I think you're letting your imagination run wild. Besides, Mrs. Weatherbourne was released from the hospital. Perhaps you could ask her about all this."

The kids were disappointed that Mike Kelly didn't believe them, but they were excited at the mention of Mrs. Weatherbourne's return. Asking her about it sounded as good an idea as any. They weren't giving up. The Cape Cod Daily wasn't their last hope.

If anyone knew about Milton's treasure, it would be Mrs. Weatherbourne.

Amy, Will, Dez, and Isaac stood from their seats. They left their cups where they'd been sitting. Mike stood from his seat too, walking them back toward the door. The bell chimed upon opening and the kids walked out.

"Listen," Mike called as the kids grabbed their bikes by the handles. "I don't want to freak you out, but you kids should be careful out there. Did you hear this mornings' breaking news story?"

The kids shook their heads.

"It took place in the early hours. You know that hockey player, Puck? The Greg Collins kid?"

After exchanging a glance, the kids nodded.

"Well, he was found dead. His body was located near Swan River Bridge, covered in crabs. It was low tide." The expression on Mike's face was grim, but the kids couldn't describe the newfound energy that pulsed through them at the mention of this piece of news. "We don't know if it was an accident or not. Just be careful, all right?"

"Yes, sir," the kids chorused together.

"All right," Mike nodded and turned back to his station, closing the door with yet another chime of the bell. He had no idea what he'd started by telling the kids about Greg Collins.

The story was scary, but the kids couldn't help but wonder how Greg Collins had died. Was it possible that it was just an accident or was Gorska Maika really out there, watching them? They figured the only place left to find answers was with Mrs. Weatherbourne.

They were going right to the source.

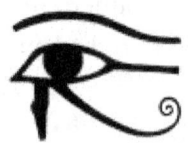

CHAPTER 21
MILTON'S TREASURE

Once they arrived at her house, the kids rushed up the wooden steps of her porch and rang the doorbell urgently, not caring if they were being rude. They heard the meows of Seymour at the door and shifted anxiously from foot to foot as they waited. Each of them found themselves glancing around to make sure that they weren't being watched.

The door swung open after some time, revealing Mrs. Weatherbourne. There didn't seem to be anything wrong with her, other than the slow way in which she moved. She looked down at the kids with confusion clearly written on her face.

"Boys?" She asked. Glancing at Amy, she added, "I see you've made a new friend."

"Hi, Mrs. Weatherbourne," Amy murmured shyly. They'd forgotten that Amy wasn't their friend the last time they'd visited Mrs. Weatherbourne. It was such a short time ago that they'd helped Mrs. Weatherbourne, but so much had changed since then. "My name is Amy Howard."

"It's a pleasure to meet you, Amy," the elderly lady nodded her head. "What can I do for you kids today?"

"We wanted to talk to you about Milton, ma'am," Dez stated. "We have some things to share with you."

"Well, then," Mrs. Weatherbourne smiled and stepped aside. "I suppose you'd better come in, hadn't you?"

The boys walked passed Mrs. Weatherbourne, mumbling appreciatively as they made their way toward where they knew her living room was. Amy followed closely behind them. Seymour found them quickly, running into the room from some other room in the house and brushing himself up against their legs as they sat down on the sofa.

Photos were still strewn across the coffee table in the middle of the room, but there seemed to be more order to them now than there had been before. It looked as though Mrs. Weatherbourne had been sorting through them. The kids wondered if that was before or after the events that landed her in the hospital. They figured that there would surely have been some signs of a struggle between the elderly woman and her attacker if they'd been sorted before the break-in.

"Would any of you like some lemonade?" Mrs. Weatherbourne offered and the boys couldn't help comparing the different situations.

The last time they were here had been the first day of the summer for them. This time, there was an urgency to their actions. They shook their heads.

Mrs. Weatherbourne raised her eyebrows in surprise. "It must be serious for you to say no to some lemonade."

"It is," Isaac confirmed.

"I see," Mrs. Weatherbourne sat down in her armchair. Seymour followed her and, once she was seated, hopped into her lap. While she stroked his back, the cat curled up and relaxed, its eyes watching the kids even as they grew heavy with sleep. "Well, then, what is it that you kids wanted to talk about?"

"What happened to you, Mrs. Weatherbourne?" Isaac asked quietly, thinking that they should probably get this out of the way. After all, it would do them no good to tell her about everything they'd discovered without first finding out what happened to her. For all they knew, she might have witnessed that it wasn't Gorska Maika. "Why did you have to go to the hospital?"

"I'm sure you kids have heard that my house was broken into," she answered. The kids nodded and she continued. "I don't know who it was. It was dark and I couldn't see them. And I can't really remember much about that night."

"Were you really hurt?"

"I had a concussion and I've still got a few bruises, but I'm still kicking, kids." Mrs. Weatherbourne winked. "Is that all you wanted to talk about?"

Isaac shook his head quickly. "We think we know who attacked you."

"Who?" Mrs. Weatherbourne leaned forward with wide eyes.

"We call her Gorska Maika. She's a Russian woman dressed in all black, roaming through the town in a black Mercedes." At the mention of the car, something resembling recognition lit up in Mrs. Weatherbourne's eyes. "We've seen her following us around."

"And we saw her here," Will whispered. He didn't look at anyone in particular when he spoke. His eyes were fixed on the coffee table, roving over the many pictures that littered its surface.

"You believe this woman broke into my house?"

"And our treehouse," Dez added with a nod of his head.

"Why would she break into my house and your... treehouse?"

"Well, ma'am," Isaac pulled his backpack off of his shoulders and unzipped it. He pulled the comic book and the magnifying glass out of its depths. The other kids looked on in reverence while Mrs. Weatherbourne only mildly recognized it as the same comic she'd given away. "We believe that the rumors about Milton's treasure are true. We think he might have hidden it somewhere. And we think it has something to do with this comic book."

At this, Will gasped and all eyes landed on him. He was still staring down at the photos on the table. He reached forward to grab one, crying out, "Look, look!"

He showed the other kids the photo. It was another one of Milton. He was sitting on a granite step next to a pile of dirt, wearing a big hat on his head. In the background of the photo was a windmill. And standing in the dirt next to him, beneath the hand he leaned on, was a shovel.

"It's a picture of Milton digging," Will cried out in excitement. "Perhaps he was burying the treasure?"

Mrs. Weatherbourne giggled and the kids snapped their heads up to stare at her in surprise. "Such imaginations!" She proclaimed. She'd been listening, simply taken in by all the excitement in the room. The young kids were so lost in their stories. "First you have all these fabulous stories about Milton's missing leg, which, I hate to pop your wildly imaginative bubbles, were wrong. He actually lost his leg due to his diabetes. Hardly as exciting as a great white shark, but there you have it."

The kids could only stare at her as they took in what she was saying.

"And now," Mrs. Weatherbourne continued. "You think that he buried a grand treasure somewhere! That's just a photograph of him at the Judah Baker Windmill in South Yarmouth. Didn't you know he'd done a lot for the community over the years?"

She looked between the kids and they remembered what Mike Kelly had said.

"He volunteered his time during the restoration of 1973." At the looks on their faces, she giggled again. "Such an imagination on you kids. God bless each of you."

Things grew silent. The kids didn't know what to say.

"You are right about one thing, though. The rumors about a treasure are true! Milton had a secret he brought home from World War II."

"What was it?" Isaac breathed.

"His treasure was a little girl! While he was away, he found a sweet, innocent girl. She was eight years old, found at sea, cold and alone." Mrs. Weatherbourne paused, glancing off into the distance and giving the kids the impression that she was remembering either the child, Milton, or both of them. "Well, she had nobody and she was scared. It was Milton's ship that rescued her and when they docked in Boston, the Navy granted Milton and I temporary guardianship over her, until she could be processed as a refugee. Now, she was a true treasure." Mrs. Weatherbourne smiled at the kids. "We enjoyed every moment we had with her before she was adopted."

The kids sat back against the sofa, looking deflated.

"No real treasure!" Dez cried out.

"How can this be?" Will asked.

Amy and Isaac looked on, their disappointment evident. They'd been so sure that they'd figured it all out. It had to be real. How else could they explain Gorska Maika? It's obvious that she was after *something*. They'd seen her following them. What about the break-in? What about Mrs. Weatherbourne's injuries? And finally, what about Greg Collins?

These kinds of things simply did not happen in Dennis Port.

"You see, kids. That was Milton's big secret. I know that it's not the treasure you were looking for, but it was a life plucked from the ruins of the war, given hope in a new world," Mrs. Weatherbourne concluded with a sense of pleasure. Then, remembering something, she sat up straight. "I actually found this letter about finding the girl at sea. I couldn't even finish reading it."

As they watched, Mrs. Weatherbourne plucked the letter from her end table. She unfolded it and handed it over to Amy.

"Here you go, young lady," she murmured. "Perhaps you can read it aloud. It might help me having all your warm hearts in the room here with me. The last time I tried to read it, I was on my own and couldn't get past the first few words."

Amy took the letter and looked over at the boys who watched with muted interest, still deflated from news they just learned, before reading it aloud;

> Dear Commander Weatherbourne,
> I leave behind the love of my daughter and an incomplete promise. I regret that I will not see the day my Sofia lives in a world where she is free of the horrors of this war. I regret that I will not see her smile again, but I hope her days are full of smiles rather than tears. I regret that I will not be able to uphold a promise that I made to another, someone whom I owe a life debt. Sir, can I, with my last breath, entrust you to complete these two duties and deliver my daughter to freedom and carry out the promise I made? If you are so willing to deliver my daughter to her freedom, her name is Sofia. She is

eight years old and the only child of her beloved Herman and Helena Katzenstein. If you are so willing to carry out the promise that I made, take this sack without ever laying your eyes on its contents, and bury it at the coordinates on the cover of this comic book. I will be forever in your debt in this life and in the next. The last request of a dying man,

~ Herman

The moment Amy finished reading the letter, her eyes growing wider with each word she read, she slapped her free hand to her mouth as she gasped. The boys were less discreet about their excitement, crying out enthusiastically. They'd been hit with a shot of energy and the disappointment of moments before had vanished. Mrs. Weatherbourne's mouth dropped open at the sight of them, aghast.

"We told you, we told you!" Will cried out. "Milton must have buried the sack. There is a treasure!"

Isaac grabbed the magnifying glass and brought it close to the comic book. "The letter said that the numbers were actually coordinates!"

Despite her doubt and equally surprised by the turn of events, Mrs. Weatherbourne stood from her armchair and walked to Milton's study and returned with a thick, hardcover map book. They'd set the comic book on the table and she set the map book down beside it, opening the book to a map of the world that spread in the centerfold.

"These two sets of six digits on the cover are some kind of coordinates," Isaac explained as she sat back down, watching with some surprise on her weathered features. "We're looking for 701965 and 416547."

"The first two digits of each number could be longitude and latitude," Dez stated.

"That's brilliant," Will began studying the map on the table. Amy and Will ran their fingers up and down the sides of the map, crossing one another's paths several times in their haste and excitement. "There are six possibilities!"

"*Latitude seventy degrees, longitude forty-one degrees…*" Amy read out. "That's somewhere in the Barents Sea. No, that's not it."

"*Latitude seventy degrees, longitude minus forty-one degrees…*" Will read the next one. "That's somewhere in Greenland. Nope."

"*Latitude minus seventy degrees, longitude forty-one degrees…*" Amy sighed as she realized it wasn't correct. "Somewhere in Antarctica. Definitely not."

"*Latitude forty-one degrees, longitude seventy degrees…*" Dez read one out. "Uzbekistan. Nah. But that's getting pretty close though!"

"*Latitude minus forty-one degrees, longitude seventy degrees…*" Will's heart raced. He knew his friend was right. They were getting closer and closer to trying all the possible combinations. He couldn't hold back a sigh as he realized his wasn't the one, however. "Indian Ocean…"

"Oh, my goodness," Amy screamed. "I think I've found it."

Everyone paid attention when she moved her fingers across the map, watching as they traced closer and closer.

"*Latitude forty-one degrees, longitude minus seventy degrees,*" she read it out. "New England! We got it!"

Mrs. Weatherbourne, rather intrigued, flipped the page to a different map. This one was of Cape Cod. The kids continued to narrow down the coordinates until finally, all four fingers slid across the map and met at one spot.

Latitude 41.6547, Longitude -70.1965. It was near Windmill Beach.

"Look," Will murmured again, grabbing the picture of Milton with the shovel. "It was true. The picture was a clue; Milton buried something at the windmill."

Mrs. Weatherbourne couldn't believe her eyes or ears. Her Milton really did have a secret after all. "He spent a month at the Judah Baker Windmill during the restoration of 1973. I never knew!"

The kids were struck by wonder. They'd had their hopes dashed by Mrs. Weatherbourne, but now they were higher than they'd ever been. They were right all along. Milton had a treasure and, bit by bit, the kids were beginning to piece it all together.

"Now, listen here, you four," Mrs. Weatherbourne wagged her finger. "If you do this, you'll want to look around the granite step. That one in the picture. He laid it himself."

The kids nodded their heads, their hearts pounding. They had a mission. It was a true adventure.

"You four have a purpose. You're the Katzenstein Kids now," Mrs. Weatherbourne's tone was serious as she took the kids in. "Whatever you do, stick together and keep an eye out for this woman in black of yours. If what you told me is true, you could all be in serious danger. Be very careful."

Mrs. Weatherbourne ushered the kids out of the house a short while later. No words were said after that, but Amy, Isaac, Will, and Dez noticed Mrs. Weatherbourne glance around suspiciously while they were on the porch. She walked back into the house less relaxed than before, her shoulders weighed down with her concern for the kids on her porch.

Still, the only reason she'd warned them rather than turned them away from their quest was because Marjorie and Milton Weatherbourne believed in destiny. If the kids had discovered this secret, there was a reason for it. She could not stand in the way of that.

As they rode away from Mrs. Weatherbourne, the four eventually reached the crossroads where they would have to split home and head separate ways.

"I say we make the trip to South Yarmouth tomorrow," Will stated at the crossroads. "Do we all agree?"

The others nodded and spoke at once, "Yes."

They went their separate ways, Will was the closest to his house, and he kept an eye out for a black Mercedes. They would heed Mrs. Weatherbourne's words and be as careful as they could be. By the time they reached their own houses, the kids were relieved to have made it without seeing the black Mercedes. In their homes, they laid low, staying inside until the following morning, out of Gorska Maika's sight.

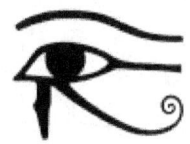

CHAPTER 22
THE HUNT BEGINS

Later that evening, Gorska Maika sat in a black car outside the Fernandez home. In her hands, she looked down at the crinkled newspaper cutting of Milton Lee Weatherbourne's obituary. Fury seethed inside her as she stared down at his photograph.

I know you're the one that found Sofia Katzenstein at sea and took her in. Your name was on all the old records, every single connection to the case connects you, Gorska Maika thought, picturing herself saying all these things to Milton's face if he'd been alive long enough to allow her to do so. *I know you hide the sack of gems and their power somewhere near here...*

The woman in black looked up toward Dez' house, narrowing her eyes as she stared at one of the windows. This night was the first one that she'd seen those curtains closed. Dez had never cared before, so why care whether or not someone could see into the room now? The Russian woman knew – she just *knew* – that those kids had found something.

They were acting strange for kids of their age, sneaking around everywhere together.

♦ ♦ ♦

Dez had been sleeping restlessly, tossing and turning, when he felt the cold blade of a knife against the front of his neck. The feeling of it pressed to his skin sent a shiver of fear down his spine and his eyes snapped open, revealing its holder. It was the Russian boogey woman, Gorska Maika.

"Give me the comic," the woman in black hissed.

"I don't have it!" Dez whispered in a panic.

He was shaking and trapped. All he wanted was to squirm away, but the smallest movements caused the blade to dig into his skin and he thought he could already feel the keen sting of it as it sliced through the surface layer of his flesh.

"Don't make a sound," she warned him as his mouth opened. "Where is the comic book?"

"I can get it for you tomorrow," Dez answered.

"What have you and your friends found? What is it that you know?"

Dez didn't want to tell the boogey woman anything. He wished that he was strong enough to resist her, to deny her the knowledge that she so desperately sought, but he knew that this was not a movie and he was not a hero. In real life, he was in grave danger. To mess with the woman in black could result in his death. Now was not the time for heroics.

"We thought Milton had a treasure," he whispered shakily. "But he doesn't. The secret he had was that he saved a young girl during World War II and brought her home with him. He and his wife took care of her until she was adopted."

Suddenly, the boogey woman released him. She stepped back from the bed, pointing the tip of her knife at Dez. "Get me that comic book and deliver it to me tomorrow. Don't even think about trying anything. I will be watching you and if you and your little friends don't stop messing up my plans, I will cut you all like pigs."

With that, the Russian woman slipped out of his room. Her footsteps were so quiet that he didn't hear her at all as she traveled down the hallway in the middle of the night. He could only imagine her fading into it, a shadow as dark as the sky.

Once she was gone, Dez realized that he was coated in a thin sheen of sweat, but he was freezing cold. Shaking, he covered his body with his covers and hid his face from the dark room. Out of the corner of his eye, everything appeared to be a malevolent figure hiding in the shadows of his bedroom. His heart pounded and his mind raced even faster than his pulse.

He couldn't sleep for the rest of the night, no matter how hard he tried to escape his fears and thoughts of Gorska Maika. He had felt her breath against his skin, heard her Russian accent in his ears, and felt the cold of her blade. She was more than an image on the cover of a comic book; she was real and she was terrifyingly so.

♦ ♦ ♦

The next morning, Dez climbed out of bed as sunlight shone through the fabric of the curtain in his room. It was his only indication of it being morning, long before his grandmother's Pomeranian woke everyone in the house with her incessant barking, whether at the birds that chirped their morning song outside or at his grandmother for food.

Dez hurried down the hallway as quietly as he could. He would have known if his grandmother was awake. Cocoa's barking was the signal. As it was, the sunshine and his lack of sleep gave him an early start. He was exhausted and sluggish, but he couldn't let that stop him. Once he was at the phone, he rang each of his friend's houses, explaining to them individually what had happened the previous evening. He told them about Gorska Maika's warning. Amy, Isaac, and Will promised to be at Dez' house as soon as they could.

By the time his friends rolled up on their bicycles, Dez was already waiting in the garage, knowing that his grandmother was going to be shocked to find that he was not only awake, but up long before she was. He ate his cereal as he waited, hoping to set the nerves whirling around in his stomach at ease.

"Dez?" He heard Will's voice at the side door. The handle rattled as Will tried to open it, unaware that Dez had locked it. He never did.

Dez stood and ventured toward the door, the keys rattling on one of his belt loops. He shoved it into the lock and unlocked it as quickly as he could. The metallic clicks within the door went off as he did. When he tugged it open, his friends tumbled into the garage and he quickly shut it behind them. He hazarded a peek through the glass, standing on his toes to make sure that there was no sign of the black car or the boogey woman.

"Dude, are you okay?" Isaac asked, staring at Dez as if searching for some wound Gorska Maika might have inflicted.

"I'm okay," Dez nodded. "I mean, I'm scared, but I'm okay. We need to come up with a plan."

"Yes, I agree," Amy spoke. "We can't let her get that treasure."

"We have more information now than we had yesterday," Isaac offered. "We could always go back to the Cape Cod Daily. Mike Kelly might believe us now. We read the letter from Milton."

"But we don't have the letter, G-man," Dez pointed out. "We have no proof to give Mike and you saw the guy yesterday. He doesn't believe us. He thinks we're just silly kids like Mrs. Weatherbourne."

"He's right. Mrs. Weatherbourne didn't believe a word of what we were saying until I read that letter out," Amy shrugged.

"Look," Will sighed. "What else are we going to do? There's not much that we *can* do. I think this is worth a shot."

Dez and Amy exchanged a doubtful glance, but reluctantly agreed with a nod of their heads.

"We have to come up with a plan to lose Gorska Maika.

She said she'll be watching last night." Dez glanced over at the door once more, as if worried that she might burst through the door right then. Of course, that didn't happen. Still, he was riddled with anxiety.

"What if we trick her?" Amy murmured. "She'll want to follow Dez, right? What if we split up? We all grew up here. We know these roads way better than her. If anyone can get her lost, it's us."

"That could work," Isaac nodded. "Dez, do you have a pen and paper?"

Dez went over to the other side of the garage and grabbed a notepad and pen. Making his way back to Isaac, Will, and Amy, he handed them over. Isaac immediately began drawing on the notepad. It took the others a moment to figure out what it was he was drawing.

They were plans. In particular, they were the streets the four kids had often travelled to get to and from one another's houses. Amy was right. They knew the streets well enough. As the others watched, Isaac drew paths that they could take to split up that would all meet up again later down the lines.

"So, Dez will be the one that she'll want to follow," Isaac began explaining the plan. "I don't think he should go alone though."

"I'll go with him," Will volunteered quickly.

"Okay," Isaac wrote their names on one of the roads, the one that left directly from Dez' driveway and veered toward Will's house. "Then Amy and I will take this path," he wrote their names on the path he indicated.

"I see where you two would split up," Will nodded.

"And we meet again up here, right?"

Isaac nodded his confirmation and glanced at the other two. "What do you guys think of the plan?"

"It could work," Amy admitted. She glanced over at Will, worry lining her features. "But we'll have to be really careful."

"Don't worry," Will whispered, knowing that she was talking about him. "We will be."

"Okay," Dez stood. The others noticed that his hands were shaky, but no one said anything. Dez was usually the brave one in the group. They couldn't take it away from him for the terrible experience that he'd had the night before. "Is everyone ready to get going?"

The others nodded and they all moved toward the door. As soon as they exited the garage, the four kids gazed around them, looking for signs of the Russian woman. Once they confirmed that she was nowhere near them, they made their way over to the maple tree and jumped onto their bikes. Together, they peddled out of the driveway.

Their plan would only work if Gorska Maika didn't catch on. For that to happen, they had to remain together. The visit from the boogey woman had all but confirmed their suspicions. She had been watching them and therefore, she knew that they travelled together. Changing their behavior now would be a giveaway. And she'd warned Dez not to try anything funny.

It was difficult for the kids to relax as they rode through the little town of Dennis Port. At every corner, they thought the car might come into sight. Each of them was fully alert, prepared for it.

After some slow cycling, taking their time so that they didn't reach the split before she revealed herself, they saw the black Mercedes. It was Gorska Maika! The black car stayed at a distance, creeping up behind them as if the kids could somehow miss its presence.

Dez shook his head at the boogey woman's silliness. Surely she knew they weren't that stupid? They were kids. That didn't automatically make her smarter. And at that moment, they were outsmarting her without her even realizing it.

As the four approached the split, they began to peddle faster, gaining momentum for their plan. The split was on a downhill trail and they allowed it to carry them. All at once, Dez and Will veered off to the left while Amy and Isaac took a right at the crossroads.

The switch clearly confused Gorska Maika. She paused, the engine stuttering for the slightest moment, before she caught herself again. Isaac found himself cursing the fact that she didn't stall the car. That would have bought them a little more time. As it was, the Russian woman did as they predicted she would; she turned left, following Will and Dez. The turn was so sudden that the tires on her black car screeched along the asphalt, making all four kids flinch as the high-pitched sound broke through the air. Amy and Isaac glanced back over their shoulders, making sure that the black car was no longer on their tail. They began peddling with all their might. Their path was longer, with more twists and a nature trail between the wooded area behind Dez' house. In order to reach Will and Dez around the same sort of time, they needed to move as fast as they could.

Meanwhile, Dez and Will cycled as quickly as they could too. Will was the only one who could sort of keep up with Dez. They darted in and out of empty suburban streets with a strange rhythm, passing Isaac's house and doubling back into a different lane. It was easy enough to remember the roads. Will and Dez had been racing up and down them since they were young kids. All they had to do was follow their instincts. The only difference was that they'd never ridden this fast and with hands this sweaty before.

Twice, the two boys thought they'd escaped the Russian woman, but she caught up with them moments later. The car roared as she drove faster and, glancing back over his shoulder, Dez could see the angry expression on the woman's face as she switched gears. Her face was curled into a snarl as she fought to keep up.

"The trail is up ahead!" Will called, as though he could sense his friend's fear. "She won't be able to follow us through there!"

In their twists and turns, the Russian woman hadn't realized that the boys had doubled back toward Dez' house. There was another path, from the opposite side of the woods, and it was too thin and rocky for cars to travel through.

"Come on!" Dez shouted. "We're nearly there. I can see the woods!"

He could. Up ahead, over the top of the hill, he could see the tops of the green trees. In the summer, they were easy to see. The thin branches blended into the sky when they were naked during the winter, the lack of leaves making them practically invisible. That wasn't the case on this particular day. They could see the greenery standing out against the bright blue sky above. As when they'd crossed Dez' backyard the previous day, the weather felt wrong.

It certainly didn't feel like they were meant to be in a car chase at that point in time. Of course, none of the kids had ever imagined that they might one day be involved in a car chase. Yet, there they were.

Gorska Maika must have noticed the trail up ahead because the car screeched as she powered through as fast as she could. The car groaned and complained as she put her foot down on the accelerator. Dez' cycled as fast as his legs could, his muscles stinging with the effort that it took to get him over the last stretch. He could only imagine how Will, whose muscles were not nearly as used to the strain as his were, was handling the ride. One thing was for sure, he would certainly feel the pain the following morning.

The bonnet of the front of the car was closing in, nearly kissing the back of their bicycle wheels as they made it over the hill. They let their bikes carry them over the rocky path, their bones jostling as they rode over the gravel and dirt. Dez was so relieved to have gotten away from the Russian woman that he screamed as their bikes rolled downhill and into the cover of the wood. Will joined in after a moment, both of their hearts pounding with adrenaline. It coursed through their veins, making them feel like they were on top of the world. No one could mess with them – not even the scary Russian woman and her sharp knife.

Forced to slam her foot down on the brakes, the woman in black screamed out for an entirely different reason from the kids ahead of her. She slammed her fists down on the top of the steering wheel. She couldn't believe that the kids had outsmarted her.

Anger pumped through her and she swore that she would make the little brats pay for their insolence. They had no idea who they were messing with. She had warned Dez, but if this was how they wanted to play, there would be no more warnings from that moment on.

Finally, Gorska Maika turned the key in the ignition and shifted the car into reverse. There was nothing she could do on that path. The car wouldn't travel down the gravelly hill and, even if it did, she wouldn't have been able to drive through the thin path between the trees that Dez and Will had followed. She would have to find another way. The kids would be on their way to somewhere else in Dennis Port.

For the Russian woman, it was a mere matter of waiting for them to reappear.

◆ ◆ ◆

Will and Dez reached the meet-up point first, as the four had predicted they would. They parked their bikes up against the nearest tree and moved off the path on the off chance that the boogey woman *did* follow them down it. The two boys wandered through the trees, hiding within their cover while they waited for their friends. It gave them the chance to catch their breath and calm down. The car chase had rattled both of them and their nerves were shot.

Rubbing a hand beneath his ribs, Will sighed. "That was

insane. I really thought she was going to get us."

"Man, Will," Dez brushed the sweat from his forehead with the back of his hand. "That's the fastest I've ever seen you ride. That was impressive, dude!"

Warmth rushed to Will's cheeks. "Thanks, dude."

"You're gonna kick my butt in one of those races pretty soon."

Will gave a chuckle, feeling a sudden burst of affection for his friend. Only Dez would be able to lighten such a tense situation in a manner of moments. They sat on the ground together, recovering from the chase.

A short while later, they heard bicycle wheels rolling over the gravel, spraying tiny stones outward in every direction as Amy and Isaac cycled through the path.

"Look!" Isaac shouted. "I can see their bikes. They made it!"

Will and Dez bounced to their feet and moved out into the path so their friends could see them. Amy's face lit up at the sight of Will and she jumped off of her bike and ran to him. The boy's breath was knocked from his lungs as the pretty, blue-eyed girl wrapped her arms around his neck and hugged him tightly.

"I'm so glad that you're okay," she murmured.

"I told you I would be," Will responded.

When they released, Will caught Dez grinning at them. Isaac had taken his comic out of his backpack as was looking down at the coordinates again. "Did everything go okay?" He asked Dez and Will.

"Yeah. She nearly caught up, but the skid at the first turn bought me and Dez some time. She didn't seem happy."

"I'll say," Dez muttered, shaking his head. "What's the next step? Are we going back to the Cape Cod Daily?

"Yes," Isaac nodded. "Who knows? He might believe us if we show him the comic."

Will wasn't so sure that they should show him the comic, but he didn't say anything about it, watching as Isaac packed it back into his bag. "Are you guys ready to ride again? We're taking this trail for a while."

"I'm ready," Dez moved to his bike.

Isaac simply nodded. He and Amy climbed back onto their own bikes and the four began cycling once again. The words of Mrs. Weatherbourne repeated itself over and over within their minds. She'd told them that they were the Katzenstein Kids now. What did that mean?

The ride to the Cape Cod Daily was far more relaxed than the morning ride had been. All of them felt the ache of their muscles. It was as though their bodies were begging them to get off the bikes. They took their time making their way to the news station. None of them were particularly excited to see Mike Kelly again. There was no guarantee that he wouldn't treat them with the same disbelief as he had the previous day.

When Bass River Bridge came into sight, the four sped up over the bridge, arrived and parked their bikes outside the station. They were greeted by the familiar ding of the bell on the door as they entered the building. Mike looked up at their arrival with a smile, which quickly transformed into an expression of concern. The kids weren't surprised by his reaction.

"Hey kids," Mike greeted them as he walked over to them. "You're back again?"

"We spoke to Mrs. Weatherbourne, like you suggested," Isaac started. There was no time to waste. "While we were there, she showed us a letter written by a dying man from World War II. In the letter, the man asked Milton if he could bury a sack for him. It never said what was in the sack, but what if this is Milton's treasure?"

Mike's brow furrowed. He thought that Mrs. Weatherbourne might deter the kids from this line of interest, and he was surprised that they'd come back with more enthusiasm than the day before – something he didn't think possible until that moment. "What makes you think that he buried the treasure? What did Mrs. Weatherbourne say?"

"There was a picture of him digging. Remember when he helped the community? He was involved with the 1973 restoration at Judah Baker Windmill." Isaac explained. "We think he might have buried the treasure there."

The news reporter looked between them, shaking his head. "I don't know… It seems a bit far-fetched if you ask me."

"But last night, Gorska Maika was in my house!" Dez yelled, throwing his hands into the air. "She had a knife to my throat!"

"And we got into a car chase with her this morning," Amy added. "We had to outsmart her so that we could make our way to you."

"You were in a car chase?" Mike repeated in a tone that didn't suit the news of a car chase. They thought he'd be more excited, but they could suddenly understand why it was so difficult to believe. Who would think that four kids would be involved in a car chase on an early summer morning?

The news reporter probably thought they were playing some kind of elaborate roleplaying game and they'd decided that he played a relevant role. He supposed he could understand how cool it would have been to add a news reporter to a game as a kid, but this was bordering on irritating. Mike and the Cape Cod Daily had more important things to do with his time.

"Please," Amy pleaded, looking up at Mike. "We're telling the truth."

"I'm sorry, young lady," he shook his head. "I just don't buy it."

"The treasure's real!" Isaac insisted. "We're going to retrieve it and prove you wrong!"

Without another word, he turned on his heel and stormed out of the station, the bell chiming as the door opened and closed. Will, Dez, and Amy were too stunned to move for a moment, but after one last look at Mike Kelly, they followed their friend out of the station. The kids all mounted their bikes and they knew that they were going to do as Isaac said. They were going to find the treasure for themselves and prove everyone wrong. After all, it was better that they got the treasure before the boogey woman did. There was no telling what she would do with it.

"So, I guess we're heading to Judah Baker Windmill, huh?" Dez asked as they began to pedal away from the station.

Amy glanced back over her shoulder to see Mike Kelly standing in the doorway, watching them leave. There was an expression she didn't recognize on his face. It was as though he didn't know whether they were messing with him or not. It would have been better if they'd had the assistance of an adult, but Amy shrugged her shoulders. It was Mike's loss. This could have been the story of a century for all he knew.

Why was it so difficult for the grown-ups to believe them?

Windmill Beach was only a stone's throw away from the Cape Cod Daily. The kids were already in South Yarmouth. All they had to do was follow Old Main Street south along Bass River.

As with all coastal towns, it didn't take long for the sea to come into sight. In the distance, they could all see the blue line on the horizon, marking the ocean somewhere dead ahead. Without planning or speaking about it, the kids began to pedal their bikes a little faster. The treasure was practically in sight.

Windmill Beach was even prettier than the one in Dennis Port, but that was because it got fewer tourists at this time of the year. In fact, the beach was so abandoned that there were still pieces of driftwood that had rocked up on its lonely shore, resembling lost planks of forgotten rescue boats. The sight of those planks of wood somehow brought the same thought to the surface of all four of the kid's minds. They couldn't help but think of the child, the little eight-year-old girl that Milton and Marjorie had taken care of named Sofia.

They knew that the Weatherbournes had taken care of none other than Herman Katzenstein's daughter. He was the author of their comic! All along, he'd been the one to give the treasure to Milton. The kids were in awe of the thought of the author. He was basically a celebrity to them and Milton had rescued him at sea.

Still, that begged so many questions and they didn't have anyone to give them the answers. Why were the Katzenstein's lost at sea during World War II? They were Jewish, but what did that mean for them? Isaac, especially, was preoccupied with thoughts of the two Katzenstein's. They reminded him, inexplicably, of his mother and her story. They were another two people who'd suffered loss at the hands of the war. Sofia had been given a second chance and the three wondered if she was still out there somewhere, alive. Who had she grown up to be? If she was alive, would she be willing to answer some of their questions? Could she clear up the confusion they felt?

They didn't know and, worse than that, they didn't know if it was possible to track her down. The odds that she carried her maiden name or that she could be traced to Sofia Katzenstein at all were low, almost improbable. The Navy, the adoption agency, or the refugee camps would have had her change her name, be it for her protection or something else. The idea of meeting Sofia was nothing more than a pipe dream, but it was one the four kids shared.

The steps that led down to the beach were not the weathered wood that they knew from the beach back home, but they were prettier. They were made of stone and it was clear they'd been standing, buried deep within the sand, for quite some time. The cool surface had been battered down, smoothing the edges of each step until they practically melted into one another.

One day, the stones would be brushed down to nothingness, leaving no trace of them having been there before. The tiny grains that blew through the air seemed to be weak, but it was apparent that they were stronger than they looked based on that set of stairs.

"I wonder if Milton placed them," Amy murmured as they climbed down to the beach. "It looks really similar to the granite, don't you guys think?"

Will, Dez, and Isaac stopped to glance down at the stone and found themselves nodding in agreement. The two did look rather similar and, with his leg, it would make sense for Milton to want to make accessing the beach easier. Everywhere they went, it felt as though they were passing little pieces of the man Marjorie loved. It was almost as if he were guiding them on their way, whispering in their ears and telling them about himself.

The treasure hunt had begun.

On one end of the beach, the kids could see the famous Judah Baker Windmill. It had been six years since the restoration and the windmill showed it. It still looked as though it had been built a fairly short time ago, but as the sand had done with the stone steps at the top of the beach, the sand had blown against the sides of the windmill, day in and day out. The wood shingles appeared to have been weathered, the kids knew that it was nothing more than the effects of nature.

As they approached it, they saw that the windmill was barely turning. The day was clear and quiet. There wasn't much wind, even with a cool brine breeze drifting off the ocean waves, to blow the big thing. It creaked as it moved slowly. Dez, being the tallest of the four kids, tried to hop up and touch the edges of the wooden blades, but even he couldn't reach them. They were too high.

"Okay," Will murmured. "Let's look around."

The four split up and began looking at the outskirts of the windmill, searching for the spot where Milton had posed for the photograph. Every side of the windmill looked the same, save for the one where the old wooden access door stood. Even so, the paint had chipped and faded away to such an extent that the first few times Will had passed it, he didn't notice the door at first since he was too busy looking down.

"Hey, guys!" He suddenly called. "I found it!"

The other three hurried over to where Will stood, and they noticed the granite step from the picture, the one Mrs. Weatherbourne had told them about, solid in the ground in front of the access door.

"It must be under this step," Will stated. "It's the same step from the picture."

"Mrs. Weatherbourne said that Milton laid it himself," Isaac added.

"Let's dig," Dez nodded and immediately got to work.

Of all the plans they'd made thus far, it occurred to the kids that they should have brought something along with them to dig. Will tried opening the access door to the windmill, in the hopes that there might be something inside, perhaps the old shovel that Milton had used in the first place, but the door was locked and it wouldn't open. Instead, the four had to use their hands to dig through the sand.

They teamed up and took the four different sides of the step, using their hands to scoop the sand out of the way around the edges of the step. It took a while for them to actually clear the ground of all the fresh sand being swept forth by the beach, but they were finally able to begin probing underneath the step with their hands. They stretched their fingers through the dirt, twisting and bending as they made their way inward beneath the step until at last, someone felt something solid.

"I got something!" Will cried out.

Together, the kids moved over to him. They could feel the hard object beneath the step too. Each of them began maneuvering through the dirt, pulling it away from the edges of the object in the hopes of finally dislodging it. At long last, the object seemed to shift slightly and Will was able to wrap his fingers around its edges, prying it from the hole in the ground.

A wooden box came out from beneath the step and each of the kids looked over at it. It was about eight inches in width and five in height. They never got a chance to open it or see how deep it was because the Will, Dez, Isaac, and Amy all looked across the beach at the familiar sound of a purring car engine. Looking back up the beach, they could see that it was the black Mercedes.

They'd led Gorska Maika right to the treasure.

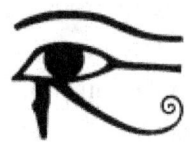

CHAPTER 23
NOWHERE TO RUN

The kids moved all at once. Dez and Will were in complete synchronization as Dez unzipped Isaac's backpack while it was still on his shoulders and Will stuffed the ditty box into the open bag. They sprang from the ground and leaped for their bicycles, running ahead of the Mercedes rather than the direction they'd entered the beach from. Their wheels were treading the roads in no time, but they knew they couldn't out-cycle a car.

Nevertheless, they were certainly going to do their best to try.

"We need to head back to the Cape Cod Daily!" Amy called out to the boys.

They nodded their heads in agreement and together, the four began to double back. They didn't know the streets of

South Yarmouth nearly as well as they knew their neighborhood streets, but the two areas worked in similar ways. It didn't take them long to figure it all out. It seemed as though they'd spotted the Mercedes before its occupants had spotted them, giving the four kids a head start on the chase.

However, it didn't take long for the engine to roar to life, speeding up behind them. They'd been spotted and a new chase was on the rise. They had to communicate with one another this time around, but at least they were all together.

"Right up ahead!" Will cried.

They sped up and weaved into the next street on the right and then the very first right after that. The houses in South Yarmouth had pretty, wooded fenced-in yards, and they were easy to dart between. The kids stayed near the water's edge, keeping it on their right side as a reference point for where they needed to go.

The car skidded into the street after them but missed the second turn. That didn't stop the kids though. The roads were all connected in some way or another and it was highly likely that they'd be seeing the Mercedes again soon, especially since it was much faster than their bikes were.

Ahead of them, they could see a dock. It was near one of the many waterfront houses.

"We can get back to the beach from here," Dez pointed toward the dock.

"Good idea," Isaac called.

They began cycling forward, Dez standing on his bike to go even faster, when the car reappeared. The Mercedes skidded to a stop right before the boat dock and the wall of a man who'd been driving Gorska Maika around when they first saw her jumped out of the car. They could see her seated in the passenger seat, staring out of the open door with unmasked contempt.

"Dez!" Amy screamed out.

There was nothing he could do, however. Dez was too far ahead of the rest of them, nearly at the boat dock. He didn't have time to turn into the wooded yard on the left. Without slowing down, Dez kept riding forward, finally sitting back down on his seat. The man in black was running at him and the other three kids could already see the imminent crash waiting to happen. Amy wanted to shut her eyes as the two approached one another and then, at the last possible second, Dez swerved to the left.

The bike spun smoothly, moving a hair's breadth away from the man in black. Dez' move was so sudden and unexpected that the man in black was knocked off-kilter. He stumbled, trying to regain his footing, but it was no use. The wood of the dock beneath his feet was slippery as the salt and water of the sea beneath washed upward. Sea mist coated its surface like a soft gloss and the next thing the kids knew, the man in black, as big as he was, toppled over and fell off the edge of the dock. They heard the massive splash as his block of a body collided with the water below.

Amy, Isaac, Will, and Dez had to resist the urge to laugh at the scene. It had been like something out of one of Herman Katzenstein's comic books. A frustrated scream rang out through the air though, reminding them that it wasn't over yet. Glancing over at the car near the dock, they watched as Gorska Maika switched seats and jumped behind the steering wheel. She shut the door and the kids looked on in horror as she started up the car. It seemed she was going to leave her fallen comrade behind and keep up the chase.

Luckily for the kids, the Cape Cod Daily was just ahead. They didn't have to go much further. They sped up and rode past the bridge and down the street. The rest of the way was downhill, and they simply let their wheels carry them on their own, rolling into the parking lot outside the news station.

The kids didn't bother parking their bikes. They simply dropped them in the lot outside and ran for the door, slamming into the Cape Cod Daily building with such force that Mike Kelly jumped up from his seat this time. All at once, the kids burst into an explanation, creating a cacophony of voices and garbled speech that Mike couldn't understand.

"Mike! We found the granite step!"

"We have the treasure and we're being chased!"

"Gorska Maika is right behind us and she wants Milton's treasure!"

"We told you we were right! We went to Windmill Beach and dug it up from beneath the granite step!"

"Whoa, whoa," Mike held up his hands in surrender. His eyes took in the state of the kids; their arms and hands were covered in the dirt they'd been digging, each of them had a pink hue to their cheeks from the exertion of the chase, and there was sweat on their brows. "Why don't you kids calm down and tell me what's going on? Maybe we can try a little *slower* this time."

"We have the treasure!" They all screamed at once, causing Mike to take a surprised step backward.

"Gorska Maika is right behind us," Amy added in a panic. "And she's going to kill us all!"

Behind them, they heard the Mercedes pull into the lot at the front of the building. They turned to see the Russian woman climbing out of the car. She walked toward the door with slow, deliberate steps, and there was no mistaking the menace on her face. Mike quite suddenly knew that the kids weren't lying about this woman. The mere sight of her was enough to instill fear into a grown man's heart.

"It's her, it's her!" Isaac stammered, his voice breaking with fear. "It's Gorska Maika, the Russian boogey woman!"

"Head down the hall," Mike whispered to the kids without taking his eyes off the woman making her way toward them. "Take the back staircase up. It will lead you to the attic. Hide there and let me handle this."

Without a moment's hesitation, the kids followed Mike's orders and moved down the hallway together, scattering from the front room. It didn't take them long to find the stairs and the moment they climbed the first one, they heard the familiar chime of the bell on the Cape Cod Daily door. They were careful to tiptoe from that moment. They didn't want to give her any indication they were there, but there was no hiding for long.

The kids had left their bicycles in the parking lot.

"Can I help you?" Mike asked as the woman entered

the newspaper office.

Gorska Maika paid no attention to Mike Kelly. He had never felt as invisible in his life as he did at that second. The woman in black ignored him, gazing around the room for any sign of the kids. When she found none, she concluded that the back hallway was the only place they could have gone and began making her way toward it. She still took the same calculated steps, the heels of her boots threatening the wooden floor.

"Stop!" Mike cried out, moving over to the front of the hallway. "If you don't leave right now, I'll call the police."

The Russian woman didn't respond at first. Slowly, she tilted her head to the side and surveyed the news reporter. Upon deciding that he posed no imminent threat to her, she kept walking past him as if he wasn't even there.

It was then that Mike knew this was a dangerous woman. He didn't know how he knew. Perhaps it was the cold stare in her dark eyes as she looked at him or perhaps it was the way his blood ran cold when she tried to move past him. Whatever it was, he knew that those kids were in danger and he had to do something about it. He couldn't let this woman kill them, and he found himself wondering if it was possible that the kids had been right about Greg Collins. Had this woman killed the boy commonly known as Puck?

Without thought, Mike dived for the woman. He pushed her out of the hallway, grabbing onto her upper arms as leverage. He'd planned on knocking her to the ground, but Gorska Maika's strength surprised him. She held her ground and pushed back against his hands until he was forced to stumble back into the nearest wall.

Mike gasped as the breath was knocked out of his lungs, crying out at the pain of being slammed into the wall. His head hit the corner and he could feel blood, hot and sticky, running down the back of his neck and soaking his shirt as a sharp pain rang out through his skull. Tilting her head in the same eerie way that she did before, Gorska Maika forced her forearm against Mike's throat, pressing him harder into the wall. His voice was cut off, replaced by gurgling noises as she strangled him with her arm. She looked into Mike Kelly's eyes as the skin of his face began to change color, turning first red and then deepening into a violent purple color as the light started to leave his eyes.

This was not how she planned to end Mike, however. She'd easily overpowered him. This was only her way of toying with him. She wanted him to know that he was about to die, but she would be the judge of the how and the when.

"Stop," he managed to choke out, spit bubbling on the corner of his mouth and dripping down over his chin.

Gorska Maika looked at him in disgust and then, abruptly, let go. She removed her forearm from Mike's throat before his saliva could drip onto her arm. In one swift movement, she pulled an eight-inch long, straight blade from her belt and drove it into Mike's abdomen. The news reporter crumpled to the ground, grunting in pain as his knees met the ground with a loud crunch of bone against wood.

Done with him, the woman in black turned and continued down the hallway as if she'd never been interrupted by the news reporter. By the time she reached the bottom of the stairwell, Gorska Maika could practically smell the fear of the kids hiding in the attic. She could hear the low whimpers and ragged breaths that they were too young to know how to control.

Using the leg of her pants, she wiped the blood off both sides of her knife and raised it to her eyes. In its shiny surface, she could see her own face twisted into a look of pure hatred. She took the first step up.

"Now, if I were a mouse," she murmured in her thick Russian accent. "Where would I hide? Perhaps the attic would be a good place…"

"We are doomed," Will muttered under his breath. "We are doomed…"

They were the only words that he could muster. He and his best friends were cowering in a dark attic room. There was no light source and they could barely make out the dust particles floating in the air, illuminated by the thin rays that broke through the vent shutters in the attic. There was nowhere to run and they could hear the distinct stomp of the thick-soled military-style boots as they closed in with each calculated step that the woman in black took, walking through the small newspaper office somewhere below.

Thump, thump, thump…

There was nothing they could do. A part of Will wished that she would hurry up and get it over with already. She could simply take the treasure and put them out of their misery without making things a million times worse by taking so long to get to them. They had failed. Mrs. Weatherbourne told them they had a purpose and that they were the Katzenstein Kids now, and they'd failed both her and Milton.

They were fools to think that they could have solved this case. The adventures they'd set out on this summer were about to come to their miserable end. And there was nothing that they could do about it all.

Thump, thump, thump…

With each rattling step, dust fell like rain from the rafters above their heads. They cowered in a small circle in the back of the attic, hidden in a shadow for as long as they could still hide. It didn't matter that there was no point in hiding and that the Russian woman already knew exactly where they were.

"Well," Isaac whispered. "Does anyone want to open the box?"

The others looked at him with wide eyes. In their fear and panic, they'd all but forgotten about the ditty box and the treasures hidden within. They nodded their heads vigorously and Isaac pulled his backpack off his shoulders. In the small, quiet space, the sound of the zip seemed louder than usual, echoing off the slanted attic roof.

Isaac reached into the bag and carefully pulled out the wooden box that had brought all of them to this place and this moment. His heart pounded and his hands shook slightly as he set it down on the floor between them. If ever there was a moment to find out what it was that they'd been searching for and what Gorska Maika was willing to kill them and others for, now was as good as any.

The kids exchanged a glance and an unspoken agreement came between them. Each of them was afraid of what they might find within the box, perhaps more afraid than they were excited, and they reached out to touch the corners of the lid. On the soft count of three, they lifted the lid off the box together. They moved backward involuntarily once the box was open, expecting something to jump out at them or some kind of explosion to go off, shutting their eyes expectantly.

Of course, that didn't happen. And for a moment, none of them moved, waiting for it.

At last, they opened their eyes and moved in again, closing the circle. None of them reached in, instead looking at the contents from the top of the box. Inside, they could see a vintage Cracker Jack box, typically filled with caramel-coated popcorn and peanuts. The box had a picture of the mascot, Sailor Jack, and his dog Bingo.

In the upper corner of the box were the words *Prize Inside*.

"I don't understand," Amy murmured, looking between the boys.

Will and Isaac seemed as surprised and disappointed as she did, but Dez had an entirely different expression on his face. He was angry. His jaw was clenched and the muscles in his cheek twitched as he stared down at the box through narrowed eyes.

"Are you okay?" Amy asked Dez.

"That's it?" He snapped. "That's what we risked our lives for? We're going to die over caramel corn?!"

Will couldn't believe it. He'd been so sure that there was more to all of this. Isaac felt much the same way, which is why he didn't stop Will from lifting the box and shoving his hand inside. Will dug around through the contents of the box, searching for something that they might have missed.

His fingertips touched something hard, but it was covered by some kind of bumpy material.

"There's something inside," Will declared.

Will looked back into the box and, now that he knew that there was something more, he could see something he hadn't before. There was a brown material at the bottom. Suddenly, Will turned the box upside down, shaking it until everything fell onto the wooden floorboards.

From somewhere beyond the attic, out in the hallway, they heard Mike Kelly crying in pain. They heard the scuffle and each one of the kids' hearts began to race a little faster. They were running out of time. On the floorboards, a small burlap sack had slid out. It hit the floor with a small clatter and, as they watched, a green glow radiated from between the lines of fabric. The kids looked on in amazement, uncertain of what to do now that they'd confirmed there was more to the ditty box than they'd first assumed.

"Don't touch it," Amy gasped.

The moment she spoke, the glow stopped, receding back through the bag. The silence that followed was thick with tension and they realized that it wasn't only the attic that had gone quiet. Outside the attic, things seemed to have come to a quiet halt. None of them moved, afraid that they would break some kind of spell and hear Gorska Maika come through the opening.

"She's going to come soon," Dez whispered. "We may

as well find out what it is before she reaches us."

"Yeah," Will agreed. "I think so too."

Amy watched on, biting her lower lip nervously, and Isaac nodded his head. Will picked it up off the floor and pulled the string that tightened it. He was interrupted when they heard the sound of someone making their way up the stairs. They knew that Mike had lost the fight because there was no mistaking the sound of the thick leather soles, complete with a slight heel, as they moved slowly. It was as if the Russian woman was taunting them.

The kids realized with a start that she probably was. In this situation, they were the mice and she was the cat. The boogey woman struck them as someone who enjoyed playing with her prey.

"She's coming," Isaac hissed. "Hurry!"

Will opened the burlap sack and dumped the contents of the bag on the floor between them without looking to see what they were first. Four metal toy trinkets fall to the floor and spread out in the circle in front of them. Dez groaned as, yet again, he was hit with a shock. Nothing about Milton's treasure had been what they expected and, now that their doom was officially upon them, they were deflated with disappointment.

The four kids met one another's eyes, best friends ready to accept their fate, and each picked up one of the small toys. There was a sense of solidarity between them as they held onto them. Disbelief etched into their features as they waited for the door to open.

BOOM!

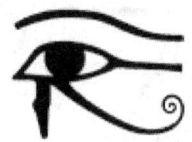

CHAPTER 24
ALL IS REVEALED

The attic door flew open nearly as soon as they'd thought about it, revealing the woman in black with a large knife in her hand. The straight blade shone and the kids were almost certain they could see the smallest hint of blood near the hilt. The handle was engraved with a falcon in a striking pose, its talons extended and ready to swoop in, much like Gorska Maika.

The end had truly fallen upon them. None of them could move. They were speechless as they watched her step into the small space, barely able to breathe, let alone able to move or speak.

"Give me my gems, you filthy little beasts," the Russian woman hissed, moving toward them.

"There is no treasure!" Dez cried out. "It was just some

Cracker Jack's trinkets!"

"You lie!" The woman's blade glinted. "I saw what those gems can do. When I was just a young girl, I saw them and the enormous power they held. They were taken from me."

The kids pushed backward on the floor, moving as far away from the crazy woman as they could. What was she talking about? If she had witnessed the gems when she was a girl, that meant that she'd been around when Milton had discovered them, let alone buried the box. She would have been a child during World War II.

The woman had a mad look in her eye as she continued. "They were taken from my father."

Amy screamed in fear as the Russian woman stomped down on the wooden floorboards. The boys huddled closer to her, suddenly feeling regret at having gotten Amy involved in everything. The guilt hit Will the hardest, causing his stomach to tighten uncomfortably.

"Where is my treasure?" Gorska Maika asked again. "Where are my gems?"

They held out their hands, each of them opening their palms for the woman to see the small trinkets they held.

"This is it," Will stated. "This is all there was."

"Please," Dez cried. "There was no treasure! No gems."

"They must be here," the woman responded. "I've been searching for the four parts of the Eye of Horus for decades! You must have them! Hand them over or I will kill each and every one of you little beasts."

The woman in black dove forward, grabbing ahold of Will by the front of his shirt and tugging him forward. He went flying into her arms and she spun him around to face his friends, bringing up the knife and poising it over his chest. "I'm going to ask you one more time," she warned, holding Will's wrists behind his back. "Give the gems to me or he dies first!"

"No!" Dez, Isaac, and Amy yelled, moving forward.

"Don't hurt him!" Amy added.

As soon as she said the words, Amy felt as though something burned her hand. She hissed in surprise, looking down at her open palm. The Toy Prize from the Cracker Jack's box was a mood ring. The heat had disappeared from the center of Amy's hand, leaving behind no sort of mark that indicated a burn, but she did see something else that was green. The gem on the ring gave off the tiniest green twinkle.

Amy furrowed her brows in surprise. She couldn't believe what she was seeing. Instinctively, Amy knew that she shouldn't pass the ring to Gorska Maika. She closed her fingers around it, clenching her hand into a fist and squeezing the mood ring tightly.

It was as if she'd activated it by squeezing it. Amy's mind was thrown backward, out of the room. Dez and Isaac faded away, the image of Gorska Maika holding a knife over Will's chest grew distant, and Amy felt as though she were floating far away from the attic of the Cape Cod Daily. Moments passed by and she thought she recognized them, images from her past. She thought she saw her mother, that last evening that she saw her and they made their pinky promise over the stars in the night sky.

Amy wanted to grab ahold of the memories, but her fingers fell through them whenever she tried to hold onto them. Tired of being disappointed, she let them pass her by without taking too much notice until she finally stopped. She knew she was in the past and for some reason, she felt connected to the vision before her.

Herman, Sofia, and the Ancient Egyptian God, Horus stood in a small room. She gasped at the sight of the half-man, half-falcon and realized that they couldn't see her. She was free to walk around and witness the scene before her in its entirety.

Amy was in some kind of grey laboratory. There were bodies on the ground and Amy had to force herself to look away from them. She wasn't sure how she knew, but she had a feeling she was in World War II. The men on the ground around her wore the grey uniforms of the Germans and she thought she even recognized a Nazi Officer uniform.

"Herman," Horus' voice echoed.

It sounded as though it was coming from inside Amy's head, but she wasn't Herman. Herman Katzenstein was the man holding onto a little girl. Realization hit Amy as she saw the girl; Sofia didn't look older than eight years old. Was this the night that she escaped?

"You are both joined in love and pain, marked for death, and yet you continue to live," Horus continued. "Hide the eye of Horus at this latitude and longitude." The Egyptian deity ran his finger up and down the Katzensteins' matching concentration camp tattoos. "Your destiny is to save your daughter and fulfill the deed I ask of you. For that, Sofia will live a full life."

Amy was thrown forward all of a sudden, the memory of the strange laboratory speeding by her too fast to see its detail anymore. She wanted to cry out, but she didn't seem to have control over her mouth in this strange vision world that she'd fallen into. It felt as though it was all in her head, but she knew that her consciousness had somehow separated from her body and that she was moving through time.

What had the mood ring done? Was that green twinkle one of the four gems that Gorska Maika referred to? Did it contain the memories of the times where they'd been?

With no time to consider the possibilities, Amy was once again unceremoniously dumped on the ground in another time. The same tug that she felt in the laboratory returned. It wrapped itself around her waist like a lasso and pulled her forward until she was a part of her surroundings once more.

Herman Katzenstein sat up in the bed. He was topless and there was a red-stained bandage wrapped around his shoulder. He'd looked gaunt in the previous memory, but in this sickbay, he looked downright yellow.

Amy realized that this was where he must have written the letter to Milton Weatherbourne. This was where he signed the last request of a dying man. Curious and tentative, she stepped toward the bed so that she could watch what he did.

The Jewish man wrote on the cover of the comic. He was the illustrator. It was easy enough for him to create something that blended in well. It wouldn't look out of place if one didn't know what the tattoos on the cover meant. However, this copy, the one that Marjorie had passed on to Isaac, was one of a kind. Herman followed the directions that Horus had given him, etching the coordinates into serial number tattoos on the forearms of the cartoon characters.

Rather than move through time again, Amy felt the pull around her waist lead her out of the sick bay and down a hallway. The pull stopped outside a door in the ship, and Amy reached out to open it. The moment she touched it and the door opened, the guide released her and left her to the new vision.

Milton Weatherbourne, a superior Navy officer, pored over a map book on his desk. Amy recognized it to be the same hardback cover as the one Marjorie had retrieved from his study back at her house. She walked over and, indeed, Milton was tracing the coordinates on the comic book cover, much the same way she and her friends had done. He looked from the cover of The Katzenstein Kids and back again, amazed by his discovery. The coordinates were only a stone's throw away from where he and his dear Marjorie lived. He had always believed in fates and destinies. At this discovery, he had a strong sense that this was his. He had been doubtful of the Jewish man they'd rescued at sea, but that faded away with the discovery that the coordinates were located in South Yarmouth.

That couldn't be a coincidence, could it?

He fetched the empty Cracker Jack box sticking out of the trash can and shoved the burlap sack into it. After that, he placed it safely inside the wooden Navy ditty box he'd removed from beneath his bunk. Milton glanced around just as Amy's vision faded, almost as if he could somehow see her apparition in his Navy quarters.

Amy opened her eyes and she found that she was back in the attic. It was as though no time had passed. Gorska Maika was still standing in front of them with her mouth twisted into a sneer, the knife held over Will's chest.

Margrit Himmel, the name echoed from within Amy's mind. She didn't know where it had come from or whose voice it was, but Amy said the words out loud.

The woman in black's head snapped toward Amy, her eyes widening in shock. "How do you know my name?"

Margrit's eyes dropped to the glow coming from Amy's hand, radiating from between her dainty fingers where they clenched onto the mood ring. The knife blade moved quickly, slicing through the air away from Will. Margrit pointed its sharp point toward Amy, aiming at the girl's exposed throat.

"You have something," Margrit murmured in a singsong voice. "I can see it glowing in your hand. Give it to me or he dies first," she repeated the threat, inclining her head toward Will. "You like him, don't you, little girl?"

Before she could answer, Amy felt the tug and realized that the lasso was still wrapped around her waist. As long as she held the mood ring, she was still connected to its power. She was still connected to the things that it saw.

And, with a start, it occurred to her that she was connected to Horus, the Ancient Egyptian deity.

"Your destinies were set a long time ago," Horus' deep voice spoke to her.

As it had with Herman, the half-man, half-falcon spoke from within her mind. Their thoughts were connected, but this time she knew the words were for her and not someone else. This vision wasn't a memory at all, not like the others before.

"The prophecy gem has shown all that was, all that is, and all that will be," Horus continued. "Use the full power of the four gems that make up the eye of Horus. They have chosen you, and you have chosen them."

Amy furrowed her brows, wondering what he meant.

"When wielded by four pure souls," Horus explained, hearing her thoughts, "the gems will grant you the power of my four sons."

"Your four sons?" Amy asked the God.

"Imsety is the Protector of the South and the Holder of the Protection Gem; Duamutef is the Protector of the East and the Holder of the Power Gem; Hapi is the Protector of the North and

the Holder of the Health Gem; and Qebehsenuef is the Protector of the West and Holder of the Prophecy Gem."

Before she could ask who they were meant to represent, Amy's eyes snapped open in time for her to see Margrit Himmel draw the blade back and drive it into Will's chest. Amy screamed at the sight, but the scream quickly ended as she watched the scene. The blade didn't penetrate Will's skin.

The kids stared down at the blade in surprise and confusion. Margrit was also staring down at the sharp point in total confusion. She drew it back again, angrier than before because it didn't touch Will, and slammed it forward with all her strength.

Again, it didn't touch Will. The woman roared in fury. She drove it forward again and again in vain. Each time, the knife stopped shy of penetrating Will's chest. Amy had to stop herself from giving a smirk of relief, knowing the blade would probably end up trained on her and she didn't like her odds.

Amy glanced down at the ring in her hand and as she took in the gem, she heard the voice of Horus. It rang out in her mind once more. *"Qebehsenuef, Protector of the West and Holder of the Prophecy Gem."*

"Imsety, Protector of South and Holder of the Protection Gem," Will heard the voice this time. He was confused, wondering where it came from and, suddenly, he noticed Amy staring at the mood ring in the palm of her hand.

Will glanced down at the toy trinket in his own hand, all while the blade of the knife continued to rain strikes that never touched him down on his chest. It was a shield, small and intricately formed. The words of the Egyptian deity whispered through his thoughts as he stared down at the trinket.

Isaac and Dez watched their friends, noticing their sudden fascination with the trinkets in their palms. Taking the lead, they looked down at their own toy trinkets, wondering what it was that had Amy and Will so mesmerized. The events that were unfolding around them seemed to slow down, allowing them to take note of more than they would ordinarily have been able to without Gorska Maika interrupting them with her fiery rage.

Dez held a toy trinket that resembled the medical bags medical officers used to carry about in the war. "*Hapi,*" Horus spoke to him, "*Protector of the North and Holder of the Health Gem.*"

Meanwhile, Isaac noticed a gun trinket in his hand. It seemed so unlike him. He was usually the shyest of them all, protected by his mother from the terrible world around them, and the quietest of all four of the kids.

Horus' voice was a mere whisper in the wind as it breezed through Isaac's mind. "*Duamutef, you are the Protector of the East and Holder of the Power Gem.*"

They didn't know that each of them heard one another's names. Amy, in particular, made it possible for all of them to hear Horus' voice, speaking through the Prophecy Gem.

"Isaac!" Amy yelled. "Use it! Use the power of your gem!"

Isaac looked down at his hand and noticed that the toy gun glowed the same green that Amy's mood ring emitted.

As he stared at it, he knew what he had to do. When there is no hero to save you then you must become the hero. He sucked in a deep breath and closed his fist around the toy gun, thrusting his arm forward. He aimed his fist at Margrit and an invisible force of power burst forth from his hand, warming the palm of his hand. The woman cried out in pain and flew backward.

Margrit screeched at them as she tumbled backward and down the stairs of the attic, rolling over as she hit each step until, with a nasty crunch, she landed at the foot of the staircase in a crumpled heap. Will, Dez, Isaac, and Amy rush forward to see her limbs bent at weird angles. Margrit didn't move at all.

"Is she... dead?" Amy asked.

Isaac nodded his head slowly. "Yeah," he whispered. "I think so."

"Whoa," Dez breathed in amazement.

The kids were stunned by what had happened. All of a sudden, they had become something else and each of them carried some kind of power in their bare hands. What on earth was going on in their small, out-of-the-way town of Dennis Port?

None of them had time to linger on the many questions they had about the events of the day because they heard the sound of someone moaning in pain at the bottom of the staircase.

The kids looked at one another and at the same time, cried out, "Mike Kelly!"

They ran down the stairs and past Margrit's body. Each of them gave her a wide breadth. They knew it was nothing more than their imagination, but they couldn't help the anxiety that filled them at the thought of her reaching out and grabbing one of them by the ankle.

The news reporter was hunched with his back to the wall, clutching at his belly. The blood soaked through his grey button-up shirt and poured over his hands. He looked paler than usual as he looked up at the kids.

"You guys got her," he whispered. "How did you do that?"

"Shhh," Amy hissed. "Don't speak. We're going to get you help."

"We need to call the ambulance," Will added. "I'll go find a phone."

"No, wait," Dez murmured as Will stood and turned away from the scene.

Dez looked down at the medical bag trinket in the palm of his hand and clenched his fist around it, taking a deep breath and hoping that this actually works. The center of his hand felt warm and he could see the green glow shining in between his clenched fingers. He held his fist over Mike's stab wound. Mike sensed that something was up and removed his hand from his abdomen. As the kids watched, the wound began to seal, the skin stretching shut over the gash in his stomach. Mike gasped as he watched his wound shut, the pain fading away. His breath slowly returned to normal, as did his heart rate.

Once the wound had shut and the pain had disappeared, Mike raised the hem of his shirt and looked down, amazed. He wasn't sure whether it was real or not, but he felt as though he was actually able to stand again.

He pushed himself off the wall and sprang to his feet.

"Go!" Mike yelled at the kids. "I'll call the police and come up with story. You won't be involved, I promise."

They knew then that Mike felt terrible for not believing them sooner. If he had and he'd contacted the appropriate authorities before, they wouldn't have been in this situation. When Gorska Maika stabbed him, Mike feared for the lives of the kids in his attic. He'd been bleeding out, riddled with guilt over having sent them there and letting the woman in black get past him. They could have died and it would have been all his fault.

The kids didn't need telling twice. Since Mike was safe and unharmed, they followed his orders and made their way out of the news station without looking back. Their bikes were on the ground where they had dropped them, right beside the black Mercedes.

They'd been inside for so long that the sun was beginning to set in the distance. The horizon was alive with beams of color, pinks and oranges bathed in a warm, golden glow. On any other day, it would have been pretty enough to make Amy's heart sing. Right then, however, it marked the fall of evening and they needed to get home.

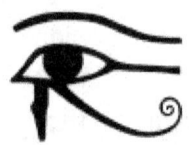

CHAPTER 25
THE FOUR GEMS

Luckily, the Cape Cod Daily was only three miles from home, little more than a pebble skipping across the smooth surface of the water. They rode home together until they reached the spot where they all had to split up. None of them knew what to say as they removed their toy trinkets from their pockets and locked them in their fists, though they were no longer glowing.

Will couldn't let Amy go home on her own. They split up and headed in different directions and after a minute of riding back home, Will turned around and followed Amy. She wasn't far off and he caught up in no time while Isaac and Dez went home.

"Hey," she gave him a small smile. "Miss me already?"

"I just didn't want to let you ride home alone. It could

be dangerous."

The smile grew wider. "It makes sense that you're the protector of us. You've come to protect me twice now."

Will grinned over at her, feeling lighter than he had in a long time. The pair rolled through the town leisurely. Unlike Isaac, they didn't have to worry about getting home early. They could ride beneath the stars, and Will liked that because Amy's face lit up each time she looked up at the night sky.

When they arrived at the Howard house, Will walked Amy to the front door. His hands were dry for once and he realized this was the first time he was alone with Amy without suffering the effects of his nerves. Nonetheless, he took a deep breath when they reached the door.

"Thank you, by the way," Amy said as they stood on the front step of her house. "Thank you for protecting me."

"Always," Will whispered, stepping closer to her.

They leaned in toward each other and their lips touched. The kiss was soft and sweet, lasting longer than the last time. Amy's stomach swirled with butterflies as Will pulled away.

"See ya'," Amy smiled when he stepped back.

"See ya'," Will breathed before walking backward to his bike, not wanting to break his gaze away from her.

When he climbed onto his bike and made his way past Davenport's back to his own house, Amy turned and walked into her own house. She didn't have to wonder if her father was around because he was fast asleep on the sofa. The TV was still on, lighting up the room.

Before she could take another step, Amy felt a warmth in her hand and a glow radiating from between her fingers. *A vision filled her head, the vision was of her father's cupboard at the back of the house. The door opened, revealing a brown shoebox hidden in the back of the storage space. She tried to move toward it, but that only brought her back to herself.*

Amy raised her eyebrows in surprise and made her way to the back of the house, toward her father's room. She could hardly breathe as she snuck down the hallway and pulled open the closet door, hoping that her father wouldn't wake up while she was rummaging through his things.

Bending down, Amy moved through to the back of the cupboard and located the shoebox hidden behind random junk and old clothes. She tugged it out with a grunt, pulling it from the cupboard. Once the shoebox was out, she sat down on the floor with it in her lap. She was afraid to open it now that she had it. What was she going to find hidden in its depths? What was her father keeping from her? Amy wasn't sure she actually wanted to know.

It's now or never, Amy, she told herself. *Are you going to let the Prophecy Gem's powers go to waste?*

With a deep breath, Amy pulled the lid off of the box and looked into it. She was surprised to find that it was filled with envelopes – dozens and dozens of them. Taking one of them out, she found that it was addressed to her from her mother.

Amy's breathing quickened as she rifled through the box. All of them were the same, envelopes addressed to her and all from her mother. The whole box was filled with letters and cards sent to her from her mother. One of them was dated only a week earlier. Tears pricked Amy's eyes and she felt them fall over her waterline and run down her cheeks, warm and salty.

It occurred to her that the ring, which she'd slipped onto her finger, had shown her this moment. The Prophecy Gem had given her this vision in order for her to discover the truth. Her mother didn't forget about her after all.

◆◆◆

Will arrived home to the sounds of fighting that he and his younger sister had gotten far too used to for his liking. His father and his mother were fighting – if you could call it a fight. Will wasn't so sure it actually counted as a fight if one was bigger, louder, and stronger than the other and it was mostly a one-way screaming match. He could already smell the vile odor of alcohol as Will walked through the door.

It didn't take a genius to put two and two together. His father had had too much to drink again and his temper was through the roof. Normally, Will would walk away from the noise, but he heard his mother scream and his feet were traveling toward the sound before he knew what was happening.

Will burst in through the living room and found his mother on the ground. His father was standing over her with his hand raised into the air. Will knew that he'd gotten physical – again. This was the second time. There was no way that he was going to let his father hurt his mother again.

Moving forward, Will pulled the metal trinket from his pocket and gripped it in his fist, feeling the warmth running through his fingertips yet again. "Stop," Will stated firmly, stepping between his mother and father. "Today, it ends. You will never put your hands on mom again!"

Will's father didn't back off. On the contrary, Will could see his eyes widen in anger. No one had ever stood up to him beneath his own roof before. He threw his arms out in an attempt to shove his son back, but Will didn't move. Again, his father shoved him – again Will didn't move. The trinket grew more green, the barrier between Will and his father prevented his father from laying an angry hand on him. Will stood his ground, staring up into his father's eyes.

Sense seemed to return to Will's father as he realized what his son was doing. He stepped backward, looking between his son and his wife, shaking off the alcohol-induced daze that he'd been under. "Son," he murmured. "Oh, my… I'm so sorry. I'm so sorry, Will."

Will took a step back and his father stopped in his tracks. He'd been about to approach Will again, but Will was still jumpy. With the scent of alcohol lingering on his dad's breath, he didn't know what to believe.

"I need help," his father murmured quietly.

Tears welled up in his eyes as he looked around at his family. Upon hearing Will's voice get involved, Beth had arrived and was standing in the doorway of the room, looking on with a fearful expression on her face.

Will relaxed his defensive stance and moved to his father, wrapping his arms around his father's waist. This was the man who'd raised him, the man who he loved dearly. Will didn't know who the monster that sometimes came out was, but he did know he was going to do everything within his power to make sure that it stayed away.

Standing up from the ground onto shaky feet, Will's mother joined in on the hug, wrapping her arms tightly around the two men in her life. Beth ran into the room from the doorway and she, too, joined it. The family clutched one another, not without several tears, and felt the warm glow of love and protection twist itself around them.

"We're going to get you all the help you need," Kathy murmured to her husband.

◆ ◆ ◆

Dez arrived home with only one thought in mind. It was one that dominated his thoughts from the moment that he healed Mike Kelly in the Cape Cod Daily. Nothing else in the world mattered more than what he was about to do as he charged through his house.

Grandma Ruth jumped in surprise as Dez opened the front door and made his way down the hallway toward the room in the back of the house without so much as a greeting. Her Pomeranian, Cocoa, didn't bark at the entry for once. The dog's intuition was alive and well, present in the soft moans she released from where she sat in Grandma Ruth's lap.

"Dez?" Grandma Ruth called, baffled. "Are you all right, sweetheart?"

Dez didn't respond. He went to his mother's bedroom and noticed that she was awake. She looked up weakly as he entered the room and walked around to kneel beside her bed. The medical bag was clenched tightly in his fist and it had been glowing for some time, long before he'd even rolled his bike down the driveway of his house.

He'd broken the rules. He didn't have time to park his bike at the maple tree as his grandmother had asked him to do so many times before. It was lying on its side in the driveway, the wheel still spinning from how fast he'd pedaled home after splitting up with Isaac, Will, and Amy.

"Mom," Dez murmured, reaching for her hands. He took one and then the other, putting them on his clenched fist. Somehow, his mother knew to tighten her hands around his fist, though she stared at the green glow with great curiosity and nervousness. "Mom, you will be okay."

"Emilio," his mother spoke softly, her voice cracking. "What's going on? Where have you been?"

"I've brought you a miracle, mom."

As he said it, the glow grew and grew, emanating bright enough that the effervescent color seemed to come from within Dez himself. It spread through both their hands, bathing the entire room in a warm, glow. Grandma Ruth stared at the green light ahead of her as she made her way down the hallway, uncertain of what she was going to find when she reached her daughter's bedroom.

Dez took a deep breath, his throat tightening with emotion because he knew that the Health Gem was about to save his mother's life and heal her.

◆ ◆ ◆

Isaac's fingers shook as he wrapped his hand around the handle of the front door. A million thoughts raced through his head at the day's discoveries. He thought back at the holocaust serial number on his mother's arm and then it hit him! One of the six-digit serial numbers on the cover did match, it was the same as the one on his mother's arm. There were certain things that his mother had told him about her past, certain things that he knew to be related to the events that he'd found out about that day.

One of the things Isaac knew about the woman inside the house was that she was saved at sea, alone and cold, and brought to America by a US Navy officer. He'd had no idea who that officer was, had no idea that they lived in the very same town and that he'd grown up with the people that saved his mother's life.

It never occurred to Isaac that the reason his mother spent so much time helping Marjorie Weatherbourne and sending him over there to help her was that Marjorie and Milton had once taken her in. Over the years, his mother had lived a life filled with secrets that she didn't want to share with her son. He was so young and so innocent. It felt wrong to spoil that with the secrets of her past as a Jewish girl who'd escaped the holocaust in World War II.

It took a long time for Isaac to build the courage necessary for entering his home. In the end, it was the weather that did all the convincing. The days may have been warm in the summer, but the nights were cold with the wind off the sea and the chill bit into his skin as he stood on the porch. He shook his head and entered the house, knowing that the events of the day – in fact, the events of the entire summer thus far – had changed things forever and there was no turning back for him or any of his friends.

They have been given the power of the four sons of Horus.

"Isaac?" His mother called from the kitchen. "Is that you?"

"Yes, mom," Isaac called, walking toward the sound of his mother's voice.

"Are you okay? It's after dark." She asked, taking in the sight of him. She hadn't seen much of him over the course of the past few days. The previous day he'd rushed out of the house and she wasn't sure what it was that was urgent enough that he felt the need to scald his throat with hot pancakes.

"I'm okay," Isaac sat at the table across from his mother.

The two of them simply looked at one another for quite a long time, neither of them knowing what to say and both having a fair amount to say. The truth was that Isaac was still sorting through his thoughts. He was envious of Amy's powers. He wouldn't have to have this discussion at all if he was able to have visions and rifle through the past, he could simply find out all that he wanted to know for himself.

He'd told his friends about his hunch as far as the concentration camp tattoos were concerned, but what he hadn't yet told them was that one of the tattoos was an exact match to the one on his mother's arm.

"Your name was once Sofia Katzenstein," Isaac whispered.

Surprised Anne replied, "It was, a long time ago," as if she'd been expecting this conversation. "I think it's time that I told you everything."

Isaac took his bag off of his shoulders and pulled out the comic book, setting The Katzenstein Kids down on the table between them. At the sight of it, his mother began to cry. It wasn't soft tears that simply rolled down her cheeks without consequence. No, these were real tears, tears that came from a thousand buried memories being brought to the surface, uncovered by the mere existence of a comic book.

The last thing Isaac wanted to do was make his mother cry. He sprang from his seat and made his way around the table, wrapping his arms around his mother. "Is everything okay?"

"Yes," she said through her tears, sobbing. "But I have so much that I need to share with you, my beautiful boy. Let me tell you about your grandfather, Herman Katzenstein."

♦ ♦ ♦

The following day, Amy, Will, and Isaac prepared to get to Dez' house as early as possible. If they had learned anything from the previous day, it was that their lives were short and they didn't know when they might end. The woman in black very nearly killed all four of them in the attic of the Cape Cod Daily.

Besides, it seemed as though all four of the kids were interested in the news that morning, but though they watched the entire news report, Mike Kelly mentioned nothing about their existence. He looked healthy and happy, albeit shaken, as he reported the news of a Russian woman being found dead at the Cape Cod Daily.

"A Russian passport, blade, and identification were found on the woman's person at the time that her body was discovered. My sources say that she was the daughter of a Nazi who managed to flee from the war and change their identities. Currently, she is the top suspect in the break-in of Mrs. Marjorie Weatherbourne's house and the death of our local hockey star, Greg Collins."

The kids were annoyed that Greg had been glorified as the town's star hockey player in light of his death, but they shoved those feelings away. It made them no better to wish someone who was already dead ill will. Once the news report was over and they had confirmed that Mike Kelly was true to his word in making sure that the four kids weren't involved in the ongoing investigation, the kids got ready to leave and hopped onto their bikes.

Dez was waiting expectantly for them, but the kids were taken aback at the sight that greeted them on the front porch of their friend's house. Isaac and Will, who had grown up with Dez, knew his mother well. She had been like a mother to them through the years too, always making sure that they tried the best Portuguese delicacies and giving them a free laugh at every opportunity she got. Amy, on the other hand, could only hazard a guess at who the beautiful woman sitting on the porch with Dez was.

The woman had long, black curls that framed her face. A once-thin face, sallow with the amount of medication she'd had to take for her sickness, glowed with life. For the first time in many months, Will and Isaac could see the rose of Dez' mom's cheeks and her eyes were alight. In her hand, she held a cup of her famous hot chocolate. Dez had one too, with marshmallows foaming on the surface.

"Hey guys," Dez smiled.

"Dez," Isaac and Will breathed. "Mrs. Fernandez..."

"Hello boys," Mrs. Fernandez smiled at them. "It's so good to see you again. Dez has been telling me all about your adventures." She turned to Amy and stood from the porch, walking over to give Amy a welcoming hug. "You must be Amy. Dez told me all about you too."

At the sight of his mom meeting one of his new friends, something that he never thought would happen again, he grew emotional. "Okay, mother," he laughed nervously. "We have to go to our secret treehouse now!"

With that, he jumped off the porch and began leading the way around the back of the house and the yard, heading toward the treehouse. The others followed him, after rushing to park their bicycles at the maple tree. They kept glancing over their shoulders in disbelief.

Mrs. Fernandez laughed, knowing that her son was growing embarrassed. She'd only gotten better the evening before and she was already slipping into the default mom role. She smiled, calling after them. "Hey, kids! While you're in that secret treehouse, would any of you like some famous hot chocolate with marshmallows?"

The kids excitedly cheered, turning to chorus, "Yes please!"

Mrs. Fernandez nodded her head and turned to head back into the house and whipped them up some hot chocolate, feeling better than she had in many months. It felt good to be able to make some hot chocolate for herself. Grandma Ruth could only look on at her daughter in amazement. The two women knew that things were only going to get better from there and it was all thanks to Dez and his friends.

Though, some credit was to be given to Milton Weatherbourne, Herman Katzenstein, and the Egyptian deity Horus.

"Dez!" Will finally cried out as they reached the treehouse. He hugged his best friend, clapping him on the back enthusiastically. "I can't believe it! Your mom... She's..."

"Yeah," Dez nodded and pulled the small medical bag from his pocket. "I healed her. She's better now."

"She's not going to die?" Isaac asked, his eyes filled with both hope and joy.

Dez' answer was to grin widely and shake his head before he climbed up the ladder and into the treehouse above. The others followed closely behind. Their hearts were filled with wonder.

The treehouse was a bit of a mess from Gorska Maika's ransacking, so the first order of business was to clean it up as quickly as they could. Will, Dez, and Isaac did their best to collect all the dirty magazines before Amy could see them, but they were pretty sure she figured out what they were doing. Her cheeks stayed red as they finished cleaning up.

Finally, when the treehouse was tidy, they sat down in their beanbags.

As Amy sat next to Will, Dez spoke. "You know," he looked over at the pair. "I think we need to get Amy a beanbag."

Amy grinned. "I would love that."

"Can you guys believe what happened yesterday?" Will asked, eager to change the topic. He quite enjoyed sharing the seat with Amy, but he didn't want to admit that to the others. "That was crazy!"

"We've been gifted," Dez added. "This gift... It's incredible."

"You know," Amy turned to look at the boys. "Horus told me that his four sons could only be of pure hearts. The only reason we're able to use the gems is because we're pure of heart."

"What does that mean?" Isaac asked.

"I think it means that we're the Protectors of the Children of Men," Amy answered thoughtfully. "We're here to help Horus."

"Remember what Mrs. Weatherbourne told us?" Will took his shield out of his pocket. "She said that we had a purpose and that we were the real Katzenstein Kids. I think she was right about that."

"I vote we all start calling ourselves the Katzenstein Kids," Amy raised her right hand and placed her palm over her heart. "All who agree with me, say aye."

The boys grinned and copied her, raising their hands and placing their palms, with their toy trinkets, to their hearts. Each trinket began to glow gently and watched as the room radiated with the green glimmering light. It was wonderful and magical and special.

"Aye," the Katzenstein Kids all stated together.

Amy felt the ring warm her finger and she looked down at it, tilting her head curiously. "My ring is the Prophecy

Gem," she murmured quietly. "Why don't we all do it together this time?"

The boys were eager to agree, sticking their hands out toward the center of the treehouse. They'd each wished they could have seen Amy's visions from the previous day. Now, they were going to get the chance.

Amy put her hand on top of the stack and suddenly, a vision blurred into sight as if they were peering through a porthole of a ship. Each of them felt the tug around their waist carrying all four of the Katzenstein Kids away from the treehouse and into another place, another time.

ABOUT THE AUTHOR

A.G. Sullivan

Award winning author A.G. Sullivan grew up on Cape Cod in the small town of Dennis Port, Massachusetts. Since his youth he loved the art of story-telling. He studied at the Boston Architectural Center and later at the University of Phoenix, earning his degree in 1999. He lives with his two children in Arizona.

Known for his **Katzenstein Kids Trilogy** as well as his phycological thriller, **Trypophobia**. His work has earned him 5-STARS from READERS' FAVORITE, as well as a FIREBIRD BOOK AWARD.

CONNECT ONLINE

www.agsullivan.info
facebook.com/agsullivanaz1
instagram.com/AGSullivanaz
x.com/agsullivanaz